Praise for *Thicker Than Blood*

Leary has a deft hand; her clear, intuitive prose offers insight into the disappointments, mystery, and beauty underlying human love.
—Janice Deal, author of *The Decline of Pigeons*

Blind to her adopted daughter's secret struggles with race, class, and identity, a mother confronts the void that is left when a child disappears. Heart-rending from beginning to end, *Thicker Than Blood* exposes the nuances of racism that make it hard for a mother and daughter to connect.
—Marylee MacDonald, author of *Montpelier Tomorrow*

Thicker Than Blood

Jan English Leary

Fomite
Burlington, VT

Copyright © 2015 Jan English Leary
Author photo: John Leary

All rights reserved. No part of this book may be reproduced in any form or by any means without the prior written consent of the publisher, except in the case of brief quotations used in reviews and certain other noncommercial uses permitted by copyright law.

This is a work of fiction. Any resemblance between the characters of this novel and real people, living or dead, is merely coincidental.

ISBN-13: 978-1-942515-12-8
Library of Congress Control Number: 2015941474

Fomite
58 Peru Street
Burlington, VT 05401
www.fomitepress.com

Cover art - © 2015 John Leary, detail from *Shore*

For John, James, and William

Acknowledgements

There are many people to thank.

Donna Bister and Marc Estrin at Fomite Press for their wisdom, guidance, and collaborative spirit.
Fred Shafer, my mentor, the most important influence in my writing and a friend for over twenty years. He taught me more than I can say about striving for emotional truth in fiction.
Kevin McIlvoy, an inspiring, revelatory teacher, who helped me carry this novel to completion. Ellen Lesser, who worked with me during my MFA program and well beyond. She knew what the stories wanted to say even when the words failed me.

Jennifer Matthews and Rene Steinke, editors who published earlier versions of chapters from the novel.
Olga Abella, Scott Anderson, Anniken Davenport, Karen Kulpa, Doug Lawson, Phong Nguyen, Melvin Sterne, Rachael Tecza, Etta Worthington, editors who've helped my short fiction reach a wider audience.
The Illinois Arts Council for support and encouragement.

The fellow writers who saw this work through its messy infancy, difficult adolescence, toward its coming of age: John Allen, Jeanie Chung, Jan Deal, Vivian DeGraff, Goldie Goldbloom, Joyce Gordon, Maggie Kast, Julie Justicz, Jackie Keer, Dragana Djorgevic-Laky, Marylee MacDonald, Arlene Brimer Mailing, Jill Pollock, Mary Beth Shaffer, Katie Shonk, Lynn Sloan, Lee Strickland, and the many members of Fred Shafer's writing groups over the years who have sustained and nurtured each other's work.

Shana Wills for her expertise about refugee resettlement.
Fidele, Sylvia, Nelie, and Anocled who continue to exemplify bravery and resilience.
The adoptive and birthmothers who shared their stories with me.

Ann Leone and Terry Zheutlin, sisters adopted by my heart.

Bill and Muff English, my late parents, whose love of words and books was forever imprinted on me.

David English, my brother, voracious reader and grammar nerd, my earliest companion in make-believe and play.

James and William Leary—our sons, wonderful men, constant sources of inspiration and pride.

John Leary—my love, my life.

CHAPTER 1
Chicago, 1992

Andrea sat at her desk, tidying up loose ends on her immigrant case files so she could hand them over to her co-worker. She changed her answering machine message: *Andrea Barton will be on maternity leave from February 5 to March 7. All calls relating to cases at Breadbasket can be handled by Dale Blank at —.* She stared at the photo taped to the bookshelf. A tiny brown baby, swaddled in a white blanket, her eyes shut, her lips full, her hair, tiny black curls peeking out. Andrea peeled off the photo and ran her finger along the surface, flat and unyielding as a pane of glass. She wouldn't actually touch the baby until tomorrow.

In her desk drawer, she'd stashed the *Tribune* article about an African-American newborn who'd been abandoned at St. Ita's Catholic Church and how the police had taken her to Weiss Memorial Hospital, where the nurses named her Baby Ita. The police had been scouring the neighborhood near the church, interviewing residents to see if they could locate the baby's mother. They needed to rule out kidnapping and wanted to give the mother time to reclaim her baby. Reading this, Andrea's heart started pounding, and she stuffed the article back in the drawer. No, the mother wouldn't come back. She couldn't.

At the end of the day, her best friend and colleague, Freya Reyes, ducked her head in the door and said a short meeting had just been called. Andrea said she was done, out of there, but Freya shrugged and mentioned something about the transition to her leave. Andrea stuffed her commuter cup and several CDs into her shoulder bag, pulled on her boots, grabbed her coat and scarf and handed a cascading spider plant to Freya to tend her in absence.

"I can't believe the next time I come back here, I'll be a mom."

"Yeah," Freya said, "Lucky you. No stretch marks or varicose veins."

They headed down the hall, Freya holding the plant up high, its shoots trailing to the floor. Andrea shouldered a canvas tote crammed with papers and books. Freya draped the plant over the reception desk and opened the door to the unlit room, then flicked on the lights. "Surprise!" yelled her colleagues, huddled together in the corner. Someone had written "Congratulations Andrea! It's a Girl!" on the blackboard and had hung strings of plastic beads from the fluorescent lighting.

"You guys," Andrea said, shedding her bags and coat. "This is so sweet of you." Her office mate, Dale, popped open a bottle of Korbel and poured it into plastic stemmed glasses, and Freya hit the play button on the boom box. Pink cupcakes with silver nonpareils sat on a platter next to bowls of chips and salsa.

"We got you a new-mother survival kit," Freya said, lifting a basket wrapped with cellophane. Andrea opened it to find diapers, onesies, blankets, formula, a steamy romance novel, and a bottle of wine. Andrea thanked them, running a soft cotton onesie over her cheek, inspecting the diapers, fingering a lurid pink afghan crocheted by Tanisha, the receptionist.

Andrea passed around the photo of the baby, and her coworkers said how cute she was and what a good mother Andrea would be. Andrea promised to bring her in, "As soon as she's settled. I promise." And she added that Pearl would go the Breadbasket's daycare after her maternity leave was up, so they'd get to see her all the time.

How dangerous to project into the future. Andrea tried to heed the caution of the DCFS worker that this might be a temporary placement, that the mother could still surface and reclaim her up to sixty days. Until then, Andrea was her foster mother, nothing more. Andrea knew the woman didn't approve of white Andrea being guardian to a black baby, even if it was temporary. Guardianship—she hated to think in terms of possession—was on Andrea's side, but she also knew the more time she spent with the child, the more devastating the loss. But how do you care for a child and not become attached?

Andrea hadn't bought a lot of baby supplies, just the basics, fearful that acquiring too many things would jinx the deal. But seeing these gifts, she allowed herself to be excited, to picture herself bathing, dressing, and feeding Pearl.

After too much cake and bubbly, Freya helped Andrea carry the gifts down to the car. "I can't wait to go with you tomorrow," she said, giving her a hug. "But are you sure you don't want your mother to come?"

"No, I'll see her in a few days. The whole adoption idea is a lot more complicated for her than I realized." She hugged Freya and drove off.

TWO MONTHS EARLIER, ANDREA HAD invited her mother on a lunch date to announce her plan to become a foster mother. She'd expected her mother, an adoptee herself, to be delighted.

3

"This doesn't sound thought out," her mother had said. "You just broke up with Jim."

"But that's why we broke up. If he couldn't commit to children, he couldn't really commit to me."

"Oh, he'd have come around." She speared a grape and popped it in her mouth.

"I doubt it. And do you mean I should have browbeaten him into the decision? And maybe end up divorced?"

"Well, you can still meet someone and have your own baby."

"I'm thirty-eight, Mom. That may not happen." She closed her eyes and massaged her temples. "I thought you'd be pleased that I'd want to adopt." Hadn't that been what she'd told Andrea and her sister, Joanne, since they were girls, that being chosen was special? This would be her child even if she hadn't given birth to her.

"Why do you have to be so damned independent?"

"And that's a bad thing? Mom, I'm not Joanne."

"You make things so complicated," she said, fixing Andrea with a stare. Andrea sat there, torn between apologizing and holding her ground. They picked at their food, the news spoiled, while they tried to find something to talk about.

A FEW DAYS AFTER THE ARTICLE on the abandoned baby came out, Andrea received word from DCFS that an infant was available for foster placement. She called her parents, hoping that her mother would come around when it was a case of a real flesh-and-blood child. Instead, her mother sighed and said, "Well, if that's what you want," and her father, not one for effusive displays, asked, "So what will you be, her mother or her guardian?"

"First her guardian, and if all goes well, then I'll file to adopt."

"That's the baby from the paper, isn't it?" her mother said. "The abandoned one." Andrea didn't answer. "Oh, Andrea, are you sure about this? Doesn't this put you in limbo?"

"No, Mom," Andrea said, adrenaline zinging through her. "She abandoned the baby. She's not coming back."

"It happens."

"Mom, please. Don't make this harder for me."

"I just don't want you to be devastated if you fall in love and then lose her."

"I have to do this. I'll take her home and love her. She needs that."

"I hope you know what you're doing."

Andrea asked if her mother had known what she was doing when she had Joanne, but her mother said that was different. Andrea didn't see how.

Her mother retreated into silence, and Andrea finished the conversation with her father, although she had a hard time concentrating because she could hear her mother's breathing. Her father told her about a letter he'd written to the *Chicago Tribune*, taking issue with an editorial about a controversial City Council decision. Andrea half listened as she stared at her bookcase, imagining it filled with children's books and toys.

HER SISTER'S REACTION DIDN'T SURPRISE her. "You don't know what you're getting," Joanne said. "The child could be special needs. What will you do then?"

"I'll deal with that. You were lucky with Gary and Blair. But no one knows what they're getting, even with your own genes." She knew what Joanne meant, that if you picked the right man, you'd have smart, attractive children. Joanne's husband, Mitchell, was smart, tall, and naturally thin and athletic. Except for a receding hairline, he was perfect—kind of a creep—but with the right genetic material. And they had made beautiful babies who'd had all the advantages of good schools, lessons, a large house and yard. How could Joanne understand what it meant to Andrea to raise a child who wasn't born to any of this privilege?

Joanne had escaped diverse Hyde Park for lily-white Winnetka, so her attitudes were predictable. Their parents had remained South Siders, living in the same apartment their whole marriage. Why was there doubt in her mother's mind about Andrea's decision? Was she protecting Andrea or betraying a secret belief that adopted children were cast-offs? And what did that say about her mother's sense of self? Hadn't she been raised in more fortunate circumstances than if she'd lived with her own birth mother?

CLEARLY, FREYA WOULD BE THE one to accompany Andrea to the agency. She stood solidly behind the guardianship and had an unshakable faith that the adoption would happen without a hitch. Andrea needed this kind of unconditional support right now. Freya, with four children of her own, was a more-the-merrier kind of mother, always ready to thin the soup, to re-patch a pair of jeans, to put two kids head-to-toe in the same bunk to make room. Never overwhelmed, never thrown by chaos, in truth, embracing it, Freya was Andrea's model for the kind of mother she wanted to become.

At home that night, Andrea placed a bassinet from K-Mart in her bedroom. She'd ordered a crib and had started to clear out her home office for the baby's room, but she could do that gradually. She laid out the gifts from the Breadbasket co-workers, the onesie with green and pink stripes, the purple pajamas, Tanisha's pink afghan, not Andrea's taste, but a very sweet gesture. A stash of diapers and wipes, cans of formula and bottles. She sat in bed and flipped through a picture book she couldn't resist buying about an African girl from a village who learned to tame wild animals.

The next morning, she drove to Freya's, and they installed the car seat, stained and well-worn, but still usable, having served all of Freya's children. And then they set off for the DCFS office.

They met with Dorothy, the still-skeptical caseworker, whom Andrea tried to reassure that she was ready for the challenges of a transracial placement. She signed the papers, her hand shaking, and followed Dorothy down a hallway to a room where another woman sat holding a tiny brown child in her arms. The child was wailing, her lower lip quivering, and Andrea reached for her and folded the bundle into her arms, surprised that a small baby could make such noise. The baby turned her head toward Andrea's breast, and Andrea took a bottle of formula from Dorothy, placing the nipple in the baby's mouth. She latched on and started to suck.

"This child likes to eat," Dorothy said. "A very good sign."

Andrea ran a finger over the mossy covering of black curls and studied her tiny, shell-shaped ears, her wide-spaced eyes, her skin, a beautiful tawny brown. The baby looked up at her with large, not-quite-focused eyes and shut them again.

When she saw that Freya's eyes had filled with tears, she allowed herself to cry as well.

"Baby Ita," said Dorothy. "What an angel."

"I'm going to call her Pearl."

Out front of Andrea's building, Freya showed her how to detach the car seat carrier from the base, and then they took Pearl up to the apartment, home at last. Freya had taken the day off to help Andrea. Pearl had slept during the ride home and continued to sleep while Andrea made lunch and sat with Freya, talking. When Pearl woke up crying, Andrea gave her a bottle, and she fell asleep again. Andrea found that her babysitting experience kicked in. She could hold Pearl until she slept, then place her carefully back in the bassinet without waking her. It felt right, two best friends hanging out, the baby asleep in the next room. But when Freya announced that she had to go home, Andrea panicked.

"You're a natural," Freya said, smoothing back Andrea's hair. "Just let her guide you." Andrea watched Freya disappear down the stairwell and out into the street.

She sat alone, afraid to make a sound, then she tiptoed into the bedroom and watched Pearl while she slept, her little fingers curled shut over her palms, her head turned to the side, her tiny chest rising and falling. Andrea crept into the kitchen to prepare the next bottle.

Pearl woke up and Andrea changed her diaper, running her fingers down the silky skin of Pearl's legs, over the folds at the knee and hip. She carried Pearl over to the window and stood, looking out at the sliver of Lake Michigan that her view afforded, rocking from one foot to the other, breathing in Pearl's powdery smell. She fed Pearl again, and, as she held her, Andrea tried to imagine what it must feel like to sustain a child from her own body, to feel the milk flow out of her into her child. Although she regretted not growing Pearl inside of her, she knew she could do this. It felt right.

But that night, Pearl awoke and cried, refusing to be soothed. Andrea fed her, changed her, rocked her, walked up and down the hallway, bouncing her, as Pearl screamed, her cries echoing. The only thing that worked was to walk around the living room in a circle, the baby hot against her shoulder, as she sang, "Here We Go 'round the Mulberry Bush." Finally, Pearl dropped off to sleep around four a.m., and Andrea sank onto the sofa for a nap, pulling a blanket over herself. When Pearl woke her again two hours later, she resumed her circle around the rug until Pearl quieted and Andrea stood, bouncing her, looking out the window as the sky pinked up. Were other sleep-deprived mothers up at this hour, holding babies, staring at this view with red-rimmed eyes, wondering what the day would bring, knowing that every day from now on would be different? Over the next couple of days, Andrea traced the same circle on the rug over and over, grabbing sleep when she could, wearing the same formula-stained clothes day and night, her eyes scratchy and red, her teeth unbrushed, her nose filled with the smell of diapers and formula.

When Andrea had received the news about Pearl, she'd planned a little family party for a week after her arrival. But she'd barely had a minute to herself since then and hadn't cleaned up or shopped. She'd thought of cancelling, but was determined not to give Joanne reason to feel superior. The morning of the party, she put Pearl down for a nap and jumped in the shower, then gathered up the mess from the living room and threw it into her bedroom, grabbing a box of crackers and some cheese and chilled wine and juice. It would have to do.

When her parents arrived, Andrea waited for her mother's usual complaint about the third-floor walk-up, asking why, for once in her life, she couldn't live in an elevator building. Instead, her mother rushed past Andrea over to Pearl, leaving behind her a wave of perfume, which Andrea feared would overwhelm Pearl. She'd awakened from her nap and was fed, dry, and quiet.

"Look at you!" her mother said, voice pitched high. "You're beautiful!" She reached for Pearl, cradling her, putting her face down close murmuring in a singsong voice. So much for her hesitation.

"Hey, Dad," Andrea said, giving him a hug. A patch of whiskers missed in shaving scratched her cheek like sandpaper. She took his coat, which smelled of damp wool and aftershave.

"Andie, girl." He pointed to his wife, sitting on the couch, bouncing Pearl. "Look at her. This is all she's talked about since you told us."

"Really?" Andrea asked.

"Is she getting enough to eat?" her mother asked, breathless.

"Of course, Mom. Every two hours. Demand feeding."

"You have to make sure she's eating enough," she said, eyeing the half-full bottle next to the rocker.

"Not a problem, Mom. I'm looking forward to the time though when she sleeps more."

"Now, don't wish her life away."

Andrea swallowed back the dig and took her father's arm, showing him the food she'd laid out. He placed a wedge of cheese onto a cracker and examined her bookcase for a moment, fumbling in his shirt pocket for his reading glasses. He walked around, inspecting a frayed wire, a broken light switch, a crack in the dry wall, things he'd offer to repair. Now it was important to keep Pearl safe, and it would give her father something to do on his visits. Andrea sat watching her mother hold Pearl, swirling her index finger, whistling down the scale until she touched the tip of Pearl's nose. "Where's your nose? There it is!" Her mother's skin next to Pearl's looked mottled, ruined.

When Joanne and her kids arrived, Pearl had just pooped, and Andrea was in the middle of changing her diaper. Her mother buzzed them in. Five-year-old Blair raced under her grandmother's arm over to where Andrea was changing the baby, her ankles in the air, her bottom slick from the wipes. "I want to see her!"

"Take it easy, Blair," said Joanne, shrugging off her coat. "She's a little baby."

"Show me, show me!" Blair said, her hands flapping.

"Let's go sit down, okay?" Andrea said, guiding Pearl's legs back into the sleeper. "And you can hold her." Blair did an excited dance, hopping from foot to foot. Bending over Pearl's face, she spoke in a high, squeaky voice. "Hi, Pearl. I'm Blair." She looked up. "Why doesn't she look happy to see me?"

"She will soon."

Blair took one of Pearl's hands and played with the fingers. Pearl's tiny brown fingers were dwarfed, even by Blair's small white hand.

Seven-year-old Gary stood next to the sofa, his eyes riveted on a video game in one hand, the other lifted in greeting. "Hey, Aunt Andrea."

"Hi, Gary, how are you?" Gary was the boy version of his father with his narrow nose and seal-brown hair, whereas Blair was a mini-Joanne—blond with fine features. At his age, he'd have no interest in a baby. Mitchell, of course, hadn't come along. No surprise there.

"Why is she brown?" asked Blair.

"I told you, Blair," Joanne said. "Andrea is her guardian. And she's African-American."

"Or black," said Andrea. "Either is fine. And I'm going to adopt her."

"Couldn't you find a white baby?"

"Blair!" said her mother.

11

"No, that's okay. I wanted a baby who needed a home, and Pearl was the one who did."

"Why did she need a home?"

"Sometimes moms can't take care of their babies," Andrea explained, "and they need to find new homes."

Blair shot her mother a worried look. Joanne patted her on the knee. She hoped Joanne wouldn't poison Blair's relationship with Pearl from the start.

"You and Pearl can grow up together as cousins," Andrea said.

"Please don't confuse my children."

"Joanne, don't ruin this."

"Get some sleep, Andrea. You're grouchy."

Andrea felt her face redden and, determined not to let Joanne see her upset, she excused herself to get some juice for the children. In the kitchen, she patted her eyes with a wet paper towel. By the time she returned, Pearl had become fussy. Her mother was bouncing her, but it only made Pearl cry louder. Gently, Andrea pried Pearl from her mother's arms and put her in the bedroom. Pearl shrieked and Andrea passed around the cheese plate, her head aching from fatigue and the effort of it all.

Finally, when Pearl quieted down, her mother handed Andrea a small, narrow box. "This is for Pearl down the road. I couldn't resist, even though she won't be ready for it for years." Hearing her mother talk about Pearl's future made Andrea want to hug her.

"Oh, Mom. That's sweet," Andrea said, tearing off the paper. It was a thin gold chain with a single pearl. "How beautiful."

"It's an Add-A-Pearl necklace," her mother said. "I'll give her a pearl every year for her birthday. By the time she's grown up, she'll have a necklace. I mean, with the name Pearl, how could I resist?"

It was a sweet gift, a bit old fashioned—did anyone wear

pearls anymore?—but it was what Andrea needed to hear, that there'd be years ahead for them to add pearls.

"Is it natural or cultured?" asked Joanne.

"Joanne, come on," said Andrea, looking at their mother, who'd flushed red, a sheen of sweat on her upper lip. "Well, I think it's lovely," Andrea said, fingering the pearl and tucking the necklace back in its case.

"Blair, why don't you give Aunt Andrea the gifts from you and Gary?"

Blair jumped off the sofa and picked up two wrapped packages, one big, one small. "Open the little one first," Blair said. "It's from me."

It was a squeaky giraffe. "It doesn't look like much," Joanne said, "but babies love them."

Andrea hugged Blair and thanked her.

She opened the larger package, a soft yellow pashmina that looked expensive and not machine washable. "Oh, Joanne, it's beautiful. Thanks." How typical of Joanne to give her something that would show every stain and have to be dry-cleaned. At least Tanisha's afghan, though tacky, was practical.

Pearl never completely settled down for her nap and had worked her way back into a wail, so both Andrea and her mother took turns rocking her, but nothing worked. Gary held his hands over his ears, and Blair grew antsy, so Joanne announced that they'd let Pearl and Andrea get some rest, and they left. Andrea apologized for the crying, and her mother reminded her to feed Pearl enough.

After her parents left, Andrea felt vaguely sad, like the day after Christmas when all the gifts had been unwrapped. Joanne's coolness had hurt her feelings, and she wasn't sure her mother believed she could do this on her own.

Although she hadn't welcomed her mother's comments, during the long, sleepless nights that followed, Andrea found herself wishing for her mother's help and advice. Pearl cried for hours at a time, sleeping only fitfully during the day. At night, Andrea walked around the Mulberry Bush, singing to Pearl, bouncing her, afraid that her neighbors would complain about the noise. For short periods, while Pearl napped, Andrea would drop off a cliff into a deep sleep, only to be awakened by Pearl ramped up into a crying jag. Andrea existed from nap to nap, barely taking time for a shower, uncertain how she could manage to shop or do her laundry. She called Freya to ask about the crying, whether it could be colic, even placing the phone in the bassinet so Freya could hear the wail.

"If regular crying is a five, colic is an eleven," said Freya. "You'd know. Julio had it. I thought I'd lose my mind. But you survive."

"I just wish she'd get a schedule."

"She will, then she'll change. Get used to it. Her whole life she'll be changing on you. It's continual catch-up."

"My family thinks I'm setting myself up for a big letdown, that I'm getting ahead of myself."

"But you have to connect with her. I'm praying that it all works out for you." Pearl lay in her bassinet, screaming, her eyes shut tight, her legs pumping. "Andrea, you can't hold back. You're in it for the long run. And you can do this."

PART OF HER WISHED SHE could share these days with Jim. She fantasized that he'd call her or show up and fall in love with Pearl on sight. He'd realize he really wanted children, that he'd just been scared but was ready now. He'd cart her around in the Snugli on walks, take naps with Pearl in their bed, feed her while he watched TV, urging Andrea to take a bath. But no, more likely he'd have been jealous of Pearl's hold on Andrea, eager at first to help, but weak on the follow-through. Best not to weave a fantasy about him. Jim's departure had been necessary for Pearl to come into her life.

GRADUALLY, BY THE END OF two weeks, Pearl found the semblance of a schedule, her naps stretching out longer, her hunger coming at more predictable intervals. Andrea learned to jump in the shower when she had the chance, knowing that just having clean hair and skin made her feel human again. When Pearl woke up at two or three o'clock, wailing, Andrea would heat up a bottle, go around the Mulberry Bush, then bring her back to the big bed for the rest of the night. As Pearl drank her bottle, little beads of sweat broke out on her forehead. Andrea would stare at her, stroking her forehead and cheek until the sucking slowed and Pearl's eyes started to droop. Very gently, Andrea would lift Pearl to her shoulder and coax out a burp. At times like this, she could imagine staying home with Pearl and never working again, never leaving the apartment even. But when Pearl started to cry, her doubts loomed large.

Twenty-one days had passed since the abandonment, and Andrea thought about Pearl's birth mother every day, wondering if she regretted giving her up, fearing she might still come forward to claim her. But also, Andrea worried. Had she eaten right? Had she been a drinker? A drug user? Was Pearl the child of incest? Pearl didn't look like the Fetal Alcohol Syndrome children Andrea had seen, but she worried that some serious condition might still surface. But if the birth mother had been competent, she wouldn't have abandoned her. Thank God this woman, this girl probably, had recognized she was unfit before it was too late.

15

On Day Twenty-Five, Andrea woke up in the morning, realizing she'd slept for six hours straight. Panicked, she raced in to find Pearl on her back in her crib, sound asleep.

A couple of days later, a mid-winter thaw arrived, the kind of cruel tease that Chicago tossed up each year to lure its residents outside, only to smack them down again with a deep freeze. Andrea took Pearl out in her Snugli, walking south on Broadway, stopping at a used bookstore and a Thai restaurant for curry, the kind of thing she didn't have time to do when she was working. It always surprised her to see so many people on the street in the middle of the day. Some of them, dressed for work, walked with purpose. Others, clearly jobless, stood or leaned against buildings, smoking or staring at passing cars.

One day, as she sat at a café near Loyola, the baby seat tucked in beside her, she noticed an older woman studying them from across the room. Andrea gave her a quick smile, then went back to her book, jiggling the seat with her knee.

The woman asked, "What kind is your baby?"

"Excuse me?" Andrea said, feeling her face flush.

"Your baby, what kind is it?" she said, pointing. "A girl or a boy?"

"Oh, she's a girl," Andrea said, angling the seat so the woman could see her better.

"Adopted?"

"Sort of." She busied herself checking Pearl's diaper bag, telling herself to get used to it. *No, my husband isn't black. No, I didn't give birth to her. Yes, I'm her mother.* She wanted to wear a sign that said, "I'm adopting her. Deal with it." Or maybe it could say, "Obviously, her father is Chinese."

Reactions to Pearl ranged from the over-compensating

good-for-you kind of cheeriness to outright disapproval. All she wanted was a simple, "Your baby is beautiful."

As her maternity leave dwindled, she felt both a loosening in her chest as they inched closer to the magic Day Sixty, when her guardian status would be solid, and a sense of sadness that she'd soon have to go back to work. She took Pearl to the pediatrician for her one-month checkup, and she weighed ten pounds, four ounces. Perfectly healthy and thriving.

One day, when Andrea was bussing her on the tummy, massaging her arms and legs, she looked up, and Pearl's lips parted in a grin. Andrea let out a little yelp of delight, which startled Pearl, the smile disappearing. Scooping her up, she hugged Pearl tight, doing a little happy dance around the room.

Andrea dreaded leaving Pearl in daycare, even though Breadbasket's Child Center was steps from her office. At first, she'd welcomed the diversity that Pearl would encounter there, children from all over the world, built-in playmates, cultural richness. She couldn't afford to hire a nanny, so daycare was the only option, but what about all the exposure to viruses? Would Pearl receive enough attention? Would she, on some unconscious level, experience this as a second abandonment?

The Sunday before Andrea returned to Breadbasket, Day Forty-Five, she took a walk along the lakefront. The wind was still chilly, but the weather was tipping toward spring. She stood looking at the horizon and made a silent wish that Pearl wouldn't be scarred by the adoption, that she'd be okay being raised by a woman who didn't look like her, who didn't have a husband, who was just doing her best. Would that be enough?

The next day, she packed the baby bag full of bottles, diapers, and wipes. Pearl lay on the bed in her snow suit, her face peeking out of the pink hood, her big brown eyes wide. Andrea imagined she was staring at her warily, as if to say, "Where are you taking me, huh?" Andrea blinked back tears.

At Breadbasket, colleagues rushed over to greet them, gushing over Pearl. When she walked into the Child Center, Kaila, the young Haitian woman in charge, made a beeline for Pearl. "Can I?" She gathered her up and started to bounce.

Andrea had to restrain herself from putting her hand behind Pearl's head to anchor it. A runny-nosed toddler, maybe a Hmong, walked up and touched Pearl's leg, saying, "Bay-bee." And for the first time, Andrea found herself wondering whether the other children, whose parents were immigrants taking ESL and job-training classes, had received their vaccinations, or if they'd been checked for head lice.

"Andrea, she'll be fine." Kaila reached for the baby bag. "Go to work. You can check back any time you want."

"Her bottles are prepared. She should need one in about two hours."

"I know the signs." She was patting Pearl's back. "Do you want to stay a little longer?"

"Yeah, maybe." Pearl had fallen asleep again in her snowsuit. Andrea unzipped it and guided her arms and legs out, easing the suit out from under her. Andrea could smell that she needed a new diaper. "Let me change her before I leave."

"No, I'll do that. She's asleep. This is a good time for you to go."

Andrea left the room, her throat tight, and headed toward her office. Her caseload had been cleared in her absence, so she had to start with new families. She placed the stack of files on her desk and opened the one on top. A refugee family from Burundi was due to arrive in Chicago that week and needed help settling into their apartment in Uptown. Five members: a father, age thirty; a mother, age twenty-five; two daughters, ages three and two; and a son, age seven months. The father knew French and Kirundi; the mother only Kirundi. The younger child was still nursing, and neither of the older children was up to date with immunizations. Andrea stared at the smeary ID photos in the file. The father, handsome with prominent cheekbones and large, serious eyes, the mother, her hair wrapped in a scarf, her eyes sad, the older girl peering up from a lowered head, the younger one, out of focus, and the baby, eyes closed, held up by one of the parents. What would they think when they encountered Chicago's weather? She'd gather coats, gloves, and hats from the stockpile of donated items to take with her to the airport. Breadbasket had a van equipped with car seats for the children. She hoped the apartment would be warm enough. The building where many of the resettled families lived had spotty heat and leaky windows, but the rents were low and there was a community of other African families.

Several times that morning, she peered through the window to check on Pearl. She didn't want Kaila to catch her spying. It wasn't really spying; she just wanted to see Pearl without interrupting. One time, she saw Kaila change Pearl's diaper, clasping her tiny feet in one hand as she wiped her bottom. It wrenched Andrea to see someone else touch Pearl's skin, to soothe her, to look into her eyes. Kaila guided Pearl's legs back into the onesie and held her over one shoulder as she gathered the dirty diaper. Pearl's head settled next to Kaila's neck, brown skin against brown. Would she forget that Andrea was the one who loved her best? She stuck her head in the door to Freya's office, but she was on the phone and held up a finger for Andrea to wait. Andrea waved and went back to reading files.

At the end of the day, she rushed to the daycare and found Pearl on her back in a crib, staring into the air. Kaila said she'd just awakened from a nap, having slept most of the afternoon, and had eaten well. "What a good girl she is!" Kaila said, handing Andrea the baby bag. As Andrea guided Pearl's arms and legs into the snowsuit, she concentrated on slowing her breathing, on reacquainting herself with Pearl's skin, her smell, her weight on Andrea's shoulder.

That night, she put Pearl into bed with her, resting her hand on Pearl's tummy, rising and falling, matching her own breathing to the rhythm. She forced herself to slow down, to leave thoughts of the day behind, to focus only on her daughter next to her, so that she, too, could drift off to sleep.

CHAPTER 2

Chicago, 1992

On Wednesday, Andrea reluctantly left Pearl at Breadbasket and drove out to O'Hare to greet the Burundians. She knew they'd have taken several flights—the refugee camp to Dar es Salaam, then London, New York, and finally Chicago. They'd be dead on their feet. And so scared.

Standing in the arrivals area of Terminal 5, she watched for the family, checking their photos clipped to the file so she'd recognize them, wondering if they'd get through customs without a snag, wishing they didn't have to deal with all the paperwork. These were people, not merchandise to be checked on delivery.

A flurry of Asians arrived, among whom walked several Western couples carrying Chinese babies, and she again marveled at her incredible luck. She'd have gone to China, to Russia, wherever, if she'd had the money, but Pearl had been born right under her nose. As one woman passed by, carrying a tiny Chinese toddler in pink pants and purple jacket, Andrea smiled at her brightly, hoping to catch her eye, to forge a bond of recognition. The woman was folded into a group of cheering family member who held signs, "WELCOME LULU!!," and waved stuffed pandas and Chinese flags.

The African family appeared, easy enough to recognize for their shell-shocked faces, the baby strapped to his mother's back, the older children zombies led by the hand. Andrea greeted them, showing them her credentials, helping them into gloves and coats and leading them to the Breadbasket van. As was the case with most newly arrived refugees, they had no English, so she spoke French, and the husband answered, although his accent was hard to understand. As she drove into the city, she talked, and they sat, silent, exhausted, as they stared out the window at passing billboards: one for Hooters with a busty waitress in a tight tee-shirt offering wings on a tray; another one where an over-fed child bit into a donut, his eyes popping greedily. She didn't know how much they understood—her French was decent, but not fluent--and knew she'd have to wait until they were less tired to start the business of acclimation.

She'd settled many families and knew the routine by heart, the papers they needed to sign, the explanation of the locks, the flush toilet, the gas burners. She'd stocked the refrigerator with the food items supplied by Breadbasket—bread, cheese, fruit, milk. Today, she found herself going through the motions because she was distracted, impatient to return to Pearl. She waited while the mother nursed her baby before she could show her the basics, remembering to drink a glass of water herself from the tap to show them it was safe, reminding them to hang onto the key, knowing she'd have to repeat the lessons over and over until they sank in.

Pulling into the parking lot at Breadbasket, she was breathless with anxiety. As soon as she saw Pearl dressed up and ready to go home, all the tension flowed out of her arms and legs, and she scooped Pearl up into a big hug.

Thursday night of that week, Pearl fussed and wouldn't settle down. The next morning, she woke up with a fever and a runny nose. Maybe it was that Hmong kid, thought Andrea, hating him for infecting Pearl. Andrea planned to take Pearl to the doctor during her lunch break and made arrangements to reschedule a meeting for the early afternoon. By the time she checked mid-morning, Pearl labored to breathe. Andrea sat with her in the daycare rocking chair, Pearl's hot little head nestled up against hers.

The doctor said a cold was to be expected now that she spent time in daycare. Andrea asked about Pearl's stuffiness, and the doctor gave her a saline solution with a bulb to suction out her nose. Pearl hated it. Andrea slept sitting in a chair with Pearl in her Snugli. Pearl's breathing rattled, and Andrea slept poorly, waking up when her head nodded forward. In the morning, Pearl was still stuffy but didn't have a fever anymore. Andrea felt like a crumpled paper bag.

A week later, Andrea woke after a night of troubling dreams where Pearl was washed out to sea by waves, and Andrea swam out as far as she could, but she failed to save her. Pearl's little hands reached up above the waves and somehow she could talk and was crying "Mama!" Andrea shook herself awake, trembling, afraid to go back to sleep. When she turned on the TV, she realized that it was Day Sixty, the last day the birth mother could come forward. They'd reached the line of demarcation, and she was one big step closer to adopting Pearl.

At Breadbasket, Freya greeted her with an azalea plant and a big hug, asking how it felt. Andrea said it hadn't sunk in yet. Could she trust that nothing would go wrong? Freya invited her to dinner to celebrate. "Ramón and the kids will watch Pearl, and we can have cocktails."

Andrea called her parents and Joanne to tell them about the milestone. None of them seemed to share her relief at this date.

"This is very good news," Andrea said, pushing back thoughts of the birth mother and how she'd felt these past two months, wondering about what happened to her baby.

After work, Andrea put on jeans then changed Pearl and put her into a new six-month sleeper since she'd outgrown the smaller size. She packed a bottle of wine along with diapers and two bottles in the bag. An evening out, what fun.

On their way to Freya's, the rush-hour traffic slowed to a crawl, and when a cab cut her off, she slammed on her brakes, narrowly missing an accident. "Fuck you!" she yelled, her voice trembling, and she vowed to curb her swearing from now on. Her throat was scratchy, and she feared she'd caught Pearl's cold. At a stoplight she fished a napkin from an old take-out bag and blew her nose. When she tried to draw a breath, her chest tightened, her lungs unable to take in air. Fighting for breath, she signaled to pull over, out of traffic. She cut the ignition, her chest heaving with loud wheezes. She leaned her head against the steering wheel and forced herself to slow down, to lengthen the breaths, not to pass out. Cars rushed past as she counted, slowly, her eyes closed, trying to breathe, her hands gripping the wheel.

Starting the car, she eased back into traffic, taking side streets with fewer cars. Only a couple more blocks.

When finally she parked close to Freya's two-flat, she burst into tears, hugging the steering wheel, gulping air. Pulling herself out of the car, she grabbed Pearl and forced herself to take careful steps toward Freya's front door, ringing the bell, catching the door as Freya buzzed them in. By the time she reached the second floor, her arms felt rubbery, and she was afraid of dropping Pearl. Freya answered the door and asked what was wrong.

Her heart thumped, and she was bathed in sweat. "Can't breathe."

Freya took Pearl in one arm, reaching for Andrea's wrist with the other hand. "Your pulse is racing. You're having a panic attack. Come inside. Sit down." She called her daughter, Rosa, who took Pearl into the family room where she and her sister and brothers were watching TV with their father, Ramón. Freya led Andrea to the couch and unwound her scarf, helping her out of her coat. Andrea laid her head back and forced herself to breathe as deeply as she could. Freya returned with a wet washcloth and put it on her forehead. "How does that feel?"

"Good." She shut her eyes for a moment. She could breathe better now. "What happened? Why would I have a panic attack today of all days?"

"Are you kidding me?" Freya grabbed two wine glasses and an open bottle and poured some for Andrea, sitting down next to her on the couch and testing her pulse again. "Think about it. You've probably been holding yourself back so you wouldn't be disappointed if Pearl left, but now that obstacle has been lifted."

"And now the worries really begin," Andrea said, breathing in deeply, pushing back another wave of panic. Now what?

Freya took her hand. "All I can say is buckle your seatbelt."

"For the rest of my life."

Freya lifted her glass to Andrea and they clinked. "The bumps are part of the fun." She folded her feet under her, swirling her glass of wine. "You okay now?"

"Oh, yes," Andrea said. "We're doing okay."

Andrea looked up and caught sight of Rosa dangling a plastic set of keys over Pearl, who stared at them, arms and legs flexing. Rosa, every bit her mother's daughter. Andrea wasn't alone in

25

this. She had friends to help her and Pearl. They were lucky. She leaned back, slipped off her boots and put her feet on the coffee table, taking a big sip of the wine. Just breathe, she told herself, breathe.

CHAPTER 3
Chicago, 1993

Andrea held Pearl under her arm as she wrestled the stroller through the turnstile at the Berwyn El station, then repositioned Pearl on one hip, the stroller on the other, and climbed up the steep stairs. Before they left the apartment, Pearl had been cheerful, babbling, playing with her favorite rubber giraffe, Twiga, so Andrea thought it would be a good day for an outing, despite the July heat. "Hey, Pearl, let's go to the park," she'd said, promising a treat. "Ice keem!" Pearl had shouted, hopping to her feet. But up on the El platform, when Andrea opened the stroller and placed Pearl in the seat, Pearl arched her back and shrieked, "No!" She wanted to walk, but Andrea knew from experience that Pearl would conk out, and she'd grown too heavy for Andrea to carry for long. She picked Pearl up and bounced her, singing in her ear. Maybe she was teething. Andrea gave her a bottle, which Pearl threw, and it nearly toppled onto the tracks. Andrea retrieved the bottle and tried again. "What's the matter, Pearl?" The El usually lulled Pearl to sleep, and a nap would take the edge off her mood. Andrea decided to wait until they reached the Fullerton stop, and if Pearl were still fussy, they'd cut their losses and head back home.

When the train came, she lifted Pearl, wriggling and squawking, into the car. Usually, Pearl liked to look out the window at the rooftops as they passed by. Today, with her eyes squeezed shut, she'd have none of it.

A few rows ahead, facing them, sat a young black woman with a daughter, maybe four years old, who was staring at Andrea and Pearl intently. Andrea smiled at the child and nearly pointed her out to Pearl to distract her from crying, but the girl looked to her mother, who frowned and shook her head, scootching her back in the seat. Andrea lifted Pearl onto her knee, hugging her, as she looked out the window. She'd grown used to black women narrowing their eyes at her, thinking she'd stolen one of their men to make this baby. Fine, let her think what she wanted.

She watched the familiar scenes go by: the Graceland Cemetery surrounded by razor wire, the city skyline as they lurched east at Sheridan, the roof-top bleachers at Addison with blue and red fans streaming to Wrigley Field. When they reached Fullerton, Pearl's cries had dropped to sniffling hiccups, and by the time the El went underground, she'd drifted off to sleep. Andrea shifted Pearl's hot head into the crook of her arm and peeled the damp linen tank from her chest. She'd dressed Pearl in pink shorts and a yellow tee-shirt, and had brought a wide-brimmed sun hat to sneak onto her head when she was napping. Andrea knew to be careful with the sun, even with Pearl's dark skin, much less likely to burn than her own. Pearl's face was wet from tears, but she slept, breath rattling, her nose stuffed, and Andrea tied the hat on, double-knotting it under her chin so Pearl couldn't yank it off.

At Jackson, she placed Pearl in the stroller, following the mass of people exiting the train. A man in a White Sox cap and low-rider jeans lifted the front end of the stroller to help them up the stairs. Andrea averted her eyes from his butt crack and thanked him when they reached street level.

They followed the fried-food smells and the sounds of piped-in music to Grant Park, where rows of cloth-covered booths stood near Buckingham Fountain. She pushed the stroller along with parents toting children, couples with arms entwined, groups of rowdy teenagers. Since Pearl had come to her, Andrea hadn't gone downtown more than a couple of times. But it was summer, and they were a family, and families go to the Taste of Chicago. Andrea tried to emulate Freya, who went wherever she wanted, her four children tagging along, napping at their mother's feet while she worked, playing quietly in the corner, doodling on paper placemats at restaurants. Andrea could barely manage to shuttle between work and home. It frightened her to think of where she'd be if Pearl's birth mother hadn't decided to walk away.

Andrea wondered if Pearl would stay in Chicago when she grew up or if she'd move far away. Would it be important for her to separate in ways Andrea hadn't from her own parents? She'd gone to Northwestern and spent a semester in Kenya, but she'd decided, after graduation, to settle in Chicago. Would Pearl, being adopted, need to cast her net wide in order to find herself? She certainly had a willful streak, which could either serve her well or cause problems.

Andrea had hoped there'd be a breeze, but the sun beat down with no wind off the lake. She adjusted the sun hat and stroller roof. Pearl's pink-painted toenails winked from her sandals. They were in no hurry; she could get a drink and sit in the shade while Pearl slept. Andrea bought a strip of tickets and started down a long alley between rows of booths selling hot wings, pizza, pierogis, and gyros. The oily smells coated the air, making it dense. The heat had cut her appetite. Maybe she'd bought too many tickets. She hadn't been to the Taste since she and Jim had gone a few years earlier, and she didn't remember it being so hot. But Jim was now just a memory, a figure pushed to the back of the photo box to make room for Pearl.

When Pearl calmed down, Andrea gave her a sip of lemonade, finished the cup, and rose onto legs that felt heavy and thick, pushing the stroller as she carried Pearl. With her social-worker eyes, she assessed the family groupings around her: white couple, working class, four children; mixed-race couple, Asian and Hispanic; black mother with two small children, whining, pulling on their mother's arms; a skinny young man drinking a beer, holding hands with a hugely pregnant woman eating an ice cream cone. Before she became a mother, she never paid much attention to how families with children negotiated crowds, if the fathers pulled their weight or left the job to the mothers. Who meted out the discipline or tended to scrapes? Of course, all the jobs fell to her, and she felt a twinge of envy to see couples working together. When Pearl became too heavy, Andrea placed her back in the stroller and gave her a baggie of Cheerios, and braced for crying, braced also for more nasty stares. But Pearl didn't complain, and Andrea started walking again.

Up ahead, she caught sight of a brightly-colored piece of fabric wrapped around a women's trunk, a matching scarf covering her head. A child's head of black hair peeked from the top of the cloth, and little brown legs straddled the woman's back. The man with her wore an African dashiki. Like the child, he had his hair short, and when he turned his head, the bow of his glasses glinted gold against his dark face. A wave of dizziness swept over Andrea, sweat prickling the back of her neck, so she stopped and lowered her head between her knees, feeling the crowd part to push past her. Finally, her vision cleared. She straightened and looked in the direction of the couple, but they'd moved out of sight.

Daniel?

She wove the stroller through the crowd searching for bright clothes, breaking through a line of beefy men waiting for turkey legs, past a booth where the cooks were shrieking "Cheeboiger!" At the intersection of two paths, she caught sight of the women's yellow and blue cloth. The man was handing her a sno-cone. As if aware of her presence, he turned toward her. It wasn't Daniel.

WHEN ANDREA MET DANIEL KOTUUMBA in 1979, she was a couple of years out of college, stuck in a dead-end job as the gate-keeper at a public-aid health clinic catering to homeless and indigent men in Uptown. She spent her days passing out pamphlets for STD testing and homeless shelters, poised to call her supervisor if one of the men proved violent, which rarely happened, bored out of her mind answering the same questions over and over.

On a bulletin board, she'd seen a notice of a benefit to raise money for Doctors Without Borders. She had no money to contribute, but it sounded like a chance to break out of her usual rut. That Friday, she dressed up in heels and a silk top, put on makeup, and after work, took the El downtown to the Hyatt.

She found herself standing alone, a glass of wine in one hand, a stuffed mushroom in the other, in front of a wall display of blown-up photos showing Sudanese women holding skeletal children, displaced people walking barefooted on sand, a family in dust-covered robes, eyes staring balefully out at her. A bite of mushroom sat heavily in her stomach, so she wrapped the remainder in a napkin and tossed it. Her glass empty, she looked for someone to fill it up again. A man—he was very dark, clearly an African native—appeared across the room, his smile broad, his cheekbones prominent, teeth white and straight. He threw his head back in a full-body laugh, and she drew closer.

Someone handed him a guitar, but he shook his head, lifted his hands in surrender, put down his drink, and placed the strap around his neck. Strumming rapidly, his head slung low over the guitar, he started to sing, his voice a high, sweet buzz, punctuated by clicks like hiccups. When he finished the song with a flourish, hand lifted at the final chord, the crowd applauded. He shyly thanked them and then sang another song, this one slow and mournful, his fingers strumming and keeping beat on the wood of the guitar. He was trim but solid and wore wire-rimmed glasses, a white shirt, khaki pants, and a tie. His hairline traced a perfect horizon across his forehead.

After he finished singing, she got up the nerve to approach him at the bar. She assumed he was South African because he'd mastered the click sound, but he said he was from Uganda, but had left during Amin's reign of terror. He'd been targeted for death because of his vocal opposition to the regime. Through his network, he'd received advance word of the danger and had made a quick escape via Tanzania. He pronounced it Tan*zay*nia in his clipped British English. Struck by his engaging smile and the pink of his tongue between white teeth, she guessed he was in his late twenties. No more than thirty. What a lot to have lived through by that age.

When he asked what had brought her to the benefit, she said something about the work the doctors did, how she couldn't do much, but she cared. Her voice shook as she fumbled for words.

He pointed to her wine glass and smiled. "I know you just came to drink wine and eat hors d'oeuvres, yes?"

She felt her face grow hot. "I didn't plan this event. I just wanted to show support." She palmed the glass with a sweaty hand and looked for a place to put it down. "How am I supposed to do anything?" she asked, her voice fighting not to falter.

"I am sorry," he said softly. "I did not mean to offend you." When he asked what she did, she told him she worked as a receptionist for the Uptown Men's Health Center, but was disappointed with the job and had hoped to do more. "But don't you meet a lot of people with urgent needs?" he asked.

"Usually, they need a fix and I can't help them with that." His eyes widened, and he nodded slowly. "I'm sorry," she added. "I do care what happens to them, but it's an endless parade of pretty hopeless people." And she stopped, feeling herself sink deeper into a hole.

She told him she'd spent a semester in Nairobi, that she'd just scratched the surface but was fascinated by Africa. She told him she was interested in working with refugees, but feared her current job would lead nowhere.

"If you want to do those things, Andrea," he said, pronouncing her name *Ahn*drea, "you will."

"I'm sure it's hard, being so far away from home."

"It is, but I have learned to make the best of what has been given to me." His face clouded over for an instant. "That is an African trait, actually," he said.

When she said she'd love to hear him sing again, he mentioned his weekly gig at a Nigerian restaurant on the far north side. They paid him in food, he said, laughing, so they couldn't get rid of him. "Over here at least, we Africans stick together. Strange how we have to come all this way to get along," he said with a rueful smile.

They talked for the rest of the evening, and he seemed to be interested in her time in Africa, generous with his full-throated laugh when she tried to be funny. He linked his hands over crossed knees, and she longed to reach over and lay her hand on top of his but didn't dare.

When the party ended, he held out his hand formally, said goodbye and left. She wished he'd asked for her number and wondered why she hadn't made the initiative herself, but that might come off as pushy. Maybe he wouldn't be interested in a white woman.

ONE EVENING AFTER WORK, SHE went to the public library and read about Uganda, Amin's strange personality, and the brutality of his regime—the expulsion of Indians, the slaughter of the Langis and the Achiolis, the rumors of cannibalism, his obsession with Scotland, the Entebbe stand-off. The more she read, the more questions she had. What ethnic group did Daniel belong to? Was he Muslim or Christian or something else? Did he still have family there? How did he escape? She felt silly and ignorant, resorting to books when she'd had no experiences, reading about life rather than living it. Spending a semester in Africa wasn't the same thing as living there. What had she done of importance in her life?

The following Saturday evening, with nothing to do, Andrea left her apartment and drove around until she found herself parking out front of a restaurant with a hand-painted blue, green, and white map of Africa with a gold star pasted over Nigeria. She hesitated outside before entering to find a smoky room filled with Africans, eating and drinking. Seeing that she was the only white person in the room, and one of the only women, she lost her nerve and headed back to the door.

"Andrea! What a surprise!" She turned to see Daniel sitting at a table with three men. Smiling widely, he stood and took her hand in both of his. "I cannot believe you came to hear me sing."

"I was out anyway and saw the restaurant," she said, feeling herself turn red at her obvious lie.

He tilted his head, smiling. "Huh." Her face burned. "Come sit and have a drink. Let me present Mamadou and Aimé. This is Andrea."

She offered a clammy hand to two men with dark skin and high cheekbones and said, "*Jambo.*" They shook her hand but gave her wary looks as Daniel motioned for her to sit and offered a glass of wine. The men were drinking something cloudy. "I am on a break. We can talk for a few minutes." The men pushed aside their chairs to give her a place to join them, still staring. Daniel asked her a couple of questions, but mostly, he talked to the men in what she knew to be Kiswahili. Her command of the language was shaky at best, so her tongue froze, and she couldn't remember anything beyond her simple greeting.

Daniel wore a short-sleeve shirt, his arms lean but muscled. "Sit and relax," he said, "and I will be back after a couple of songs." The men had begun stamping their feet, calling out "Dani, Dani." He stepped up onto a small wooden platform with his guitar slung over his back, hand raised, a broad smile spread across his face. He launched into a Kiswahili ballad. She felt the men's eyes on her, but after a few sips of wine, she relaxed, managing to recognize a few words: tree, heart, canoe, forever. She smiled at Daniel, letting the music wash over her and even started to fantasize that the lyrics held a personal message for her. When he finished, she clapped and joined the others chanting his name, then gave his hand a squeeze when he sat back down, accompanied by smells of fresh sweat and shea butter.

At midnight, Daniel walked her to the car, but, instead of opening the door, she faced him and leaned back against the car. He placed both hands on her face and kissed her, tasting like wine. In a rush of alcohol-fueled bravery, she invited him to her apartment. His face brightened. "Oh, Andrea," he said, kissing her again. "That would be lovely." She drove him back to her place and they tumbled into bed, and all the time, she marveled that this was actually happening.

The next morning, she woke up, her eyes bleary, to find Daniel sprawled on her bed, his smooth skin dark against her sheets. Daniel was the first black man she'd slept with, and unlike most of the men she'd known, he had little body hair. She studied the tan skin on the soles of his feet and palms, his solid thighs. His fingers fluttered lightly, as if playing music in his dream. Peppered across his smooth back were keloid scars, half-moon slices with raised edges. She nearly touched them, but drew back.

WHEN SHE WAS IN NAIROBI, she'd studied alongside several African men, and there was one, Jerome, whom she'd found attractive, but nothing romantic had developed between them. She'd had a boyfriend back at school, and since she was there for such a short time, she'd decided not to complicate her life. She loved the sinuous way African men moved, the evident ease with which they held their bodies, how, unlike American men, they didn't feel they always needed to prove their masculinity.

Daniel woke up and smiled, "Hello, lady," and she shut her eyes, embarrassed that he'd caught her staring at his body. He ran his arm down her hip, and the tips of his nails made her shiver with pleasure.

Later, as he dressed, she gently fingered one of his scars. "What happened?"

He sucked in his breath. "Oh, those." He shrugged on his shirt and started buttoning it. "A souvenir of a bad time."

"What bad time?"

He shut his eyes and sighed. "The police paid me an unpleasant visit. But I managed to evade them."

"How?"

"That will be for another time. I don't want to dwell on such things with you now." Pulling her toward him, he kissed her, and the questions slipped away.

They started spending several nights a week together, always at her apartment because his place—a monkish studio with a single bed, a table with two straight-back chairs, and a lone cross tacked to the wall—proved too bare-bones. Her apartment seemed overcrowded, and she debated what to do with her touristy wooden giraffe and ostrich egg, tokens that she feared betrayed her as a dilettante.

He sang to her in bed, used her mother's old cast-iron pot to make beef stews and thick pumpkin soups with peanut butter, which he called groundnuts. He urged her to dance, to take naps next to him while he read, to sing with him, even though she was embarrassed by her off-key croak. Everything seemed so easy with him.

AFTER A DIZZYING MONTH TOGETHER, going out to small bars to hear music or staying home and cooking and heading to bed, she decided to ask her parents if she and Daniel could meet them for dinner at Greek Islands Restaurant, a neutral location, less pressured than their homes. She thought they wouldn't mind his being black. Her mother was hard to predict, open-minded about the big social issues like reproductive choice but judgmental when it came to her daughters. She'd have been furious to learn about Joanne's abortion during her freshman year in college. But her mother took to Daniel, turning on the charm and monopolizing his attention during dinner. Andrea found her mother's social affectations annoying, as if she were trying too hard to make a good impression. "What is the state of human rights in Uganda?" "Is that one of the places where they perform cliterodectomies?"

"Mom, please."

"Oh, don't be so squeamish. It's okay for me to ask that. Right, Daniel?" He nodded. How did she get away with such probing questions when Andrea could barely get Daniel to talk about his past? But her mother's questions teased out things Daniel had never told her, that he was one of six children, the only boy, and the youngest by seven years. Three babies had died between him and his next oldest sister. His parents had farmed coffee as did his sisters and their husbands. When he was ten, his mother and the baby died in childbirth, his father dying soon afterward, so Daniel went to live with a local priest, Father Patrick, a good man, who worked hard to get Daniel an education. He went to Catholic schools, after that to a boarding school, and then to the university in Kampala, something his sisters could never have dreamed of doing. Andrea didn't understand how her mother could ask so many questions without Daniel shutting down.

He seemed comfortable telling her anything she asked. Andrea turned to her father, who never seemed to mind that his wife did most of the talking, and she whispered, "Mom's showing off again. Why does she always have to make a statement?" Her father shrugged as he speared a ring of fried calamari. "So?" she asked, "What do you think of Daniel?"

He chewed, swallowed, and said, "Smart, solid, impressive."

The questions about Daniel's life were one thing, but after an Ouzo, her mother started in on Andrea. Still addressing herself to Daniel as if Andrea and her father weren't there, she asked, "Now, Daniel, don't you think she's wasting her time at this job?"

"Mom, please," Andrea said. "Don't start."

Her mother waved Andrea off. "But Daniel has an opinion, I'm sure."

"I'm sure that Andrea could do any number of things well," Daniel said, glancing at Andrea.

At the end of the meal, as they were waiting for their cars, Nancy hugged both Andrea and Daniel, saying she'd had a wonderful time and that the next dinner would be at their house.

On the way back to her place, Andrea apologized for her mother's behavior, but Daniel said that she was charming and that he could see a lot of Andrea in her.

"Oh, please," she said, the blood banging in her ears, "We couldn't be more different."

"No, she's smart and funny. Like you."

"When she started complaining about my job. She's embarrassed that I'm a receptionist. But what has she done for work?"

"She wants the best for you. Don't you think?"

"It's way more complicated than that." Her head was muddled from the wine, and she cracked open the window for some air. "I always felt she wanted me to do things because she hadn't, not because I wanted them. She always talks about her ambitions, how she was going to be a doctor, but she gave up her plans and got married instead. She wanted to travel, but I'm the one who actually did it. I feel as if I had to succeed for her, not for me. And Joanne was the one she butted heads with all those years, saying she'd never get married, never have children, and she ended up doing just what Mom did. If Mom had any idea how wild Joanne was in college, she'd faint.

"Maybe Joanne wanted to please her."

"That's my point. But there was no pleasing her."

"Maybe they both got what they wanted."

"I don't know. I always feel as if there's a trap. Do this, but no, she wanted that. Go here, but no, I should have gone there. It's exhausting."

After driving in silence for a few minutes, Andrea said she couldn't believe how much he'd told her mother, things *she* didn't even know. He said that those were not the most important things about him. "I'm just amazed, that's all," she said. He took her hand; she held it a moment before slipping out of his grasp to hold the wheel. He folded his arms and leaned his head back for the rest of the drive back to her place.

When they went out with groups of her friends, he told stories with great flair, but she noticed he was careful to limit them to his leftist political beliefs and general issues pertinent to Africa. Sexually, they had a great connection, and they laughed together, but she couldn't penetrate the wall he'd built around himself. Sometimes, she suspected he thought she couldn't handle hearing his story because her life had been so trouble-free. She wanted to know what he'd been through, longed to pierce through his resistance, because she felt part of him needed to talk. She tried to be patient, to give him time to open up to her. She found that he could talk better when the lights were out, so she took to asking him questions late at night.

Little by little, she pulled details from him. He explained that as Langis, his family was targeted for oppression. After Amin expelled the Indians, he targeted Daniel's ethnic group and the Achionis.

She asked how they could tell the ethnic groups apart, and he said that it was complicated, there'd been a lot of intermingling. Daniel had left behind much of his tribal identity when he went to live with the priest.

One night, she asked if he'd lost anyone close to him.

"Actually, my cousins were murdered, and their house was burned." He took a deep breath before continuing. She stroked his back as he talked. "They did brutal, unspeakable things." He stopped and asked if she wanted him to continue. She nodded. He told her that as part of his job, he reported on the killings, so he took that opportunity to look for his cousins. But it was impossible to recognize them, even to distinguish one body from another. Instead, he found piles of severed hands, feet, heads. "Those butchers took everything human and left food for buzzards."

In a hushed voice, she asked again about how he came to leave.

He sat up. "It became too hard for me to stay and when I had the chance to leave, I did." And with that, he grabbed his glasses, pulled on his boxers, and slipped into the living room.

"Daniel?" she said, following him. "But how did you come here?" He was staring at the TV screen, flipping through channels. "Daniel?"

"Sorry, Andrea." He stole a quick glance at her. "I just cannot talk about it anymore." She studied his jaw muscles clenching, his face, splashed with light from the TV, before she went back to bed alone.

AT WORK, SHE FOUND HERSELF more attentive to black men who came into the office, attuned to their physical features—tall, maybe a Tutsi; short, a Hutu; and wondered about their ethnic origins—Nilotic? Bantu? Luo? Their national origins—Ghanaian? Cameroonian? Were their ancestors slaves? Were they immigrants themselves, African and not yet American? How little she knew and how much she wanted to learn. She tried to apply Daniel's uncritical appraisal of people, but found the same questions grate on her nerves—"Where's the shelter?" "Can you spare some change?" She wanted to find a more meaningful work where she could actually do something and prove herself worthy of Daniel.

SEVERAL MONTHS INTO THEIR RELATIONSHIP, on a muggy July late afternoon after a particularly frustrating workweek that included a run-in with a schizophrenic off his meds and the failure of her supervisor to support her, she suggested to Daniel that they take a walk to the lake before dinner. The streets were crowded with commuters heading home or out of town for the weekend, and she held Daniel's hand as they walked south from Belmont along the path in the park and wove around joggers and bicyclists. One of their favorite places to sit was the grassy area overlooking Diversey Harbor. They walked to a spot where they often sat to gaze out at the lake and face the cooling breezes. A cluster of small sailboats followed each other in a circle, bobbing up and down in the calm water. To the south, the western sun bounced off the glass high-rises in the skyline. Daniel put his arm around

Andrea, and she nestled up to his neck. Overhead, a small plane chugged along, trailing a sign advertising a car dealership. Daniel took Andrea's hand and brought it up for a kiss. "I want to quit my job," she said. "It's boring and pointless."

"I am sure you would be great at any number of jobs," he said, rubbing her hand.

"I have some experience in journalism, you know." She looked at him as he stared out at the lake. "Daniel? I have this fantasy."

"You do, huh?" he said, running a finger down the side of her neck, smiling at the idea of a fantasy.

"You may feel it's crazy, but I think about going back to Africa and working there. You know, the two of us together. Would you ever think of doing that?"

He looked at her, eyebrows drawn together, eyes flashing. "No, I never want to do that."

His refusal hit her like a slap. She stood and started walking back toward the street, taking deep breaths to keep from falling apart.

"Andrea? What's wrong?" he asked, following her. A flock of geese were pecking at seed on a patch of grass, and when she cut through, they startled, flapping their wings. "Stop and let us talk." He caught up and grabbed her hand, but she yanked it away. She pumped her arms, heading back toward the Inner Drive where she could catch a bus. "Andrea, come on. Please? Talk to me." She stumbled to the nearest bench and sat down opposite an elderly couple doing Tai Chi on the lawn, stepping as if in high water. Daniel joined Andrea on the bench and grasped her shoulders. "What is the problem?" he asked, looking worried. "What did I do?" They sat for a moment as he rubbed her back while she wiped at her face and tried to catch her breath.

"All you do is shut me out."

"Just because I do not want to go back to Africa means I am shutting you out? How is that? You sprang this on me without any warning." He took a handkerchief from his pocket and mopped his brow. "Why would you suggest such a thing?"

"How would I know what to suggest?" she said, saying he never told her what he was thinking, that she'd tried every way she could think of to get him to open up about his past and now he didn't even want to think about a future.

Daniel screwed up his face. "What are you talking about?"

"Don't you think I can handle what you've been through?"

"Andrea, I have told you; there are things I cannot tell you, things that would change how you feel about me."

"That's not possible. What could you have done?" He shook his head. "I know you were in danger and maybe you had to fight. I understand that. Desperate times."

He said she was making excuses for him, excuses he did not deserve. She said he couldn't feel guilty about things he was forced to do, but he said no one forced him to do anything.

"Did you kill someone?"

He sighed. "Of course not."

"Then what is it?" She fumbled in her bag for a tissue, but he offered his handkerchief, and she dabbed at her eyes. Handing it back to him, she asked, "How can we be together if you don't trust me?"

"I do trust you."

"Not enough to let me in." She said she felt as if she could never measure up, that it wasn't her fault she was born in Chicago and hadn't seen as much as he had. But she could learn. "You sleep with me but you won't let me into your life. How screwed up is that? You don't want to work with me, you don't want to think of a future."

Daniel shook his head. "I want a future with you." He tucked flyaway strands of hair behind her ear. "You have to trust that there are things about me that I want left in the past."

"I can't be with you if you can't be honest with me. I just can't."

He sat for a moment without speaking, his fingers thrumming against his knees, and she was afraid she'd gone too far, drawing a line in the sand. "Andrea. Do you want to know? Do you?" He turned to face her full-on, and she held her breath. He took a few deep breaths, shook his head, and, with his eyes closed, said, "I have a child."

His words spilled over her. "What?"

"A girl. Her name is Saran. She is nearly three now."

"Why didn't you tell me?" Because, he said, it would lead to more questions. She asked him if he was married. He wasn't. She was a woman from Kampala, a Langi like him. Of course, he'd known women before her, but the fact that one had borne him a child socked Andrea squarely in the chest. When she asked where they were, he hesitated a moment, then admitted that he had lost track of them. He stared at the ground, his fingers twisting.

She touched his arm to make him look at her. "Daniel, when was the last time you saw them?" she asked, feeling her voice shake.

"Two years ago, the day I left."

"Why didn't they come with you?"

"Andrea, please do not press me. I cannot tell you anymore," he said, his voice a whisper. "I just cannot." A ratty-looking woman in dreads and torn jeans headed toward their bench, shaking her paper cup of coins. Andrea waved her away brusquely, but the woman stood for a moment, staring at them, before moving on.

"But you had to leave," she said. "Your life was in danger." He sat, his head lowered. She tilted her head to catch his eye.

A tight smile played across his face before vanishing. "I had to hurry. That is true. I got word of my transport an hour before I had to leave, and I seized the chance. I thought of Bintou and Saran and thought about how hard it would be for the three of us to leave the country together, that it might be dangerous for a nursing mother and baby."

"Of course, it would have been dangerous. You were thinking of their safety."

A couple of teenage girls walked past them, laughing.

"I cannot talk about this anymore. Not here. Let's go back."

She stood up and offered her hand to him. They walked silently back to her place passing cars, stuck in traffic, wavy fumes of exhaust spilling into the air.

Back at her apartment, she grabbed a loaf of bread and some cheese for sandwiches, but he said he wasn't hungry and went into the living room to sit in front of the TV. She joined him and suggested they watch a movie. She chose a romantic comedy, something light with a happy ending. But a few minutes in, Daniel clicked it off. "Should we find another movie?" she asked.

"There's more," he said. She nodded and he continued. "To be honest, I could have taken them. It would have been riskier, but I could have tried." His voice was almost a whisper. "But I did not. As I was packing my bag, I looked out the window and saw Bintou walking on our street, Saran on her back, howling, no doubt hungry. Bintou stopped a few doors away and sat down on a bench, lifting Saran off her back. She put her little finger in Saran's mouth to fool her into thinking she was nursing. But no, Saran would not be calmed, so Bintou bent over to offer her breast to the baby." Andrea flashed on an image of Daniel and Bintou's bodies, looking alike, dark against white sheets. "I could see her rocking Saran and talking to her. It was then that I knew I couldn't bring them."

"It's true," Andrea said. "It would have been hard."

"No!" he said, pounding the sofa with his fist. "They could have come with me. I just did not want them. I picked up my bag and left." There was a hitch in his throat, a sob caught and swallowed. "They never saw me leave. I took half of the money and left half for them. I had planned to write to explain, but when I arrived at the safe house, I was too ashamed, so I never wrote. Once, I sent some money in an envelope, wrapped in a plain sheet of paper, knowing she would understand it had come from me. I told myself it would be better for them not to be linked to me, a target for brutality, but I really knew it was my chance to be free of them, that I had never intended to take them with me. And then I knew that I was a coward." He leaned forward and buried his face in his hands. "There, I have told you." He sat up and touched her shoulder, and she made herself look into his eyes, which were rimmed with red, the irises dark and watery. "And now I feel such shame that you know it too. Now do you see why I did not want to tell you?"

With the blood thrumming in her ears, she looked at Daniel, whose face was glistening with sweat. He was rubbing his hands as if they ached. "Yes, I see." She reached over and took them, and found his fingers icy cold. She sucked in her breath, and he folded his fingers over hers. As she pulled back slightly, he clutched them tighter. So she leaned toward him and put his head on her shoulder.

"I came here to start a new life, and now it has followed me here."

"I'm sorry I pulled it out of you, but it's better to know. We can still make a good life here."

But he was right; they'd crossed a line. He'd opened up, and the truth had pushed in between them. She'd told him it didn't matter what he'd done in the past, but he said it had changed everything. He said he needed some time alone, that they'd talk soon. First, they spent a night apart, then two, then a week, until they'd drifted so far apart, there was nothing left.

"Mama, out." Pearl was awake, leaning forward, straining at the stroller straps. Andrea bussed her on the cheek, wiping a tiny grain of sleep from Pearl's eye, asking if she'd like some ice cream. Pearl frogged her legs happily. Andrea unbuckled her and lifted her, damp and wriggly. She held Pearl's hand and pushed the stroller with the other.

If that had been Daniel today, what would she have said to him? That she'd found the resolve to go to graduate school, to find a career? That he'd inspired her? He would have loved seeing Pearl, and she'd have been so proud to show him her daughter. They'd have admired each other's children and they'd have exchanged numbers but would never see each other again.

But if Daniel had gone on to have other children, what thoughts did he have about the daughter he left behind? How could he ever have left his child like that? How could he have put his own safety above that of his child and her mother? Andrea could never, under any circumstances, imagine leaving Pearl behind. How could a parent leave except to make the child's life better? It was the only explanation for why Pearl's birth mother had given her up, yet Daniel had chosen to make his own life better. She saw now that he was right to feel anguish about his choices, to judge himself as a coward. As she did now. Why hadn't she seen this about Daniel before? She'd spent so much time blaming herself for their break-up.

She looked at Pearl, sucking her thumb, and offered her hand, and she matched her steps to Pearl's as they made their way to the ice cream stand. She bought a cup of rainbow sherbet, grabbing several napkins before heading toward a bench near Buckingham Fountain. The spray from the fountain cooled their hot skin. They sat down, and Andrea alternated spooning sherbet into Pearl's mouth, then her own. "Good, huh?" she asked. Pearl nodded.

She sat Pearl on her lap and hugged her, resting her chin on top of Pearl's head. Their bench faced Lake Shore Drive, filling up now with traffic. The northbound cars were moving steadily, but the southbound lane had clogged and someone was honking with repeated bursts of the horn. Out beyond the Drive, sailboats bobbed in the wake of motorboats that zigzagged among them, creating waves. As a child, Andrea used to stand at the lakeshore, straining to discern the roundness of the earth at the horizon. If she concentrated hard enough, she thought she could make out the hint of a curve. Today, the horizon looked metallic and flat. No sign of anything beyond, not Michigan, the East Coast and certainly not Europe or Africa. A breeze blew in off the lake, covering them with a cloud of fountain mist. Looking around them, she blurred her eyes so that the families and couples and solitary people gathered on the lawn were all taking part in a village banquet—mothers and fathers surrounded by children, village elders resting on a bench, women dancing and singing, children kicking a homemade ball around in the dust, instead of what she knew to be the case, that they were tired people who didn't know each other, who would crowd into cars, the bus, and the train, jockeying for position, impatient to make their way home to the ones they loved.

CHAPTER 4
Chicago, 1998

Andrea held Pearl's hand while crossing Foster at Broadway, on their way to Argyle Street for lunch. In recent years, the neighborhood had seen the influx of Southeast Asians providing needed stability: upgraded storefronts, community murals, restaurants replacing seedy bars and liquor stores. As they passed the Dunkin' Donuts, the Vietnamese Center for the Elderly, and the African-Jamaican grocery store, Pearl jabbered happily about first grade, her favorite activities, things she had learned.

"Mama," Pearl said. "Can I have my birthday party at American Girl like Megan?" The store had just opened downtown and had become the "it" spot for upscale girls' birthday parties.

"I don't know," Andrea said, surprised that Pearl would even be interested in such a girly place. She was a Legos-and-clay kind of kid, not one drawn to dolls. Andrea's niece, Blair, had several American Girl dolls, including one that had her same upturned, freckled nose, blue eyes, and pale blond hair. Andrea found the frozen, plastic likeness unsettling. Appealing to a girl's narcissism by a mini-replica seemed creepy, and they were ridiculously expensive.

"We'll talk about it when it's closer to your birthday," she said, cupping Pearl's cheek in her hand. But there was no way she'd have that kind of party. Too expensive, too patently commercial. She'd hoped to get away with a small group at home with cake and games. But would that make Pearl stand out from the others in her class? Because she worked, Andrea couldn't invite girls over after school the same way as other mothers or their full-time nannies, so Pearl didn't go on many play dates. Her friend Willa had come to their apartment a few times on a Saturday, and Pearl had gone to Willa's house to play after school. The balance was off though, and it worried Andrea that Pearl might not be included by the others.

Andrea had chosen Crofton School for its good reputation and progressive mission, which strived for racial and economic diversity. The school's high tuition meant though that Andrea and others in the same boat had to vie for the few financial aid slots.

Early on, Andrea explained to Pearl about her adoption, but Andrea didn't know how much Pearl understood about racial differences. Now with school came issues of money and class, and Andrea worried about how Pearl would react both to looking different and having less. Pearl liked school though and talked about girls, particularly Willa, so Andrea felt she'd made the right decision.

Pearl swiveled her head left and right as they crossed at the light. "Hey, Mama," she said, pointing to her favorite store, a tiny gift shop on Argyle whose window was stuffed with gaudy items. "We can get Megan's present there." So much for American Girl.

"Well, we can look at least," said Andrea, certain they wouldn't find anything that would be appropriate for an American Girl party.

They entered the shop and were enveloped by the tang of incense, which Andrea feared would trigger Pearl's asthma. From floor to ceiling shelves sat crammed with Chinese and Japanese trinkets—Buddhas next to Hello Kitties, plastic flowers next to Bonsai trees, jade elephants facing down gold-painted plastic cats. Row after row of rooted bamboo stalks stood like sentries. "Mama, look." She pointed to a display of cats with hinged arms, their paws saluting like the faithful at a rally. "This is what I want to give Megan." The hand-painted sign read "Maneki Neko—Beckoning Cat." The Go-Away-or-I'll-Scratch-you gesture looked more like a rebuff than an invitation. On the side of the box, Andrea read, "Inside attaching poly luck-beckoning lyrics, sticking them for immediate realizations." Hmm.

"I'm not sure this is Megan's kind of store." Pearl looked at her, puzzled. Andrea liked that her daughter didn't require high-end toys, that she'd be happy with an inexpensive Japanese cat. She hated falling prey to the pressure to buy something too expensive just for Pearl to fit in among her classmates. Still, she couldn't let Pearl be the only one to give a tacky gift. "Do you think Megan would like this?"

"Yes, she loves cats."

Andrea knew that Pearl loved cats. "Listen, I think we need to keep looking, okay?" Pearl stood transfixed in front of the bobbing cat paws. "I could buy you a small one."

Pearl looked at her and smiled. "That one." She pointed to a large cat painted a lurid gold, its face, stolid and foreboding.

"I think this one might be better." Andrea picked up a smaller ceramic cat, white and black with pink features.

"But the arm doesn't move."

"I know, but I'm afraid the other one will break. You couldn't play with it. It would have to stay on your dresser."

"I want this one." Her face clouded over, and Andrea knew that Pearl was digging in her heels for a struggle.

"Come on, now."

Pearl's jaw was set. "I want a *real* cat."

So *that* was it. "Oh, Pearl. I wish we could. But you're allergic."

"I don't care."

"The cat would make your asthma worse. We can't have that," she said, pulling Pearl close to her, flashing on a memory of Pearl at fourteen months, gasping for breath as Andrea rushed her to the hospital in the middle of the night.

"Then I want that one," she said, pointing to the big cat.

On the way out of the store with the box in a plastic bag, Andrea said, "So let's go to lunch. Thai Avenue or Tank Noodles?"

"Tank!"

Andrea preferred Thai Avenue, but she felt like indulging Pearl. "I'll bet I know what you're going to order."

"Wonton soup!"

"I was right." She followed Pearl, who had run ahead of her to the corner restaurant.

As was her ritual, Pearl knelt before the miniature plate of plastic food in the corner of the entry, her fingers itching to play with it. Andrea had forbidden touching it, having seen the owner crouch down before the plate and pray before unlocking the restaurant. They weren't toys. "Are you sending a good wish?"

Pearl shut her eyes and nodded.

Asian families huddled at round tables over big bowls of Vietnamese Pho topped with basil leaves and wedges of lime. When Andrea and Pearl walked in the door, the customers looked up from their soup and stared at them, a white woman with a black child. Andrea glared back and steered Pearl to a table where she could look out on the street and not face those rude glances.

As soon as they sat down, Pearl took her cat out of the box. "You should wait until we get home to do that," Andrea said. "And there's no battery in it yet."

"I want to see how it works." Andrea agreed to let Pearl place it on the table for a couple of minutes until their food came. Pearl started pumping her arm the way the cat had in the store.

Andrea looked at her daughter, her pudgy tummy bowed out, her sturdy brown fingers curled over the palm. That morning, Andrea had oiled and parted her hair into quadrants, then made braids, attaching pink barrettes. Pearl hated having her hair styled—every day brought a teary struggle--but Andrea refused to let her go off to school with it unbraided. She planned to take Pearl to a place where she could get a professional braiding so it would stay in place and they could skip the battle. If she wanted it natural when she was older, that would be her choice. Pearl loved to comb Andrea's straight, fine hair. Did Pearl believe this hair was better than her own?

"I can call it 'Hello Kitty.'"

"Okay, it is a Japanese cat, but we bought it in a Chinese store, and now we're in a Vietnamese restaurant. Maybe we can look up some names when we get home."

"Hello, Kitty," Pearl chirped, patting it on the head. Andrea wished they could have a cat. Pearl would welcome the companion.

In addition to wonton soup, Pearl wanted a mango bubble tea. Andrea ordered Pho with beef, the most basic soup, careful to avoid extras like fish maw and tripe.

Andrea enjoyed the sun streaming in the windows as Pearl burbled to her cat, "Hello, Kitty, hello," as she hoisted her water glass, taking a sip. An old Vietnamese woman at a neighboring table had continued to stare. Andrea turned and fixed her with a fierce glare until the woman looked down at her plate.

"Mama? Mama? Look." Pearl was pointing out the window at a boy, about eight or nine years old, standing at the bus stop with a young, dark-skinned woman. His face was scarred, no doubt from burns, with patches of tan covering his brown face, as if someone had splashed bleach on him. Andrea felt a swoop of sympathy in her gut. Poor child.

"Pearl, don't point. I'll explain." Pearl pressed her face to the window. "Sit down, please." She laid her hands on Pearl's shoulders. "Come on." The woman, who looked to be in her early twenties, had a beautiful, angular face with prominent cheekbones. Seeing Pearl gape at them, she frowned and turned away, craning her neck in the direction the bus would come. "Sit down," Andrea said. "You don't want to make him feel bad."

"But what happened?"

"I think he was burned, and his skin healed that way."

"How did he get burned?"

"I don't know." Pearl sat back on her heels, but kept staring at him.

"Pearl, look at me. Now."

Pearl turned her head toward Andrea but looked out the corner of her eye toward the boy, who was unaware of being watched. "But what is he?"

"What do you mean?"

"Is he black or white?"

She took Pearl's hands. "Pearl, ssh. Listen, he's black, but his skin was hurt, and he has scars that took away the color."

The waitress came with their food. Pearl speared a wonton on a chopstick, took a bite, then let it splash back into her soup. A young couple sat in the corner, wormlike noodles trailing from their mouths. A young Vietnamese man lined up the bottles of

55

pepper, soy, and oyster sauces, and the ancient woman pushed up from the table, her spine curved like a crook, her head dipping below the shoulders. She shuffled toward the bathroom in the back of the restaurant.

"Will the scars go away?" Pearl asked.

"No, I'm afraid they won't."

Pearl stole another look at the boy, who was bobbing his head to music streaming in through his earphones.

"Pearl, please. I asked you not to stare at him."

"Did it hurt?"

"I'm sure it did." She touched Pearl's cheek, guiding her back into eye contact. The softness of Pearl's skin. What would she do if Pearl were burned? Black skin was so vulnerable to scarring. She remembered the half-moon scars that peppered Daniel's back. He told her they were the work of the police back in his native Uganda, but he'd refused to say more than that. She ran her finger over Pearl's cheek and smiled at her.

The young woman picked up her bag and called to the boy, who was studying a parked BMW. The bus pulled up and she slapped her thigh, shouting at him. He shuffled over, following her onto the bus. Andrea saw the boy plunk down in a seat before the bus lurched forward.

Pearl sat back in her seat. "Mama?" she asked, her face serious. "What am I?"

"What do you mean?"

"Am I black?"

"Well, yes, of course." She pushed the bowl aside and wiped her hands. "We talked about your birth mother, right? That she was African-American and so are you."

"Am I a little bit white?"

Andrea always tried to be honest with Pearl, particularly about her origins, what little she knew of them. "Probably some. A long time ago, some of your family came from Africa. I don't know what country or what area. And you're probably part white also."

Andrea had put up maps around the apartment. In the kitchen, next to the table, she'd posted a relief map of the world that Pearl stood in front of, running her fingers over the bumpy mountain ranges. Andrea had made a point of telling her about Africa in particular, about the refugees she worked with at Breadbasket and where they'd come from. Pearl could name the continents and locate countries like Bosnia, Somalia, and Sudan on the map and she'd spent many hours in daycare playing with the children of these refugees. With no clue about Pearl's birth family, Andrea had nothing to go on except her skin color, a beautiful chocolate brown.

"Are you a little black?" Pearl asked.

Andrea sat back. "Sure. I may be a bit black. Most of my ancestors came from England and Ireland, but some might have been African." It was way too early to talk about slavery. Or genetics. Or racism. Or sex. How would she deal with those questions when it was time? Andrea thought for a moment. "What do you want to be?"

"I want to be like you."

"Oh, Pearl, we *are* alike. We both love animals and ice cream and grilled cheese. And we're both ticklish, hmm?" She spread her fingers like claws and Pearl squirmed, giggling.

Pearl went back to eating her soup, struggling to wield the chopsticks before giving them up for a spoon, intently fishing for meat and wontons in the broth. When Pearl smacked her lips, Andrea gently tapped her own mouth to remind Pearl, who promptly clamped her mouth shut, taking a few deliberate closed-mouth bites. Andrea took a mint leaf from the garnish and tore it, dropping it into her water glass, taking a sip. Tapioca balls lay at the bottom of Pearl's bubble tea glass in a scrim of foam.

Pearl put down her spoon. "How did that boy get burned?"

"I don't know, sweetie, but it was an accident, I'm sure."

"Was that his mama?"

"I don't know. She's pretty young. Maybe his sister." Or his mother. "Hey, if you're finished, let's get going." She handed Pearl a second napkin.

"Okay." Pearl wiped off her face and reached for the cat, patting it on the head. Andrea helped her replace the bubble wrap and put it back in the box. She paid the bill and they left.

At the corner, they passed a middle-aged black man standing outside a convenience store, counting coins in his hand, and Andrea felt guilty about not giving him some change. Didn't everything make her feel guilty? Unlike the children of Andrea's immigrant clients who attended the Chicago public school in the neighborhood with overcrowded classes and too little money, its students milling around a broken slab of concrete during recess, Pearl's private school gave her art and music and plenty of her teacher's attention. Of course, Andrea wasn't willing to make an example of Pearl by placing her in a public school. She knew the district school wasn't up to snuff, and Pearl hadn't gained one of the coveted spots at a magnet school in the CPS lottery. It wasn't fair, but she couldn't sacrifice Pearl to an altruistic ideal.

Crofton had given them financial aid, but it was still a stretch to make up the difference, so Andrea's parents had helped her out, and they'd also set up a college fund. She worried that Pearl would get a taste for the kind of life her classmates' parents were able to provide—American Girl dolls, dance lessons, vacations—and she'd resent being deprived. Was it better to expose her to luxuries she couldn't attain for the education or to surround her with a more diverse group in the underfunded public schools? Andrea felt that, whatever sacrifice it took, whatever other less desirable side effects of rubbing elbows with the wealthy, Pearl needed to go to the best school possible.

"Can we go look for Megan's present now?"

"Sure. I'm thinking a book. Or maybe art supplies."

They headed toward a stretch of Clark Street lined with small shops. This neighborhood was a patchwork of smaller communities with a wide range of cultures and incomes, where Single-Room-Occupancy hotels stood just blocks from mansions with landmark status.

Pearl took her time, circling each tree, scrambling over the exposed roots, babbling to herself. Andrea wanted to finish the errand and go back home. She had some paper work to do so that her next day at work wouldn't hit her like a two-by-four. "Can you pick up the pace, Pearl, please?"

"Can we walk by the enchanted house?"

"It's not really on our way."

"I want to see the enchanted house."

"Okay, turn here." They walked up Magnolia as Pearl counted the houses, four frame, two stone, three brick. The enchanted house, actually a three-flat, stood behind an ornate wrought-iron fence in the middle of the block on Berwyn. The current owners had embellished the front with stone sculptures and busts of stern men. Some windows were covered with tapestries and others had stained glass. A turret jutted from the third floor, and Pearl pretended that a princess lived imprisoned there. One day, while standing in front of the building, Andrea had seen a shock of white curly hair pop up over the bricks on the roof, then back down again. A crazy old woman? The princess grown old and forgotten in the tower? A child wearing a wig?

"I want to live there," Pearl said.

"I do too. It's amazing, all right."

"Look. There's a cat in the window." Pearl waved. "Hi, kitty. Hi."

Andrea wanted the building to be enchanted, the inside luxurious, some place she could live one day with Pearl, but she knew that the perpetual presence of a For Rent sign out front meant that there were untold stories about that building. Crazy landlords, bad plumbing, noxious mold. The inside rarely lived up to the promise of the outside. "Let's get going," she said, taking Pearl's hand and guiding her toward Clark Street.

Women and Children First offered one of the best children's book selections in the city. Pearl ran to the back, pulled a few picture books off the display, then plunked herself down on a chair and began sounding out words to herself. Andrea loved that Pearl was such a book girl, feeling proud for having instilled this in her child.

"Okay, let's find a book for Megan."

Pearl found a hardbound copy of a picture book she owned, which featured an African-American boy and his grandfather. "I want to give her this one."

"I don't know, Pearl," Andrea said, cautiously. "Maybe one that's more for girls."

"I'm a girl, and I like this one."

"I know, but we have to think about what Megan might like."

"I'm sure she will."

"I'm going to look around." Andrea found a richly illustrated copy of *Grimms' Fairy Tales*. Too expensive, but more likely to be appreciated by Megan. She held it up to Pearl.

"No, this one," Pearl said, her voice hoarse. When she was tired, her asthma tended to flare up.

"Pearl, come on," Andrea said, reaching for the book, which Pearl clasped tight. "You can't give her that book. It's just not for her."

"Yes! I want to give her this one." Andrea worried that Pearl would rip the cover and they'd have to buy it, giving them two copies of the same book. "The boy and the grandfather go fishing together and they're happy."

"I think we may need to go home and forget about the present today. Maybe you're too tired to be pleasant."

"No! I want to get her this book." Pearl said, wheezing. Andrea tried to pry the book from her hands. She stopped. "Pearl, what's going on? Why are you so insistent?"

"Mama, I want to give her this book. I know she'll like it. I do. Please?"

Andrea realized that Pearl needed to give Megan this particular book.

"Okay, we can get it for her."

They paid and had the book gift-wrapped. Andrea rolled her eyes for the sales clerk, then felt ashamed of herself. Pearl, her forehead beaded with sweat, stood next to Andrea breathing through her mouth. "Let's go home and take a rest." Andrea guided her toward the door.

Back at their apartment, she made Pearl lie down, and she worked while Pearl watched a videotape. Andrea wished she hadn't questioned Pearl's choice of book, that she'd been confident enough in Pearl's choice to give it to Megan even if, particularly if, Megan didn't like the book. She made a mental note to ask Freya, her touchstone for all matters of motherhood, what she'd have done in that situation.

Over the past six years, Andrea had developed a thick skin in the face of the doubters who didn't approve of her adopting a black child. She'd been able to stand up to them, whether they were openly hostile or well-meaning and ignorant. But since Pearl was now out in the world, a largely white and privileged one where a mother couldn't always run interference, Andrea'd had to strike a balance between urging Pearl to stand firm and encouraging her to fit in. She didn't know in fact how well Pearl got on with the other girls, and she hated to think that Pearl was out there mostly alone.

On the day of Megan's birthday party, they headed downtown on the El. Andrea had suggested that Pearl wear a dress, but she'd refused, choosing a pink shirt and her new gym shoes with flashing lights. Pearl bounced on the seat of the El, jabbering away, swinging the plastic bag with the book wrapped inside. Andrea was happy to see her so excited, but she still worried about the party and wondered if Pearl would even tell her if the girls had been mean.

When they got off at Chicago Avenue, they blended into the crowd of mostly white shoppers wielding huge bags and walked toward the American Girl store. Although Pearl had been excited up to that point, when they arrived at the store, she held back a moment, her hand gripping Andrea's tightly. "Here we are. Let's go inside." Pearl ducked her head and hugged the gift bag. "I'll go in with you, okay?" Pearl nodded.

The first floor featured dolls with historic personae—the plucky frontier girl, the Swedish immigrant, the nineteenth-century Mexican girl, the Civil-War-Era slave girl. Pearl made a bee-line for Molly, the Irish doll with braids and glasses, bypassing Addy, the only black doll. "Oh, Mama, look at Molly." Andrea knew the doll alone would be expensive, but was startled to see that the doll, book, and accessories would cost more than two hundred dollars. Would she really want a doll?

"Yes, that's really cool. Maybe we can get one of the books, okay?" Pearl stood, her breath fogging the glass of the display.

They headed upstairs past the doll hair salon and the photo booth to the café, where they saw a group of girls from Pearl's class, each one clutching an American Girl doll. Oh no. Was having a doll one of the requirements for the party? Nina Berger, Megan's tall, elegant mother, breezed over. "Pearl, you're here. Good. Aren't you excited?" Pearl stood mute, her chin tucked. "It's going to be a lot of fun. Did you see the Addy doll? Isn't she adorable?" Pearl was staring at the group of girls, and she ran up to them, thrusting her gift at Megan, who glanced at Pearl, then turned back to the friends clustered around her.

Andrea felt the same dread when she'd dropped Pearl off at preschool the first day and wished she could stay during the party and help in case Pearl needed her. "It was lovely of you to invite Pearl," she said to Nina and added that Pearl had been looking forward to the party.

"Yes, it's going to be *very* special for the girls," Nina said. Andrea was certain Nina prided herself on being the first mother in the class to host a party there.

Andrea took Nina aside and asked if she'd mind keeping a watch out for Pearl's breathing, giving her the inhaler in case she needed it. "I hate to ask, but it's best to head off an asthma attack."

Nina blinked, gave a little sigh before smiling brightly, saying of course she'd watch out for Pearl. Not to worry. Andrea asked what time she should pick Pearl up and gave a last look as an employee dressed in a pink hoodie with purple trim herded the girls into the café, Pearl at the end of the line.

On her way out, Andrea stopped to look at the display of "Just Like You" dolls. Although there were no specific references to race, the pigments ran from light to dark. Just a hint of slant accented the Asian eyes and the African-American noses were a touch wider than those with European roots. You could choose a light-skinned girl with freckles, an upturned nose, and straight blond hair or a dark-skinned girl with a slightly wider nose and "textured" black hair or other variations.

A mother and daughter, both blond with matching headbands, stood in front of the display, talking to a saleswoman. "My daughter hates freckles, but all the light-skinned dolls have them. Is there anything you can do about that?" Stupid woman, Andrea thought, as she pushed through the shoppers out the big doors onto the street.

Andrea headed over to a Starbucks. She sat, book opened in front of her, unable to concentrate. Instead, she watched the people walking past with shopping bags and roomy purses. Since she rarely came to this part of the city, it always surprised her to see how many people were out and about, spending piles of money, the kind of money she herself didn't have. The economic boom had largely passed her by, and she didn't regret how she'd chosen to live, but when faced with all this disposable income, it made her think about those things she couldn't give to Pearl.

Would it be better for Pearl to be around girls from more similar backgrounds? Was she making it doubly hard for her daughter both to look different and to have less money? Joanne's kids went to suburban public schools that looked like small colleges, where the students floated around in clouds of utter specialness. At least Crofton was in the city and had minority students. And wasn't it important for Pearl to have all kinds of experiences, even those that might be uncomfortable? It was a birthday party, for God's sake. Fun, games, cake. What was she afraid of?

At two o'clock, Andrea headed back to American Girl, eager to see Pearl, worried that she'd be the only one without a doll, annoyed that it would even be an issue. Before leaving the store, she'd bought Pearl a Molly McGuire book, which she hoped would make her feel better about not having a doll at the party.

A group of mothers from Pearl's school, most of them wearing workout clothes, stood near the café, talking. They all knew each other, played tennis together, volunteered at the school. She approached Simone Parker, whom she knew through her daughter, Willa. Andrea tried to make eye contact, but Simone was involved in a conversation with Susan Gross, complaining that Willa's ballet teacher, played favorites. "Wait until they get up en pointe," said Susan, the mother of three daughters. "It gets worse. If she doesn't think a girl has the talent, then forget about it." She made a slashing motion across her throat. "My middle one might make it, as long as she doesn't get too busty." Suzanne herself was gaunt. "I mean, her bras are already bigger than mine." They laughed. Simone scanned the room, her eyes passing over Andrea, seeming not to recognize her.

A petite woman with a jet-black bob complained that American Girl hadn't made a Jewish doll yet. "Shanna's a voracious reader, and she has all the books. But what am I supposed to tell her? That there's no doll with a story she can identify with?" The others agreed it was really unfair. Andrea rifled through her purse and took out her notebook, where she jotted down a shopping list, just to give herself something to do.

The door to the café opened, and a dozen girls streamed out, Megan in the middle of them toting a huge red shopping bag stuffed with gifts. Finally, Pearl emerged from the café, shirt untucked, hair escaping the barrettes, cradling an Addy doll with a pink dress and straw hat. When she saw Andrea, her face lit up, and she ran smack into her, bumping her back a few steps.

"Mama, look!" She held up the doll. "Addy!"

"Where did this come from?" Andrea asked, figuring the store had lent it to her for the party so she wouldn't feel left out.

"Megan's mom gave it to me."

"Are you sure?" Pearl nodded, hugging the doll. "But you can't accept this. It's too big a gift." Did her mother expect Andrea to reimburse her, she wondered, feeling a wave of heat roll over her.

"She said I could keep it." Andrea felt Pearl's hot cheek, noticed the sweat on her brow.

"It's very nice of them to offer, but it's too much." She reached for the doll, but Pearl held it tight.

"Mama, it's mine," she said, her voice a croak. "She gave it to me."

"Let's go talk to Mrs. Berger and Megan." She took Pearl by the arm and walked over to Megan and her mother.

Nina looked up and said, "Pearl, don't you just love her?" Pearl nodded. Andrea offered to pay for the doll, but Nina said she wouldn't hear of it. "I hope that was okay," she said, laying her hand on Andrea's arm. "And I know she loves Addy. I just didn't want Pearl to feel left out. It was *so* special to have Pearl here. Right, Megan?" She nudged Megan, who smiled mechanically, then went back to passing out goody bags. "Bye, Pearl," said Nina. "Thanks so much for coming."

Andrea's face felt frozen with a smile she knew must look forced. They thanked Nina and Megan and Andrea steered Pearl out the door and onto the street.

As they stood at the bus stop, Andrea fought back her fury and embarrassment. She'd been ambushed. Nina had no right to spend so much money on Pearl. And giving the doll to Pearl without asking Andrea was inexcusable, as was assuming Pearl would only want the black doll. Pearl stood next to her, breathing heavily, snuffling. Andrea stroked her head, stuffed the book into her bag for later. Several buses passed but theirs wasn't one of them. Pearl's breathing grew more labored, and Andrea made the decision to splurge for a cab. She'd forgotten to ask Nina to return the inhaler and worried Pearl would need it before they reached home.

The cab driver was black with a Muslim name, and he'd hung one of those pine-tree fresheners that coated the air with thick, throat-tickling scent. Andrea cracked open the window, hoping the smell didn't irritate Pearl's lungs. She wrapped her arm around Pearl and pulled her close, asking, "So how was the party?"

"Good." Pearl swiped at her nose and fiddled with the buttons on Addy's pink striped dress.

"Tell me what you did."

"We ate...cupcakes and had...tea. Even the dolls...had plates and cups."

"Pearl, slow down and take your time. Okay? You can nod if you want."

She bobbed her head, mouth open, gulping in air. Andrea sat rubbing Pearl's hand, forcing herself to calm down, to let it go.

Back at their apartment, she gave Pearl a puff of a new inhaler.

She made a nest of comforters on the couch and tucked Pearl in along with her Addy doll, the hat and boots removed and sitting on the coffee table. When Pearl asked for the Japanese cat, Andrea placed it on the coffee table in front of her, setting the paw in motion like a metronome.

Andrea offered to read her new Molly book, and Pearl scooted up, her head leaning on Andrea, her mouth open, her breathing a rattle. When she finished the book, Andrea said she'd read anything else Pearl wanted. Of course, Pearl picked the same book she gave Megan.

"Did Megan like her book?" Andrea asked.

"Yeah. She got Nintendo games and clothes and DVDs."

"My, that's a lot of stuff, huh?"

"Yeah."

"Did that make you feel bad?"

"No."

"Pearl, it's okay to let me know if something made you feel bad."

"Mama, I don't…feel bad." She'd pulled the corner of the afghan over her mouth to hide the fact that she was sucking her thumb, a habit she'd largely given up, except when she was tired. She continued to wheeze between sucks, her breath liquid and uneven.

Andrea read about the boy, his grandfather, the afternoon they spent together, and the stories he told about his job with the railroad. Pearl stroked Andrea's hand, and Andrea kept her voice soft as she read the familiar words, hoping to find some solace, to dispel her own discomfort about the party. At first, Pearl's breaths came faster than the beat of the cat's paw until they grew slower. Eventually, Andrea was left listening to the tick, tick of the cat's paw as it waved to them, a sleeping girl and her mother.

CHAPTER 5
Winnetka, IL, 2002

Nancy and George Barton were driving up to Winnetka to Joanne's place for Thanksgiving dinner. That is, Nancy drove because of George's glaucoma, and he sat holding her pea and cheese casserole in his lap, even though Joanne had said they wouldn't need it this year. But that dish was her specialty, and her granddaughter, Blair, the vegetarian, couldn't eat most of the other dishes. Joanne would knock herself out on frou-frou dressing and fancy side dishes and more pies than an army could eat. Nancy had reminded Joanne that she and George couldn't eat rich food—his blood pressure, her cholesterol—and everyone except Joanne's family needed to watch their weight. Andrea's waist had thickened, and she should certainly keep a rein on Pearl's eating. That beautiful child had packed on the pounds. But no, Nancy couldn't mention that. Andrea stomped on her when she'd made the tiniest comment about Pearl taking a third brownie. Joanne, on the other hand, exercised every calorie off her body. Being so thin made her look older, not better. And what kind of example did that set for her fifteen-year-old daughter? The girl barely put enough in her stomach to survive. Blair was always leaving the table to go to the bathroom, and Nancy had asked if she was one of those purgers, but Joanne wouldn't hear a word of it. She just closed her eyes to problems. At seventeen, her son, Gary, didn't have to worry about his weight. Naturally lean, he took after his father. Mitchell was a puzzle—handsome, sure, and a good provider, but Nancy had never warmed up to him. If he made Joanne happy, then so be it. A good provider; you don't sneeze at that. At least Joanne still had choices, even if she didn't think so. She could go back to work or get her real estate license. Anything really. Nancy wished she herself had stuck it out all those years ago and become a doctor as she'd planned, but then she wouldn't have had Joanne and Andrea or her grandchildren. Or George, of course. Things happened for a reason.

Nancy didn't understand the fuss about Thanksgiving and wished Joanne wouldn't go to all that trouble. They hadn't done it up big when the girls were younger—strictly turkey and a few sides—not like when she was a girl and the whole Perillo clan would gather for a gut-busting meal: lasagna on top of turkey, and a pie from each aunt that had to be sampled or feelings were hurt. What a colossal waste of food. And there would sit Nancy, the only strawberry blond at the table, the obvious interloper, more guest than family. Even as a child, Thanksgiving made her sad--the shortened days, the dead leaves, the chilled air. Although her parents had claimed to know nothing about her birth mother, when they died, Nancy had found the adoption papers, learning that her natural mother was poor and had died in childbirth. Up until then, Nancy had thought that her natural mother didn't want her.

On top of those childhood Thanksgivings came that first one back home from Smith—her nausea, the effort to hide her growing stomach from her suspicious mother, the fear of disappointing her parents, of proving she came from bad blood. Add to that a do-over she didn't deserve and didn't want, leaving her with a corrosive secret she'd held inside all these years.

GEORGE STARED AHEAD, POUTING AT being forced to give up driving, but after he'd sideswiped a car, Nancy didn't trust him to be safe. "I see the car, goddammit!" he'd say despite his glaucoma-blurred vision. Grateful to the eye doctor for telling George it was just a matter of time before he caused a serious accident, Nancy had felt sad for him as he sat there, his chin raised, shaking his head and saying, "Well, I guess I have no choice, do I?" A surge of love for him, more like a deep kindness, a desire to protect him, the sweet man who loved her when she most needed someone, never knowing what he'd saved her from. It was now her turn to be that support.

"Is that new man coming with Andrea?" George asked.

"Mike? I'm sure he'll be there. Why?"

"Just wondering."

"Don't forget his name."

"I won't." He stared ahead as he reached into his pocket for a Hall's, fiddling with the wrapper. She hated the medicinal smell that lingered around him, but he insisted he needed them for his throat. All those years of smoking had caught up with him, leaving his lungs stiff and scarred. Luckily, she'd quit her smoking habit in time to escape any serious damage.

"Maybe Mike's the one," George said. "She seems pretty smitten."

"Has she stopped to think about how Pearl feels about him? You don't blithely bring a man home to a ten-year-old adopted child, who's insecure about where she comes from. What will she do if they break up?"

"I suspect they'll work that out."

"There you go, Mister Optimist, Mister Head-in-the-Clouds."

Nancy exited the Edens at Willow and drove past the athletic fields toward the enclave of McMansions along the golf course. Joanne and Mitchell had torn down a perfectly good house and designed a monstrosity—a fake chateau with turrets and round windows and a two-story foyer. God-awful. Nancy and George's vintage apartment in Hyde Park had plenty of room, but Joanne just had to live in a showplace. Nancy pulled into the circular driveway, ringed by arrangements of gourds and Indian corn, making their brief appearance between the Halloween pumpkins and the lighted Christmas lawn deer.

She stopped the car and hurried around to help George out, pretending she'd come to get the casserole, really making sure he was on good footing. He shuffled to the front door with her behind him, holding the foil-covered dish.

George opened the door and hoisted himself over the threshold. He never knocked. "Hello?" he croaked, clearing his throat like ripping Velcro.

"We're back here," Joanne called.

The smell of turkey and pumpkin pie filled the house. They crossed the foyer and walked down the long hall to the kitchen, which opened into a cavernous great room. Joanne stood over her stove, all six burners going at once. Mitchell sat in his recliner watching football on their enormous TV, a drink tipped toward his mouth. He didn't get up to greet them, didn't help his father-in-law to the other recliner. Unbelievable.

Nancy asked where she could put her dish.

"Mom," Joanne said, her eyes narrowing, her forehead flat and shiny. "I told you there'd be enough food. You shouldn't have gone to all that effort." With the inside of her wrist, she pushed back a strand of her fine, blond hair and leaned in for a kiss. Joanne stiffened as Nancy kissed her daughter's temple. Well, sorr-ee.

"It was no effort. I know you said you were set, but I couldn't resist." She stood for a moment before setting her Pyrex dish next to the china platters. Joanne was using Nancy's mother's Haviland. Because Nancy and George had eloped, her mother never offered her the china, and Nancy wasn't sure if was her bad behavior or the adoption that had made her unworthy of the family heirloom. Nancy gave the china to Joanne after clearing out her parents' home. Through the years, Nancy had acquired her own everyday china, more practical after all, replaced every few years as pieces broke. With her huge table and hutch, Joanne was the logical person to inherit the china. Andrea hadn't married yet and lived in a small apartment. What would she do with twelve place settings? It was gold-edge Haviland with a string of three-leaf clovers ringing each plate. Although not usually superstitious, Nancy wondered if things might have gone better if there'd been four leaves on the clovers. Her mother brought out the china for holidays and her horrible garden club meetings. Nancy was pressed into service, made to serve the ladies tea and sandwiches. She hated these women who put on airs of social prominence. More than once during these meetings Nancy had squelched the urge to over-pour hot tea into some biddy's lap. But Joanne didn't know any of that and loved the china. All's well that ends well.

"Now, what can I do? Put me to work."

"You can mash the potatoes and whip crème fraîche into them when they're done, but not yet. And you can put out the crudités for the men. There's a dip to go with."

"Where's Blair?"

"Mom, please."

"What do you mean? I just wondered where my grand-daughter was."

"In her room. She'll be down in a minute."

"Hasn't she been helping?"

"Mom, don't start in on me about Blair." As Joanne opened the oven to baste the turkey, Nancy could see the bones of her spine through her knit dress. "She has a paper to write. Please, just give me a break."

"I wish you hadn't gone to all this trouble."

"It's Thanksgiving, " she said, squirting turkey juice into the gravy, shutting the oven door, tossing the baster onto the granite counter.

"Where'd you get the turkey this year?"

"At Harrison's. Fresh. I brined it."

"Joanne, your father can't eat that much salt."

"Mom," she said, her tone brittle, "It's just one meal."

Nancy told herself to let it go. One day of indulgence wouldn't kill either of them. She looked at Mitchell, who still hadn't acknowledged their arrival, and wondered if she and George had interrupted an argument between him and Joanne.

Nancy peeled a corner of foil off her casserole to check the temperature. It needed reheating. "When are Andrea and Pearl and Mike getting here?"

"Who knows? I asked them to pick up rolls on their way. It shouldn't take that long. She said she'd come early to help out. " Joanne was such a control freak.

"There's time. And I can help. Don't worry. It'll all get done. We could have driven up together. All this way in two cars."

"All this way. It only takes half an hour." After Joanne checked off an item on the list posted on the refrigerator, she arched her back, grimacing. Nancy was tempted to give her a neck rub, something she'd liked as a girl, but wouldn't welcome now. "You make it sound as if it's a burden to come out here."

"I didn't mean that," said Nancy, feeling her face flush, sweat blooming on her scalp. She grabbed a catalogue and fanned herself. "Where do you think things are going with Andrea and Mike?"

"Going? I don't know." She said, leaning over to check the height of the flame. "I hope he feels comfortable with us."

"Well, I plan to make him feel welcome."

Joanne grabbed a whisk and started to stir the gravy furiously.

The doorbell rang and Joanne handed the whisk to Nancy. Joanne opened the door to Andrea, Pearl, and Mike. Nancy heard Joanne say, "That's not the kind I asked you to get."

"I tried three places and this was all they had," Andrea said, her voice pinched tight. Already pushing each other's buttons, those two. Joanne wanted these big dinners, but she knew that wasn't Andrea's style. But Andrea gave as good as she got.

The gravy bubbled. As Nancy dipped her pinkie in to taste it, two sturdy arms encircled her waist, bumping her up against the stove. Pearl. "Wait a minute. I have to put this down." She dropped the whisk, turned, and opened her arms. "Now, a proper hug." She pulled the soft, dark girl to her. "How are you, darling?"

"Good."

"You say either 'fine' or 'well'."

"Okay, fine, Gram." A big smile. Jack-o-lantern teeth. The awkward stage. There were serious braces in Pearl's future, but that smile melted Nancy's heart. What a dear child.

"What have you been up to?"

"School mostly." She wore jeans and a sweater that strained across her stomach. "Oh, I brought my scarf." Over her shoulder, she carried a nylon bag with knitting needles sticking out. "Can you help me with it?"

"Of course. Let me finish this and we can sit down and have a look." She stroked the top of Pearl's head, her wiry hair pulled tight by a hair band, then left to frizz in back. She and Andrea fought all the time about her hair and it showed. This was a fright wig. That sweet child under all that hair. "But first, go say hi to your grandfather." Pearl walked over to George and put her head on his shoulder. Did he even recognize her? He always seemed surprised to see he had a black grandchild. He gave her an awkward pat, and Pearl perched on the arm of his chair, then slipped off and sat down with something that looked like a comic book. Mitchell kept his eyes on the TV.

Andrea breezed into the kitchen, her face flushed, smiling. She gave Nancy a kiss, then took the man's arm and introduced him. Mike was white, about her age, not too tall, with graying hair and glasses. The start of a paunch, but not fat. A pleasant-looking man, more conventional than some of Andrea's previous boyfriends, who'd been exotic—African, Asian—as if she'd gone out of her way to avoid anyone like her father. "Pleased to meet you, Mrs. Barton," he said, offering his hand.

"It's Nancy, please." She took his hand in both of hers. "We don't stand on ceremony. Andrea, get Mike a drink." Andrea handed him a beer, took him by the hand and introduced him to George and Mitchell. Mike pulled up a chair next to George and sat down.

Joanne slipped buttery brown puffs off a cookie sheet onto a plate, then called Pearl over and handed her the plate, asking if she could pass the hors d'oeuvres to the men. Pearl reached for one herself. "Serve the others first." Pearl drew back her hand.

"Tell Grandpa they're hot inside and not to pop it whole into his mouth," Nancy reminded her.

"Really, Mom," Joanne said. "He's capable of eating without your supervision,"

"Well, he doesn't always pay attention."

"Can I help?" Mike asked, back in the kitchen. Nancy was impressed; no man she knew ever offered to help.

"Mike," Nancy asked, taking a sip of her wine. "Does your family live out of town?"

"My parents have both died. They used to live just north of here, actually. I have a brother in San Francisco."

"No children?"

"Mom!" said Andrea.

"That's okay," Mike continued, "No children. An ex-wife who moved to D.C. and a few cousins scattered about. We've largely dispersed."

"That's a shame. Well, you're certainly welcome here with us."

Nancy wanted to find out more about him, but Joanne interrupted them and sent Mike back to the men again. He walked over and sat down, leaning in to listen to George, who turned his head, nodding, pointing to the TV.

"Mom, really? The third degree?" said Andrea. "Did you expect he'd have no past? He's not a boy."

"I just wanted to get to know him. Touchy, touchy."

"No, you wanted to know if there were resentful children hanging around. No, just Pearl. And they get along fine."

"I won't say another word." She clicked an imaginary lock over her lips.

"You know what I mean."

Andrea pulled apart the store-bought rolls and put them on a cookie sheet. Nancy worried that she and Pearl ate mostly frozen dinners, although she did make a mean chili. Maybe Mike knew how to cook.

Andrea had tied on one of Joanne's tiny aprons, which cinched her loose tunic around the middle, revealing a slight bulge above her waist. Both of her daughters were middle-aged now, showing it in different ways. Where had the time gone? Seeing both her daughters together, Nancy thought about how different they were—one too thin, one settling into middle-aged spread. Joanne blond, Andrea brunette like her father in his youth. But mostly it was their personalities that had diverged over the years—Joanne, type A perfectionist, athletic, doing everything by the book. She married Mitchell, her college sweetheart, then worked for a few years before having Gary, and two years later, Blair, before moving to the suburbs. Everything according to plan. No room for messiness in that household. Andrea, on the other hand, could stand to be more driven, less soft-hearted. From an early age, she was the kind of child who cried whenever she saw a panhandler in the street or an ad on TV for rescue dogs. They got the dog, and, of course, she left it behind when she went to college. She was the bleeding heart of the family, all that do-good work, even though it barely paid anything. Finally, at nearly forty and without a man in the picture, she decided she finally wanted to be a mother. Soon after, Pearl appeared, though that turned out to be the best thing Andrea ever did, bringing Pearl into their lives. She loved Gary and Blair, but Pearl was her favorite. Such a dear child, so sweet and open. Andrea was doing a fine job raising her. Nancy was just sad that Pearl would be an only child.

Shouldn't Joanne and Andrea's shared blood and childhood make them closer? Nancy couldn't have raised them that differently. She'd always tried to give them equal amounts of her love and time, but they didn't look alike and never really got along. Joanne had always resented Andrea as if she should have been an only child. Andrea seemed to see what path Joanne took, taking pains to follow the other. What Nancy wouldn't have given for a real blood sister in her own life instead of cousins, who always made a point of letting her know she wasn't a real Perillo like they were.

"Mom? How's Dad doing?" Andrea asked in a whisper.

"Not here." "You're always talking about how he can never hear you anymore. How's his glaucoma?"

"Oh, you know. It's progressive. But that's not the real problem."

"No?"

"His hands have started shaking so much he can barely hold a fork. And of course, he takes it out on me."

Andrea didn't answer, which meant she disagreed. She never chose to see her father's failings.

"It's not easy, you know," Nancy said. "You don't live with him."

"Andrea," Joanne said, "I could use some help."

Nancy stood there empty-handed as Joanne and Andrea wove around each other, wielding spoons, checking pots, arranging platters. Every time Nancy approached a dish, Joanne nudged her aside to do it herself. Just who did she think had taught her how to cook?

She drifted into the great room and sat down next to Pearl, rubbing her back, but she kept her eyes on the men. Mike sat with George, asking him questions, drawing him out. George's back hunched and his hand trembled as he brought a drink to his mouth. When he spilled, Mike wiped it up without calling attention to the accident. What a nice man.

Andrea asked about Blair and Gary, and Joanne snapped at her. "Just asking," said Andrea, shrugging when Joanne's back was turned. Nancy wondered if either of them would make an appearance. Blair so skinny and Gary wound too tight. A perfect student, Eagle Scout, nothing about Gary wasn't straight-A, first place, honors this, accelerated that. Joanne and Mitchell accepted nothing less than excellence from their boy. So much pressure.

Joanne hoisted the turkey out of the oven with her sinewy arms and checked the temperature. Then she tented it with aluminum foil and slid dishes into the oven to warm up. Nancy wandered back into the kitchen and re-arranged the parsley garnish on a platter of carrots.

"Hey, Grandma," said Blair, swanning into the kitchen, baggy sweater, sleeves down over her hands. Nancy could see that under loose jeans, Blair's thighs were sticks. Her long sandy blond hair hung wet and dripping, her eyes were smudged with black liner, and she smelled of some thick, aggressive perfume. Blair leaned in for an air kiss, and Nancy thought she smelled cigarettes under the perfume. She gave Blair's bony back a squeeze, alarmed at how thin she felt.

"Blair, sweetie," she said, grabbing a plate of olives. "Eat something, please."

Blair's mouth twisted into a moue. "Not a big olive fan, sorry."

Before Nancy could suggest that she help out, Blair slunk into the great room, past Pearl, who said hi, her eyes following her cousin across the room. Blair answered in a sleepy, distracted voice, "Oh, hey, Pearl."

"Blair?" Pearl continued, holding up the book she was reading, "Do you like manga?"

Blair flopped into a chair, nearly disappearing into the cushions. "Kind of. Well, I used to."

"This one is really, really good. I could give it to you when I'm done."

"Thanks, but I have a lot to read for school right now." She studied the tips of her hair, a tiny ballet slipper balancing on the toes of her bobbing foot.

"I'll leave it here, and when you're free, you could read it."

"Sure, okay." She sat wrapped up in herself, arms folded, knees pulled up toward her chest, and if she were going to take a nap. Rude girl. Couldn't she give her little cousin the time of day?

"Blair, come help, will you?" Nancy asked.

"Mom, we have enough help," Joanne said. "Why don't you go sit for a while? I'll call you when we need you."

"You sure?" Joanne nodded impatiently, so Nancy tapped Pearl on the shoulder and motioned toward the living room. "Bring your knitting."

Nancy and Pearl settled on the huge sofa where no one ever sat in front of the piano that no one ever played. Pearl was chewing a sweet, nauseating wad of gum. "Now let me see what progress you've made on that scarf."

Pearl held up a foot and a half of ribbing with dropped stitches and added loops. "It's kind of messy."

"Hmm. You seem to have dropped a stitch back here." She inspected it, poking a finger through a hole halfway down. "See? Do you mind if I unravel it a few rows?"

"Gram, no. Can't you just fix it?"

"You see this hole?" Pearl nodded glumly. "If you don't fix it, it'll go all the way to the beginning. It's like a run in your stocking. You don't wear stockings yet, but you'll see what I mean."

"Okay," she said, uncertain.

"Other than that, you're doing a fine job." Not true, but it was important to encourage her. Nancy unraveled to the row with the dropped stitch, then picked up the rest of the stiches and started knitting again.

"Gram, don't do it all yourself. Let me."

"Just getting you started," she said, quickly finishing a row. "Now, there you go." Nancy handed the needles to Pearl, who clutched them in her fists. Pearl inserted one needle into the first stitch and wound yarn around it, slipping it onto the right needle. "You'll get the hang of it. It took me a while before I could do it easily." Pearl smacked her gum, and Nancy told her to close her mouth. "Do you want to look like a cow chewing its cud?"

As she watched Pearl struggle with the needles, Nancy remembered the crafts class she'd been forced to take at the home, which she'd hated at the time. But now she was glad she could teach Pearl this kind of handwork. Andrea didn't have the time or patience to teach her. Besides, she was all thumbs.

Nancy felt a twinge at the thought of the baby booties that had been her first completed project, fifty-eight years ago. Counting the stitches, starting over until she got the two little yellow booties just right, promising to give them to the adoption agency, but at the last minute, stashing them in her suitcase and taking them back home with her. She'd kept the booties hidden, never letting Joanne or Andrea wear them. Where was that child now, maybe a grandmother herself? At the time, Nancy had sworn she'd never pick up knitting needles again, but several years later, while pregnant with Joanne, on bed rest and bored to tears, she'd been glad to have some way to occupy her hands.

"That's it. Good job. You'll have that done before the really cold weather." She fingered the multicolored yarn she'd bought for Pearl, an inexpensive acrylic, the right material for her first project. With big needles and bulky yarn, the project would go fast and the uneven technique wouldn't show too much.

She stroked Pearl's back, and as she did, she pulled down the sweater that had worked its way up, showing a roll of bare skin. "So, how's school?"

Pearl said good, then corrected herself. Fine. Pearl focused on her knitting, her tongue out, breathing through her mouth. Nancy tore off a shred of paper and told Pearl to spit out her gum.

"That's better. Now, tell me. Do you like your teacher this year?"

"Teachers. We have specials. Art, P.E., science, music, drama."

"What's left for the main teacher?" All the money she and George had given to help pay for private school, not that they begrudged it, but she wondered if they spent enough time reading.

"Language arts, social studies, math. You know."

"What's your favorite subject?"

"I don't know. Art?"

"I thought you liked science."

"I do, but I also like art."

"You know I just love that drawing you did of the girl under the rainbow," Nancy said, tucking a strand of hair behind Pearl's ear. "It always makes me happy to look at it." She wanted to encourage Pearl. Andrea had no interest in the arts. She was holding the Third World on her shoulders.

Nancy asked Pearl if she liked Mike and if he spent much time at their place.

"Duh. He moved in." Pearl caught herself. "I mean, he didn't really. I made a mistake." She was covering up, poor child. Imagine being asked by her mother to lie like that.

"Don't worry, sweetie. I won't let on." Pearl said okay. Nancy wondered what this could mean for Pearl, having a man live with them. Did Andrea know him well enough for that step? What if Pearl became attached to him, then they broke up? What if she didn't like him and she felt replaced in Andrea's affections? Growing up adopted, Nancy had always felt she might at any moment be replaced by someone more suitable, more loveable, more like her parents. Pearl was guileless, a pure heart, and she hoped Pearl's spirit wouldn't be crushed by the world.

"Mom?" Joanne called from the kitchen, her voice tense. "I could use your help in here."

"Okay, coming," she said, patting Pearl's arm. Pearl stuffed her knitting into the bag and followed her.

"Andrea, can you pour the ice water please?" Joanne asked. That should really be Blair's job, but she clearly wasn't going to help, and Joanne wouldn't want Pearl plunking ice cubes into the Waterford by herself. Why use such fine glasses anyway with kids? Andrea filled a pitcher and showed Pearl how to place each cube into the goblet with tongs.

Joanne had drained the potatoes, and she handed Nancy the masher. She tossed in a generous portion of butter, alternating with dollops of crème fraîche, the steam fogging her glasses. Might as well go all the way and make them good and rich. Joanne was mashing sweet potatoes, stepping out of the way as Andrea put the rolls into the oven.

"Blair, go call Gary. Please."

"He'll be down."

"Do. It. Now."

Blair threw back her head and unfolded her legs, slapping her feet to the floor as she vaulted out of the chair and stomped past the kitchen to the bottom of the stairs, where she shouted, "Gary! Mom says to come now!" She returned to her spot in front of the TV.

"I could have done *that*," said Joanne.

Mike brought two empty beer bottles to the sink, saying that everything looked and smelled wonderful. Could he help? Joanne said he could carry dishes to the dining room and gave him instructions on where to put them. As he passed Andrea, she tilted her head toward him, beaming, and he gave her a kiss behind the ear. The dining room table was now completely laden with china serving dishes. Nancy noticed that her casserole had ended up on the sideboard with the water pitcher and extra rolls.

Gary showed up, even taller than the last time Nancy had seen him, handsome like Mitchell, with the same sharp profile, but so pale, barely needing to shave yet. And thin, but not like Blair, whom you could knock over with a sneeze. "Come on, boys," Nancy said, clapping her hands, then feeling silly. They weren't children. George turned and gave her a blank stare, as if he were trying to place her. His unfocused eyes, his mouth hanging open. Please, no. Not this. She wasn't sure how she'd cope with dementia on top of blindness. Mike walked over and took George's arm and led him to the dining room, chatting him up as if they were taking a walk in the park. She liked this guy. Mitchell hadn't moved, his eyes on the football game. "Mitchell?" No answer. Okay, be that way. Let Joanne deal with him.

"Where's Mitchell?" Joanne barked.

"In front of the tube," said Nancy. "I told him we were sitting down."

85

Joanne stormed into the great room, and Nancy could hear furious *sotto voce* back and forth. A minute later, Joanne appeared, pinch-lipped, followed by Mitchell, drink in hand, a smile plastered on his face. "Sorry about that," he said, pulling out a chair for Nancy to sit down, laying on the charm when he chose. "I wanted to wait until the end of the down."

Joanne had put Nancy next to Mike, with Andrea next to her father on one side, the grandchildren on the other, and she and Mitchell at each end of the long table.

Mitchell started to carve the turkey with his electric knife, making slow swipes along the breast. George, a steel-knife carver himself, shook his head in disgust. He sipped his drink, the ice cubes clinking from his trembling hand.

"We can pass the sides in the meantime," Joanne said, handing the chestnut dressing to Mike and the green beans to Blair, who took out three beans and arranged them side by side. Andrea served her father, mounding his plate. No one had bothered to get Nancy's pea casserole from the sideboard, and Nancy didn't want to be the one to fetch it, but clearly, she'd have to, so she stood, scooped up the dish, and plunked it down on the table next to Blair. "I brought a vegetable casserole just for you, Bear."

Blair stuck a spoon in and sniffed at it, her face scrunched up. "I can't eat this. It has dairy in it."

"Oh, for God's sake," she said, feeling her pulse flutter in her neck. "And why can't you eat cheese? No animal died to make it."

"I'm vegan now. No dairy."

"Well, what's left? Rabbit food? That's not enough to keep you alive."

Joanne explained that Blair was committed to a vegan lifestyle.

"She doesn't have to be rude about it."

"You kind of ambushed her with that dish, Mom."

"What are you talking about?"

"Here, I'll have some," Mike said, reaching for the dish and spooning some onto his plate. "Pearl? How about you?" He winked at her, and she took the dish and served herself, looking at Nancy hopefully. Nancy approved of the easy way he dealt with Pearl and how she clearly liked him.

Blair dipped her spoon into a brown oblong blob in front of her.

"What on earth is that?" Nancy asked.

"It's Tofurky."

"Want some gravy with that?" Gary asked, wielding the silver ladle.

"Shut up, Gary."

"What's Tofurky?" asked Pearl.

"It's tofu, duh," said Blair. "That's what vegans eat on Thanksgiving."

"Here, Pearl, have a taste," said Gary, and he forked off a glob and dropped it on her plate.

Pearl took a tiny bite, giving her mother a worried look. "It's okay." She reached for her water glass.

"So now you're a vagun," said Nancy.

"It's pronounced vee-gan, Gram, not vay-gun."

"Is there anything on this table besides that Tofurky you can actually eat?"

"There's salad and plain beans. Just no meat, no dairy."

"No food," said Gary. "She cuts her peas in half," and he leaned over his plate to mimic the delicate surgery.

"Stop it, both of you," said Mitchell. He yanked the cord from the wall and wrapped it around the knife, then whipped out his napkin to sit down.

"Okay," said Joanne. "Let's all go around and say what we're thankful for." Andrea motioned for Pearl to put down her fork.

"Mom," said Gary. "Not that. It's so lame."

"No, it's not. It's important," she said with a tight smile. "Maybe you aren't thankful for anything, but I am." She looked at Mitchell, who said nothing, but waved her on with a you're-going-to-go-it-anyway gesture.

She asked Mike, the newest guest, to start. He said he was glad to be included in such a great family, "the first Thanksgiving of many I hope to spend among you." He winked at Pearl, who ducked her head but smiled. Nancy saw Andrea smile, blushing. So maybe they would get married.

Joanne sat up straight, adjusting a pillow behind her back. "Okay, I'm thankful that you're all here, and that Dad is doing well. And I'm thankful that Gary has a good shot at M.I.T." She raised her glass, as if to toast. "In two weeks, we'll know." She gave him a big smile.

Nancy could hear him grind his teeth. "Mom, stop," he said under his breath.

"I can't help it if I'm proud of you," she said, laying her hand on his. He slipped it away and dropped his fork on his plate. He said he'd *be* thankful if everyone would stop tweaking out about college.

She turned to Blair, who said she wasn't thankful. "Blair, come on," Joanne said, her voice thin. "With all you have?"

But Blair folded her arms and passed to Pearl, who chimed in, "I'm thankful that the food is so good." Andrea smiled at her, and Pearl looked at Joanne, who gave her a brittle smile. Why was Joanne making everyone perform acts of gratitude as their food got cold?

Next was Mitchell, who took a sip of his drink, looking off in the distance as if thinking hard, then shook his head and said,

"I'll have to get back to you on that." Nancy wished Joanne would drop this game. It clearly wasn't working.

Although she hated this kind of forced sharing, Nancy said she was happy that family was together and that Mike could join them, hoping she wouldn't annoy Andrea by assuming he was a permanent fixture. Andrea tended to fire men abruptly from her life. Daniel, Jim. Maybe Mike would be different. "You've made a beautiful meal, Joanne. All this bounty. It could feed three families."

"Mom, you've already said there's too much food."

"That wasn't a criticism."

Joanne swallowed hard and took deep breaths. Nancy wasn't going to apologize for an innocent remark.

"Joanne, this food looks amazing," said Mike.

Andrea said that Joanne had made such a lovely table, and when she went on to mention the larger issues of world hunger and illness, George interrupted by rapping the table sharply with his knuckle. "Pass the gravy!" Blair let out a snort of laughter.

"Here, Grandpa!" Pearl said, shooting to her feet and grabbing the gravy boat. As she rounded the table, she tripped on the leg of Mitchell's chair, falling face first onto the rug as the gravy arced, and the china boat flew out of her hands, shattering against the wall.

"Dammit, Pearl!" shrieked Joanne, dashing to the kitchen. Pearl dragged herself up, rubbing her knee, her face and sweater splattered with gravy.

Andrea was on her feet, her arm around Pearl, asking if she'd hurt herself. Pearl shook her head, her lip quivering. Andrea crouched down and started picking up the broken pieces of china. Nancy called Pearl over and helped her off with her sweater, using her napkin to wipe Pearl's face and hands. "It was an accident, Pearl. Don't cry, sweetie."

Joanne returned with a roll of paper towels. She ripped off long swatches and started patting the rug furiously. George was the only one eating, hunched over his plate, chewing, his jaw clicking. Joanne went back to the kitchen and returned with a bowl of water and a sponge, sighing, muttering to herself.

"Joanne," Andrea said, "It was an accident."

"Yeah, well, you've never cared about nice things."

"Excuse me?"

"How is she going to learn the value of things?" She held up a broken shard. "I've had this china for over twenty years. It's been in the family for, what, seventy-five, eighty years? And this is the first broken piece. What do you think that means?"

"I don't know," said Andrea. "What does it mean?"

"Mom, just buy a new one," said Blair.

"I can't. The pattern is discontinued. It's not that easy, Blair. But you wouldn't know that." She returned to her seat and tossed the piece onto her plate. "You're spoiled, you know."

Mitchell stood up and brushed off his pants, dropped some ice into his glass before leaving the room.

"Joanne," Andrea said, patting down Pearl's ruffled hair. "Pearl didn't know it was that special. And she didn't mean to break it." Pearl wept, biting her finger, saying sorry over and over. "And why are we using this china if it's so fragile and irreplaceable?"

"She treats our home like a playground."

"That's ridiculous."

Pearl's breaths were headed toward wheezes. Would she have an asthma attack? Nancy rubbed her shoulders and told her to breathe slowly.

Joanne continued, "And besides---"

"Stop it!" yelled Nancy, hearing her voice tremble. "Stop it, stop it, stop it!" Everyone looked at her, surprised. "See what you're doing to this child?" Pearl was shaking, her breath loud and rattling.

"But this is irreplaceable, Mom. It's from your family. It's tradition."

"Joanne, it's a thing. Pearl is a person."

"Mom, don't you see?"

"Tradition means nothing to me. I don't give a fig about some old dish. It means nothing," she said, slapping her hand on the table. "Imagine caring more about a dish than your niece. I'm ashamed of you." Her ears were ringing, her pulse pounding in her throat.

Joanne crumpled, her napkin held up to her face, her shoulders shaking. Blair pushed back her chair and said she needed to go to the bathroom. Gary sat back with his eyes closed, his jaw clenched before he too left the table and went upstairs. Mike said he'd take Pearl into the other room and Andrea stayed at the table. Nancy stood up and put her arm around Joanne's bony back, giving her a hug. "Come on, Joanne. We all said things we shouldn't have. Let's not let this ruin our day."

"The day is ruined. The meal is cold." Her shoulders felt like breakable twigs. "I'm sorry. I wanted it to go so well. Sorry to everyone." Elbows on the table, she sobbed into her hands.

Nancy started to rub circles on Joanne's narrow back. "You always make things so hard for yourself. It's only a thing."

"A thing. That's right. Only a thing." Mitchell had raised the volume on the TV and they could hear the sportscasters. "I didn't mean to overreact. I feel awful."

Andrea took one of Joanne's hands and squeezed it. "You're exhausted. Just take it easy. I'll clean up."

"But we have to eat. I'll be fine. Just go ahead and eat. Please.

Call everyone back. I'll be fine." She wiped her eyes, her breath catching in her throat. "Please don't let it go to waste." She hadn't eaten a bite yet. "Pearl, please. I'm so sorry. Come back to the table." Nancy caught Andrea's eye and nodded. Andrea called Mike and Pearl in from the other room and they returned, Pearl looking red-eyed with a stuffy nose. Mike sat and took a sip of his wine. Through it all, George had continued to eat, stabbing at the food and forking it into his mouth, his head a few inches from the plate. Pearl sat at her place, wheezing and chewing, her mouth open, shoveling in food as if every bite could make her a good girl again in Joanne's eyes. Across the table, Nancy could see Blair's plate, which held two mangled beans and a slab of Tofurky with an X smeared through the middle. Nancy had no appetite, but she swallowed dry pieces of turkey through a tight throat, rubbing Joanne's hand, wishing she could rewind, but how far back should she go? A few minutes? A day? Years? And do things over again.

CHAPTER 6
Chicago, 2004

Pearl sat up front in her mom's car while Willa and Jessica huddled in the back, whispering. She pressed her cheek against the cool window, looking out at the mist over Lake Michigan. Today was the seventh grade's community service morning, and they were going to spend it at Breadbasket, where her mom worked. Pearl had wanted to work in an Uptown soup kitchen near their apartment, but her advisor, Ms. Tiller, had said no, of course she'd go to Breadbasket because her mom had volunteered to lead a group. Pearl knew her way around; she could show the others the ropes.

When Pearl heard that Willa had been put into her group, she was excited, but then Jessica Baird pushed her way in, ruining everything. Jessica always made such a big deal about her summer house and her clothes, and everyone liked her. Pearl didn't know why; Jessica wasn't all that great. Her hair was good—long and thick--and she had boobs, but so did Pearl, although her hair sucked. But even Willa had started sitting at Jessica's lunch table instead of with Pearl. Why did Jessica have to be in their group today? So unfair. Willa had been Pearl's best friend since kindergarten, but with new sections this year, they'd been separated, and so they hardly saw each other during the day anymore. Without Willa, Pearl hated seventh grade.

"So, Willa, how do you like your teachers this year?" her mom asked, looking in the rearview mirror, a dorky smile pasted on her face. Don't push it, Mom.

"Mr. Martin's cool, but our math teacher, Mrs. Cutter, is really hard." Pearl could smell Willa's gum and wondered how her own breath smelled.

"Do you have them, Pearl?" her mother asked in the same chirpy voice she got when she was trying too hard.

"No, Mom, I told you I have Mrs. Riley," Pearl said, her face burning. The slow math section. Pearl hated math, couldn't do it, despite all the help she got from Mike. And even though she was good at English, the math class meant she had to be in the lame English and Social Studies sections, so she spent the whole day with dumb kids like Brendan Satz, who used to make fun of her in lower school. Gram told Pearl to ignore him. "Stupid *and* mean? Not a good combination." Pearl missed Willa and worried they wouldn't be best friends anymore if they weren't together. Something about Willa seemed different. She'd gone to camp all summer and had come back taller and thinner. Today, she wore low-rider jeans and a plush hoodie with Uggs. Her long, red hair hung loose instead of pulled back, and she flipped it behind her ears when she laughed. Pearl envied Willa's long, silky hair and hated her own, which was kinky and stiff.

Her mother reached over and touched Pearl's arm, nodding at her to join in the conversation. If Jessica hadn't come along, Pearl would be in the backseat with Willa. Pearl hugged herself, closing her eyes, hoping for a quick nap. This morning, her good jeans were still in the dirty clothes hamper, and so she'd had to put on a pair that pinched her waist and made the skin itch, especially since it was the first day of her period when she always felt gross and fat. And she hadn't had time to do anything with her hair except pull it back with an elastic. She wanted to have her hair relaxed so she could wear it down, but her mother said the chemicals were too harsh. She was all about natural. As if. Her own hair was dyed to hide the gray.

Pearl remembered the first time Willa came over to their apartment in kindergarten. As they pulled up out front of the building, Pearl said, "We live on the third floor, and there're a lot of steps."

"Oh, that's okay," Willa said, "We have three floors at home." Later, Pearl found out that Willa's family owned an entire house by themselves, and they had a housekeeper who made snacks, whatever they wanted, and she cleaned up after them. In Willa's room, there were mountains of toys, a TV with video games, and her own movies. Willa also had a big bed with a top over it and pink blankets. Compared to Willa's house, there was nothing to do at Pearl's apartment. The next time Willa came over, Pearl apologized that there wasn't a Nintendo or a TV in her room. Her mother showed up with lame snacks and milk, which she made them eat at the kitchen table. She brought out the old box of Playdoh and paper and markers like they were in pre-school. Mostly, they played at Willa's house.

They'd build pillow forts in Willa's room and sit inside, where it was cozy and warm and they made Cootie Catchers to tell their fortunes. Willa was good at things like Origami, and she added new fortunes with each new catcher. Usually, the fortunes were things like: You will be rich one day or You will get a big surprise or Be careful not to fall down today. One time, Pearl picked her color—blue--and her number—6— and Willa opened and closed the catcher B-L-U-E and then 1-2-3-4-5-6. When Pearl lifted the flap, the fortune said, You will meet an interesting stranger. "Ooh," Willa said, smiling. "I wonder who it is." That gave Pearl the shivers, because she'd just been thinking about her birth mother and wondered if she ever thought about Pearl.

"Promise you won't tell anyone?" Willa did. Pearl told her that she had another mother who'd left Pearl at a church when she was a baby. "I don't know. Maybe she just forgot me for a moment. But the police took me, and she couldn't find me."

"Maybe your mother is looking for you," said Willa. "Maybe she's been looking for you since you were a baby." Was that true?

"I don't know. I don't think about it much." But she did, all the time, even though it made her feel bad for her adoptive mom, who'd really wanted a child but she wasn't married, so she couldn't have one. "Please don't tell anyone about the church. I'm not supposed to talk about it." Willa promised.

IF PEARL DIDN'T GO OVER to Willa's, she spent her after-school time at Breadbasket in the playroom with the children whose parents were taking E.S.L. classes. She'd play with the same broken puzzles or Legos, trying to avoid the kids who coughed and had snotty noses and who yanked toys out of her hands, shrieking in their weird languages. By the time Pearl got too old for daycare and play dates, most of the girls in her class were taking after-school lessons—dance, guitar, karate—so they all hung out together. Pearl took swimming lessons for a while at the Lincoln-Belmont Y, but the locker room totally froze, and the teacher was mean, so she quit. Pearl would come home after school and watch TV until her mother and Mike returned from work. She liked having the place to herself because she could make herself a snack like ice cream or peanut butter toast and watch shows like *Maury* or *Rikki Lake* without her mother telling her to turn it off and read a book or something.

When her mother pulled into a parking spot on Ravenswood between the train tracks and Breadbasket's building, she was talking non-stop. "You're going to be sorting old clothes into categories to be distributed to immigrants, people on public aid, the homeless. The clothes come in so fast, we really need some organization before we can distribute them." Mom, so boring. Be quiet.

Jessica and Willa poured out of the car and linked their arms. A Metra train screeched past on the platform above them, carrying commuters downtown. Jessica waved, then so did Willa.

They took the old, stinky elevator to the third floor. Pearl noticed that Jessica held her hand over her nose. As they stepped off the elevator, Tanisha greeted them. "Hiya, Pearl. Hey, girls! You're here for the morning, right?" She held out her bowl of yucky ribbon candy. Pearl took one, just to be nice, but the others turned it down. Pearl stashed her piece in her hoodie pocket.

"Until noon," said her mother. Two black men in dirty clothes sat slumped in chairs near Tanisha's desk, arms crossed over their chests. One was snoring. The other started coughing in gross, sticky hacks. They both reeked of cigarettes and sour sweat. Jessica focused on the screen of her phone, while Willa looked around, not noticing that one of the men was staring at her as she pulled her hair from inside her jacket, fanning it out, letting it swish back and forth, before popping a new piece of gum into her mouth. Ever since her braces came off, she kept running her tongue over her teeth. Pearl couldn't wait to get her own braces off. Food always gucked up the braces, and she hated them.

Tanisha told them to head back to the room. It was all waiting for them. When she smiled, her gums showed above her top teeth.

"Come this way, girls," her mother said. Jessica grabbed Willa's arm and pushed ahead of Pearl, who followed behind them down the narrow, dark hall past stapled announcements for public aid and job training. Pearl noticed that Jessica nudged Willa, pointing to a sign about bedbugs, laughing. Willa shuddered and laughed too. "E.S.L. classes are on the left, nursery up ahead, offices to your right. Kind of tight quarters, but we manage," her mother said, looking over her shoulder and smiling. Who cares? thought Pearl, wishing her mother would stop acting like this was a place to be proud of.

Dale, her mother's annoying co-worker, a tall skinny guy with a wispy gray beard and a ring of frizzy hair, stuck his head out into the hall. "Hey, Pearl. Playin' hooky?"

"No, community service," Pearl mumbled, wishing he'd disappear.

"Court ordered? Ha, ha." He held a SpongeBob mug and wore a short-sleeved shirt with flood pants and gym shoes. What a weirdo.

"No, it's for school."

"Dale," said her mother, "Pearl and her friends are going to sort clothes for rummage." Right: friends. Did she honestly think Jessica would be Pearl's friend? Get a clue, Mom.

"Good. We need to move that merchandise. Keep your eyes out for the latest styles, right, girls? I wear a 40 long." He posed with one hand behind his head, grinning like an idiot. "What do you think, huh?"

Pearl groaned. The other girls looked at each other and laughed weakly. Pearl had cramps and wished she'd stayed home today. Even school would have been better than this.

Her mother unlocked a door at the end of the hall and showed them into a dark room with windows near the ceiling. The fluorescent lights flicked on, off, and on again. Folding tables flanked the walls and in the corner, garbage bags and cardboard boxes spilled over each other. The dust and mold settled in Pearl's lungs, and she felt her chest tighten as she wheezed. When her mother asked if Pearl had remembered her inhaler, Pearl shot her a shut-up look, and her mother shrugged.

She told them to open each bag and separate the clothes by size and category, putting them in neat piles. Dirty clothes should go in the hamper, anything with bugs in the trash.

"Bugs?" said Jessica. "Sick." And she turned to Willa for a hug. Pearl's face burned as her mother told them to throw out any underwear. Gross. Jessica asked how long they had to do this and she said until noon, but they could take a snack break in an hour. Snacks, how babyish. But then Jessica said she wasn't hungry because she'd just had breakfast, and Pearl's mother looked sad, which was the worst of all because it made Pearl feel like she had to make it better for her mother.

"Just ask Pearl in case you have questions or need anything," she said, laying her hand on Pearl's shoulder. "She knows her way around." Pearl shrugged off her mother's hand. "Okay," she said with a tight smile and hoisted her big bag onto her shoulder. "We really appreciate this, girls. See you later." She waved on her way out the door. Even though her mother was annoying, Pearl had to feel bad for her.

Willa took a pair of latex gloves and stretched one over her hand, snapping it. She sniffed and made a face. Jessica stood staring at her phone, her thumbs flying over the keys. "I'm not going to wear them," said Jessica. "I'm allergic to latex."

"Ooh, how do you know that?" Willa asked and laughed.

Pearl didn't know why that was funny, but she laughed too. "Yeah, latex is gross, right?" Jessica looked right at her but didn't laugh. Pearl stopped, wishing she could swallow what she'd said. She headed over to a cardboard box and folded back the flaps. A whiff of mildew rose into her nose, making it stuff up, and her head started to ache. Reaching inside the box, she pulled out a hoodie with a frayed bottom edge, a stained man's dress shirt, two tee-shirts with brown under the arms, a pair of leather shoes that curled up like clown shoes with clods of dirt on the soles. Gross. Then she found a pair of dingy tighty whities. Tears sprang to her eyes as she picked up the underpants and threw them into the trash bin. Pulling her inhaler out of her backpack, she turned away and took a puff.

In another box, Pearl found a candy-striped mini-dress in size XS. "Hey, Willa. You'd look good in this, huh?"

Willa stared at it, frowning, and Pearl wished she hadn't said that.

"It's probably dirty," said Jessica. "You don't know where it's been."

"Hello?" said Willa. "There's this stuff called detergent?"

"I don't do laundry. That's our housekeeper's job. Except she screws it up all the time. My mother almost fired her because she washed a cashmere sweater."

"Can you wear it now?" asked Willa.

"My dog could wear it."

Pearl snorted a laugh. Jessica shook her head and continued. "She threw it out. It was ruined."

Willa sniffed the dress, scrunched up her face and tossed it into the bin. Pearl felt a twinge in her stomach.

Jessica reached into a box and pulled out a pair of baggy jeans with a huge waist. "Hey, Pearl. What size do you wear?"

Pearl's eyes blurred. She lowered her head and took a couple of tight breaths.

"Stop it," said Willa, punching Jessica's arm, but laughing. "That's mean."

"Just kidding," said Jessica. "God."

Pearl felt a wedgie work its way into her crack, and she tried to ignore it until the girls weren't looking, then she tugged at the seat of her pants. This pair of jeans always did that. She wanted the kind that were custom fit, but her mother said they were too expensive, so she bought Pearl crappy ones from Target.

"Hey, Pearl," Jessica said as she was texting again. "You're adopted, right?"

"Well, duh," said Willa. "You know her mom."

"Do you know your real mother?"

"My birth mother?" She felt her head bead with sweat, and she grabbed a tissue to blow her nose. "No." Her chest felt tight, but it was too soon to use her inhaler again.

"Hey, Ms. Barton *is* her mother," said Willa.

"You know what I mean," said Jessica. "Aren't you curious about her?"

"Not really." She concentrated on taking slow, shallow breaths, so she wouldn't wheeze.

"Were you born in Africa?"

"No, in Chicago." She kept her head down, busying herself with sorting. She really hoped Willa wouldn't tell Jessica about how she'd been left in the church. Please don't.

"Did you ever, you know, want to meet your real mother?" asked Jessica. "What would you do if she got in touch with you? Would you be all mad?" she asked, excited. "What if she wanted you back?"

101

"I don't know. Nothing I guess." She felt hot and wished the windows would open. When she took a deep breath, all she could taste was nasty dust.

"Maybe Pearl doesn't want to talk about it," said Willa, and Jessica gave Pearl the kind of look you give to a sick person.

"I just..don't think about...it much," Pearl said. She wanted to sit down and get her breath, to stop talking about it. Every day, when she passed black women in the street, particularly near the church where she was found, she wondered, could this be her mother? She always wondered if the woman was thinking the same thing: Is this my daughter? I've been looking for twelve years.

"Your new mom is nice," said Jessica.

"She's not...my *new*...mom."

"You know what I mean," said Jessica and she sat back on the table, crossing her legs Indian style. Pearl worked for a few more minutes. Willa threw out everything, and Jessica had pretty much stopped working altogether. She and Willa were whispering and laughing. Pearl folded several pairs of men's pants and laid them in a pile.

"So what does your mother do here?" asked Jessica.

"She works with refugees," Pearl said as she kept her head down and sorted.

"Isn't that depressing? All those people without homes."

"No, she likes it, I guess."

"I couldn't do it. Be a refugee. I'd just want to die."

"But you wouldn't know any better," said Willa. "You'd just be glad to leave."

"Our housekeeper is from Guatemala," said Jessica.

"Is she a refugee?" asked Willa.

"Duh. Just because she came from another country doesn't mean she's a refugee. She might be illegal though. We pay her in cash."

Pearl told them that the refugees usually came from countries where there were wars, so they had to leave. But they weren't illegal; they had Green Cards and everything. Pearl saw Jessica roll her eyes at Willa, so she shut up, her face burning.

As she pawed through piles of clothes, she wondered what it felt like for refugees to be given clothes that were second hand, thrown away by someone else. Africans liked colorful clothes, but these were muddy-brown and stained. What must they think of Americans to see these dirty rags? Did they ever wish they hadn't left their homes?

Jessica and Willa started talking about this boy, Josh, who they thought was cute and who maybe liked Jessica. Willa kept trying to convince Jessica that he did, and Jessica pretended like she didn't already know that. Jessica said Josh was doing his community service at a nursing home with Ethan Miller.

"Text him!" said Willa. They went back and forth about whether she should text him. As she was texting Josh, Willa let out a scream and jumped back, fluttering her hands. The bag she was working on tipped over, spilling its contents onto the floor. "I think I saw a bug."

"Ick," said Jessica.

"I can't do this." Her eyes squeezed shut, and she wrung her hands.

Pearl sort of liked Ethan Kaplan, a boy in her grade, but she'd never tell anyone. What if they said he didn't like her, that she was a weirdo?

Pearl gathered up some baby clothes and tossed them into a pile. Willa had ripped off her gloves and was squeezing sanitizing gel on her hands. Jessica sat texting. Willa offered Jessica a squirt of gel, and she put down the phone long enough to rub in a blob, then she picked up her phone again.

Pearl's hands were sweating in the gloves and she peeled one off and wiped her hand on her pants.

Jessica finished her text and she started complaining to Willa about her parents, how they always used her to get back at the other. "I wish my parents weren't divorced."

"I wish my parents would get divorced," said Willa.

"No, you don't," said Jessica. "Well, sometimes, it's okay. When my mother got remarried, I started spending more time at my father's house. My father is a lot easier than my mom. He lets me do whatever I want, and he gives me money when I ask for it."

"He does not," said Willa.

"Does so. You're not there. For my birthday—" The phone beeped and they both jumped to read her text.

Pearl wondered whether she looked at all like her birth mother. She spent a lot of time staring in the mirror to see what her face really looked like—her eyes, her nose, her mouth. She hated her cheeks—too chipmunky. Her eyes were okay. She wanted to wear lip gloss and mascara like some other girls in her class, but her mother, who never wore any makeup herself, wouldn't let her yet. Not until she was fifteen. Was her birth mother pretty? Maybe when Pearl got older, her face would be thinner, and her cheekbones would look good. Like Halle Berry or Janet Jackson. They were pretty.

She could never figure out a good reason why her birth mother would leave her like that, a reason that didn't make her either selfish or a crack addict. Maybe she was young and poor, but even still, why hadn't she tried harder to keep her like a lot of poor women did? Did she change her mind and go back to the church to find her, but Pearl was gone, and she was afraid to go to the police because they'd arrest her or something? Had she been looking for Pearl all this time? Some adopted kids did searches when they were eighteen, but she couldn't even do that. It felt like she came from nowhere.

At ten, her mother brought in her dumb snacks: trail mix and juice. Jessica drank Red Bull and coffee. Maybe Willa did too; Pearl didn't know any more what Willa liked. They were polite enough to her mother, but it was the kind of polite you are when you think someone is a loser and you pity her.

After her mother left, Jessica started bragging about what she could get her parents to do, particularly if it pissed the other one off. She said that when she did something wrong, she'd cry if it was her father and be really, really sorry if it was her mother, especially if she called her Mommy. Willa said that she and her father got along okay, but she and her mother just screamed a lot.

Pearl fished her iPod out of her backpack and stuck the buds into her ears. Lately, she'd started listening to this rapper, Twista. She picked the song, "Pimp On," and went back to sorting. An hour and a half to go. Music would help the time go faster.

"Pimp onnn, pimp on, pimp, pimp on!" Pearl bobbed her head and folded to the beat. "You a ho need a pimp, I'm the one you supposed to call...The rougher I treat her she love a nigga even mo.'" She felt a hand on her shoulder. It was Willa. Pearl took out her ear buds.

"Could you keep it down, please?"

"Oh, sorry," she said, embarrassed that she'd been singing out loud.

"What are you listening to anyway?" asked Jessica, sitting on the table as she drew on the sole of her shoe with a pen.

"Twista," she said, her ears ringing.

"Do you even know what you're saying?" Jessica asked, then she hopped off the table and started to bob up and down, an angry look on her face, as she chanted, "Pimp, pimp, ho, ho, skank, skank," pumping her fists. Willa joined her, "Pimp ho! Pimp ho!" And they wiggled their butts, stomping their feet, then laughed, falling over each other. "And you're not supposed to use the N-word. Even if you're singing along. Don't you know that?"

Pearl switched off her iPod, her ears buzzing, sweat rolling down her back, as she tried to steady her breath, feeling her eyes fill with tears. "I didn't know you could hear me."

"Come on, Pearl," said Willa. "We were just kidding. It just sounded funny, the swears with no music."

"That's okay," Pearl said, feeling her eyes fill with tears as she turned and grabbed another bag of clothes. "I'm sorry I was so loud." Her voice came out croaky.

"You can listen. But don't sing," said Willa.

Pearl put the ear buds back, but didn't turn on the music. She pretended to listen, even bobbed her head, but instead, she listened to the girls in case they talked about her. Instead, they talked about where their families were planning to go for Christmas vacation. Jessica's family always went to Aspen, but Willa said she and her father and brother would probably just go to her grandparents' house in Michigan, but she hated it. So boring. Pearl looked at the clock. Ten-thirty-three.

Pearl wanted to go to Europe, maybe Rome, maybe Paris, some place older than Chicago, where there were beautiful buildings and art and good food. Maybe Switzerland or Spain. Her mother kept talking about them going to Africa someday, but everyone Pearl knew from Africa had wanted to leave. Why would she go there?

Her mother talked all the time about Africa and Nelson Mandela and about other black heroes in American history that she wanted Pearl to admire. People like Martin Luther King and Rosa Parks, and she wanted Pearl to read books like *The Color Purple* and *A Raisin in the Sun*. And always do what Oprah says. But those books were boring, and no one her age watched Oprah. Why would she want to be like that? Pearl was interested in things her mother didn't know anything about—hip hop and gangsta rap—regular black stuff. Maybe she wasn't Rosa Parks or Sojourner Truth. Maybe she was just a girl.

Pearl looked up to see Jessica putting on her jacket. She took out her ear buds.

"Hey, Pearl," she was smiling and she said Pearl's name like a purr. "Do you think your mom would sign our time sheets? We've done a lot."

"I don't know." Mounds of clothes lay all over the floor in a tangle. Her mother wouldn't like the mess. She was always bugging Pearl to clean her room.

"Will you ask her?"

"No, I can't. I have to finish here."

"Listen," said Jessica. "I've got to get a Red Bull. I'm falling asleep." She yawned.

"I need to stay here."

"Well, I'm going. Don't you tell her."

"I won't."

"Pearl," Willa said, gathering up her backpack. "Take a break, Come with us." She was acting like the old Willa. Finally.

"I'll work better if I'm not falling asleep," said Jessica. "I need some caffeine."

"We'll just be a couple of minutes," said Willa, smiling at her.

"We'll run to the 7 Eleven and be right back. Your mom won't mind." Willa touched her arm. "Come with us, Pearl. Please?"

Pearl looked at the mess and felt a flutter in her stomach. "Okay, but we can't be gone long."

Jessica and Willa headed for the door as Pearl grabbed her hoodie, following them. "Wait until no one's out there," Pearl said when Jessica opened the door.

They poked their heads out into the hall and saw a black couple leading two small children toward daycare. The woman's jacket was unzipped, a tee-shirt down over her pregnant belly. The man wore a ripped winter jacket and pink stretch gloves. Their two children, a girl and a boy, fought over a plastic bag, grabbing it back and forth. The boy squalled and the mother took the girl's hand and slapped it, yelling in their language. The boy snatched the bag and stuck his hand inside.

After the family entered the daycare room, Pearl ducked into the hallway and scooted toward the elevator. The girls followed. As they passed her mother's office, Pearl stole a glance and saw her hunched over some papers lit by a small desk light.

In the elevator, Jessica was texting again, her hair spilling forward, her thumbs flying over the buttons. Pearl wanted a cell phone, but her mother said not until she was thirteen. So unfair. How was she supposed to get friends if she didn't have a phone?

"Josh says the nursing home really smells bad."

Willa said they couldn't help it. Jessica pointed out that they could at least try to keep it cleaner, but Willa said that poor places couldn't even do that.

Out front, a group of men stood smoking in a stinky circle. One of them, a red-faced man with dirty gray hair, said, "Hey, where're you girls going? Can we come too?"

Jessica made a face. "Eew, no!" Willa and Pearl also shouted "No!" and pushed past them onto Montrose, laughing.

As Jessica and Willa ran ahead, Pearl followed, her chest tightening. She stopped and took a puff from her inhaler. Outside the 7 Eleven, Jessica and Willa stopped and put their heads together. Pearl jogged a few steps, then, her lungs aching, slowed to a walk. As she got close, they looked up from their huddle and waved for her to join them. For the last few yards, she took long strides, forcing herself to breathe deeply.

"Hey, Pearl," said Jessica, "I thought I had enough money, but I don't. Can you lend me some?"

"I...don't...have much...either." Her allowance covered the bus to school and back with a tiny amount left over.

"I really need some caffeine," Jessica said. "How stupid of me!" She scuffed the toe of her shoe back and forth in a pile of leaves. Then, looking up at Pearl, she smiled. "I dare you to take one and put it in your hoodie."

"What?" She asked, her head pounding.

"Just one Red Bull. We can share it."

Her lungs were stinging, her throat scratchy. "I can't...do that."

"Come on. It's not that big a deal. They plan for that when they price them. That's why everything's so expensive."

Pearl shrugged.

"Come on, Pearl," Jessica said. "Don't tell me you've never taken anything from a store before."

"No."

"Never? Oh, Pearl. You're such a good girl. Good girl, good little Pearl, never did anything wrong."

"Yes, I have."

"Like what?"

"Things." She remembered playing with a crystal swan from her mother's dresser and, after it broke, throwing it in the trash. Once she took a few dollars from her mother's purse. She often sneaked food late at night, and her mother usually blamed Mike for cheating on his diet. She lied to her mother all the time about her grades and where she went on her way home from school. She felt bad, but she couldn't help it.

Keeping secrets from her mother. It made Pearl feel bad, but there were things she couldn't tell her mother. For instance, the time she got lost at Marshall Field's. Every year, she and her grandmother went downtown to look at the Christmas windows and would eat lunch at the Walnut Room next to the huge Christmas tree. Blair used to go with them, but then she got too old and didn't like it anymore.

Pearl's mother was never invited. "It's Pearl and Gram time," she said. One year, when Pearl was eight, they were standing on the escalator, but two women stepped between her and Gram. When she reached the next floor, she couldn't find her grandmother anywhere. Pearl froze for a moment before approaching a saleswoman to say she was lost. The woman asked what her mother looked like. "She's my grandmother, but she and I don't look alike."

"Well, I suspect not, since you're a girl, and she's a lot older."

The woman told Pearl to stand by the counter while she called the store detective. Pearl pressed her nose against the glass counter and counted the gloves to keep herself from crying. When she heard Gram call her name, she ran over to her, only then starting to cry. The woman looked surprised to see Gram. That kind of thing happened all the time. Pearl was used to it.

"I was so worried," Gram said, her voice shaky and her face

red. "You must never wander off like that." Pearl couldn't tell if she was more worried or angry. "I have to catch my breath." She wheezed a bit, and Pearl wondered if Gram had asthma. "You scared me to death." And she hugged Pearl. "Let's go eat."

At lunch, Gram ordered the meatloaf and Pearl got what she always did, the chicken pot pie. And Gram let her order a chocolate soda. "Special occasion. And you don't need to tell your mother about our getting separated, okay?" Pearl nodded. "It's our secret. Can you do that?"

Pearl said she could, but her stomach felt funny agreeing to that. Gram said she didn't want to worry Pearl's mother, so it was best to keep it between them.

Since they had a secret, Pearl nearly confessed that she'd lost the pearl necklace her grandmother had bought for her when she was a baby. Even though she wasn't supposed to, she'd worn it out to play and the clasp had broken. Her mother still didn't know, and Pearl was dreading telling her, feeling awful when her grandmother gave her a new pearl the following year for her birthday. But she knew her grandmother would be sad to learn her gift had been lost. So she said nothing.

"Hey, Pearl, just do this for me, please?" Jessica asked. "He'd never have the nerve to accuse you of stealing."

"Why not?"

Jessica rolled her eyes. "He's just not going to accuse *you*, okay?"

Pearl could see through the window that the man behind the counter was black. Jessica leaned in, putting her hand on Pearl's sleeve. "We'll distract him. You just take it and put it in your pocket, and we'll leave. Come on. Please?" Jessica tilted her head and smiled.

Pearl looked to Willa for a clue. Willa was standing by the front door, braiding her hair and studying the ends, frowning.

"What if I get caught?"

"We'll distract him. We'll buy a pack of gum so he won't notice. It'll be easy. Do this for me please, Pearl?" Jessica said, smiling, touching Pearl's arm.

"Okay, I'll try." The blood was thundering in her ears.

The door chimed as they walked into the store. The tall, dark-skinned sales clerk wore a maroon and turquoise smock. He was printing out a string of lottery tickets for a fat white guy in an army jacket and cargo pants. Jessica and Willa busied themselves at the counter, flipping through tabloids. Pearl walked down the first aisle past the newspapers and the Tylenol and batteries toward the cooler. Walking back and forth in front of the beer, milk, soda, and energy drinks, she pretended to be making up her mind, trying to keep her hands from shaking. Carefully reaching into the cooler for a Red Bull, she slipped the cold, sweating can into the pocket of her hoodie, then crossed her hands over her stomach, her heart thumping. Up front, Jessica was talking to Willa as she paid for the gum. Jessica rolled her eyes to tell Pearl she should hurry up and leave, which she did, flinching when the door chime rang again. The girls pushed past her as she stood, wheezing again, her lungs burning. Seized by panic, she decided to put the Red Bull back, but when she turned around, the man stood at the door, waving her in. Barely able to pick up her feet, she dragged herself into the store again.

He stood over her, his arms crossed. "Did you forget to pay for something?"

"What?" Waves of electricity shot down her fingers, and her back was slicked with sweat.

"You took a drink from the cooler and walked out with it," he said, his voice deep and gravely.

She glanced outside and saw the girls running away, laughing.

"Young lady. I know what I saw. Don't make me frisk you." His dark hair was cut short and his goatee was dotted with grey.

"Oh, I forgot. I meant…to pay." But of course she didn't have the money, so how could she claim that?

"Should I call the police?"

"No, I'm sorry. Please don't do that," she said, holding the can out for him. He didn't take it. "They made me."

"I know that. I saw what they did. What I don't know is why you let them."

"I don't know." Her eyes fell on the floor where a wad of gum had been smashed into the filthy mat.

"I think you do." He was staring as if waiting for her to say something, but she didn't know what he wanted her to say. "Why did you let them do that to you?"

"What?"

"Don't pretend you don't know what I'm talking about." He took the can from her. "You need to stand up for yourself. Those white girls are not your friends. They're never going to be your friends."

Not even Willa? Pearl felt dizzy. "I don't know," she said, a catch in her throat.

"Why aren't you in school?"

"We're doing community service at Breadbasket."

"Is there an adult in charge?"

"My mother works there. Please don't call her. Please. I won't do it again. I promise." She'd started to wheeze again and struggled for breath, but her throat felt tight. She suddenly had to pee really badly and she needed to change her pad. "I've...learned my...lesson." She burst into raspy sobs. "I'm...really...sorry." Her voice came out hoarse and croaky. "I...promise."

The door chimed and a CTA bus driver came in. "Hey, Marv," he said as he walked to the soda machine and started filling a Super Big Gulp with ice.

"You stand there a minute," the clerk said to her. "Don't even think about running off." He walked behind the counter. Pearl stood there, shifting from foot to foot, worrying she'd wet her pants, worried also that the girls would rat her out to her mother.

The bus driver left and the man walked back to her, frowning. "Listen, I'm not going to call your mama. You're lucky I'm not calling the police."

She burst into tears again. "Thank...so much. I promise."

He looked at her a long time before saying, "If I ever see you in here again, you'd better be up front and center with your money. You understand?"

"Yes. Pro...mise," Pearl said, her face hot from crying, her nose blocked, her throat raw.

As she left, he called after her, "You watch yourself, girl."

She walked as fast as she could although her nose was stuffed, and her legs felt as if she was walking through snow.

Back at Breadbasket, Tanisha stood facing the fax machine, so Pearl slipped past her and into the staff bathroom, just in time. At the sink, she turned on the tap, washed her hands, and patted cold water on her stinging red eyes. "You stupid, ugly weirdo," she said to her reflection. Grabbing a big wad of toilet paper, she blew her nose, which plugged her ears. How was she going to face those girls? What if her mother had found out what she'd done? Why was Willa being so mean? Maybe she could just hide in the bathroom until it was time to leave. She sat on the toilet for a while, listening to music, but she got bored. Maybe she could go to Freya's office and sit with her. Freya wouldn't care. Pearl stuck her head out into the hall again.

"Pearl?" her mother was standing in the hall. "What are you doing?"

"I was just going to the bathroom."

"Okay, but you need to get back to work now."

"Mom, it's so boring and gross in there."

"Pearl, come on. Back in the room. I can't give you slack because you're my daughter."

"I don't feel good."

"Just hang in there until noon."

"Mom, I have cramps."

"I'm sorry about that, but you're here and you have to do as much as the others."

"I'm doing all the work. They're just throwing everything away."

"Pearl. Come on. I can't let you off the hook. I'm in charge and have to answer to the school. How would it look?"

"I don't care how it looks."

Her mother headed back toward her office, pointing to the room. "Pearl, now, please."

"Mom, I can't."

"What do you mean, you can't?"

"Please let me sit in your office. I've done more than either of them. Please." Pearl was trying not to cry. She followed her mother to the office and grabbed a seat. Couldn't her mother get a clue for a change? But she couldn't tell what happened because then her mother would know she'd stolen the Red Bull. "Please, Mom. I don't feel good. Don't make me."

"No discussion. Here, take some cookies to Willa and Jessica. It'll be noon before you know it." She handed her a pile of Chips Ahoy.

Pearl took the cookies and crumpled them, dropping the crumbs on the floor. "No one eats these stupid things."

"Hey, what's going on? Clean that up, right now." She handed Pearl the trashcan.

Pearl scooped up the crumbs and tossed them, the blood thundering in her ears. She was crying by now, her nose running, breath short and ragged.

"Come on, sweetie," she said as she ran her hand along Pearl's arm. "Your friends will wonder where you are." She gave her an encouraging smile.

Pearl batted at her, shouting, "God, Mom. Get a clue." Her mother shrank back. Pearl put her iPod buds, sticky now with Tanisha's candy, back in her ears. "Those *white* girls are not my friends."

CHAPTER 7

Endicott, NY, 1945

Nancy had been feeling cramps for the past couple of days, but she hadn't told Mrs. Gilbert since she wasn't due for another week. Girls close to their due dates were confined to the premises, but she'd felt stir-crazy and needed a walk. Because she'd read all her library books, she figured she could sneak out and pick up a few more before anyone knew she was gone. During the days, after morning chores, most of the girls took high-school courses, gathering in the common room for the afternoon. Nancy had already finished high school and preferred to read, but since they weren't allowed to go back to bed—can't wallow, have to socialize—she sat in the common room, burning through a book a day, her fingers rammed into her ears, as the other girls gabbed, played cards, and listened to the radio.

Her only friend at the Spangler Home, Maisie, whose alias was Mary—"It's a virgin birth," she joked—had delivered a week before and had gone back to Rochester where she lived with her parents. Girls often disappeared in the middle of the night. A squeaking door, a moan, whispers, and a girl would be transferred to the hospital wing for labor, never to be seen again. The rest of the girls were only allowed in the examining room for their checkups, but not to delivery or post-partum. Luckily, Maisie and Nancy had exchanged real names and addresses so they could keep in touch. Nancy had written to her—Was it a girl or a boy? Did it hurt?--but she hadn't heard back.

Since it was a beautiful, warm day, Nancy decided to take a detour to the George W. Johnson Park where the carousel had just opened for the season. American flags still flew everywhere to commemorate D-Day, a few weeks back, and the mood was upbeat with the hope that the war might soon end in the Pacific as well. On Memorial Day, the girls had gone to the carousel for a group outing, and they'd rushed to claim their horses, lumbering up onto the tall saddles, laughing, out of breath with their heavy bellies. Nancy grabbed a white horse with a pink mane like frosting. Once the carousel started, it carried her up and down and around. The air cooled her, and she felt light, almost a girl again. People stared at them, a bunch of pregnant girls from a maternity home, but she refused to let them bother her, feeling the breeze ruffle her hair. Before this all happened, her parents had planned to take her to New York for her nineteenth birthday to see the new musical, *Carousel*, but of course that plan had been scuttled, along with everything else.

If things had gone differently, Nancy would have just finished her freshman year at Smith. But instead, she'd spent the past five months at Spangler, answering to the alias of Nora, watching her body change, her breasts becoming swollen, lined with a map of blue veins, her navel popping from a huge belly, a brown line running down the center. Although she'd rubbed cocoa butter onto her dry, itchy skin, stretch marks snaked up her belly like ghostly fingers.

NANCY ARRIVED AT THE PARK and saw mothers and children heading toward the carousel up ahead, its glossy painted horses catching the morning sun. She felt sweat trickle down her sides. "Horses sweat, men perspire, and women glow," her grandmother often said. Well, Nancy was glowing all right, straight through her smock, which clung to her skin. Peeling it away from her belly, she fanned the damp cloth. Her mother had hastily packed a suitcase for her back in January and hadn't thought to include dress shields, which Nancy now needed.

A cramp rolled across her belly, so she lowered herself onto a bench, flexing her swollen ankles and feet, stuffed into tight espadrilles. Because she loved shoes, Nancy looked forward to the lifting of leather rationing, but she wouldn't buy a new pair until after the baby was born when her feet returned to their normal size. The factory in town, Endicott-Johnson, manufactured shoes, but she hadn't seen a single pair she'd want to own. They made Army boots after all, and she preferred to buy her shoes from New York department stores.

Today, her entire body felt bloated. Nothing fit anymore. The home had a bin full of discarded maternity smocks that the girls were allowed to borrow and return. With the recent arrival of hot weather, Nancy had searched for one big enough and not too ugly or stained. She'd washed it last night and hung it in her room. Still damp this morning, the seams rubbed against her skin. Taking a few deep breaths, she waited until the tightness in her belly subsided.

NANCY AND MAISIE HAD BECOME friends through a shared dislike of crafts. Mrs. Gilbert regularly herded the girls into the common room for art projects—construction paper and pipe cleaner Valentine hearts, St. Patrick shamrocks—which were then tacked to the bulletin board in raggedy rows. The smell of mucilage nauseated Nancy, and her sweaty fingers crumpled the paper and smeared glue and glitter. Nancy would slap the figures together, then excuse herself to go to the bathroom, and Maisie would follow her a minute later. "I didn't like this in kindergarten," Maisie said, lighting a cigarette. "How old does she think we are, anyway?" After much unraveling and restarting, the sum total of Nancy's creative efforts over months had been one pair of yellow booties made in knitting class.

Now with Maisie gone, Nancy didn't feel close to anyone there. The home didn't encourage closeness, as this was a place to hide away, to deny your identity, to roll yourself into a cocoon before emerging transformed, re-virginized even, months later. All the babies were put up for adoption, and the girls went back to their homes as if they'd been away on a trip. An adoptee herself, Nancy didn't want to repeat what her natural mother had done to her, but her parents had threatened to cut her off if she refused to give up the baby, and as far as they were concerned, it had been decided.

Another cramp started, and she sat down to wait it out. The cramps had alarmed her when they'd started a week earlier, but the nurse said they were just Braxton-Hicks, pre-labor, not the real thing. She'd know when the time came. She sat and watched a group of mothers, fanning themselves in the heat, talking as they watched their children chase each other around the park.

HAD IT REALLY BEEN ALMOST a year since her big argument with Bobby? Last July, they were parked in an empty lot, in the back seat of his car, about to go all the way for the first time, when he said, "I have to get something off my chest first." He sat up, raking back his tousled hair, and told her he'd slept with someone at Cornell, but it hadn't meant anything. So many girls and so few fellows on campus; he'd had to beat them off with a stick. The asthma that had kept him out of the war made him feel like less of a man, and so he'd slipped. Just once. But it would never happen again.

Grabbing her blouse, she wiggled out from under him, pushing his hands away as she struggled to get dressed. "Don't you touch me." How could he betray her like that, choosing the moment to confess when she was half-naked, her skirt hitched up, garters undone, her bra on the floor?

"Nancy, please. I want to be completely honest with you," he said, reaching for his smudged glasses. "It's been eating me up. I just had to tell you."

"You just wanted to confess so you'd feel better." She pulled her skirt down and hooked her bra. "Well, I feel a lot worse." She leaned over the seat to retrieve her shoes from the front. He wrapped his arms around her, but she elbowed him away and jumped out of the car, buttoning her blouse and stepping into her pumps. "Leave me alone!" She slung her purse over her shoulder and started to walk.

He drove alongside her on Genesee Street, the window lowered. "Nancy, please? Get in the car." But she refused to look at him, limping because her new I. Miller pumps had raised a blister. When he stopped at a red light, she darted down a one-way street. Suddenly, the reality of being on foot in downtown Utica hit her. It was several miles back to her home in Whitesboro, but she'd get there, even if she had to do it barefooted. She continued to hobble along, her head down, as she swiped at her runny nose. When she heard a vehicle pull up next to her, she thought it was Bobby, but she looked up to see Darryl Loomis, a foreman at Perillo Brewery, her father's beer factory. She knew him by sight from her summer job at the factory switchboard.

"Excuse me, Miss Perillo, what are you doing out here alone?"

She shrugged and kept walking.

"Do you need a ride?"

She stopped, thought about it. "Are you sure you have enough gas? We live over in Whitesboro."

"Oh, sure." He pulled over, hopped out, and opened the door for her. She wiped her face and hoisted herself on wobbly legs into the cab of his truck.

"I didn't know how I was going to make it home. Thanks so much."

She knew she'd be safe. After all, he was one of her father's employees. And a Negro. He'd never do anything to risk his job.

"Are you sure you're all right?" He offered her a Wint-O-Green Lifesaver, and she closed her eyes, imagining the spark as she bit down.

"Yes," she said. "But I don't want to talk about it."

She'd never seen him out of his work coveralls. He'd replaced them with chinos and a crisp white shirt, which set off his dark skin. Instead of his work hat, he was bareheaded, which made him look younger than she'd figured him to be, his short, curly hair oiled into shiny waves.

"So, how do you like working for your father?"

"It's just for the summer. I'm going to college in the fall. Dad wanted me to get some experience at the factory, so that's why I'm here." Not wanting to sound like a spoiled brat who didn't need to work, she added, "And I like having some spending money. I can use it next year." Then she worried he'd think she was treating her job as trivial. "Do you like your job?"

"It's good. I'm deaf in one ear, so the Army wouldn't take me." He told her he was twenty-three and had worked at the factory since high school. He was grateful to have a good job. She agreed.

He filled the empty space with idle talk about work, and she half-listened, her face chafed by Bobby's five-o'clock stubble, her feet throbbing, as she leaned her head against the vibrating window.

He pulled up in front of her parents' home, jumped out, and sprinted around the truck to open the door for her, asking, "You sure you're going to be okay?" His voice was deep, but gentle. He stood back, careful not to touch her arm as she climbed down.

"Yes, thanks. I really appreciate the lift. And my name is Nancy, please." She walked toward her house, her breath ragged, her thoughts jumbled. She waved, but he'd driven off.

That week at work, when she saw Darryl sitting in the cafeteria with some of the drivers, she felt her face turn red. It was awkward. He'd seen her crying, wiping her nose on her arm. He'd given her his handkerchief, and she'd washed it out by hand so her mother wouldn't find it. She planned to return it to him if she ever saw him alone again. He glanced at her but didn't nod. His crew, mostly white men, seemed to like him, and they all had an easy kind of banter. The men were older, the younger ones having gone off to war. The women workers sat at their own table, but Nancy usually ate by herself at the switchboard. Darryl had dark skin, of course, but was handsome enough, with a broad smile and straight white teeth.

Bobby called every day, but she refused to talk to him. Once, after work, she saw his car parked out front of the factory, so she ducked into the building and headed toward the loading dock in back. Darryl stood at the clock, punching out for the day.

She walked up to him and asked, "Can you take me home, please?"

He led her out the loading dock door and sent her in the direction of his truck, telling her to wait for him by the edge of the parking lot. When she climbed into his truck, he said, "I don't know what he did to you, but he won't find you here." She thanked him and gave him the folded handkerchief, which he raised to his nose, then put in his pocket before taking the wheel again.

Darryl wore his coveralls, and he smelled like hops and sweat. Tossing his hat behind the seat, he offered her a cigarette, which she took. He lit hers, then his, the cab filling with the sharp smell of lighter fluid. He pushed up his sleeves over muscled, hairless forearms. Her father and Bobby, both of Italian blood, had thick hair on their arms.

As they headed toward Whitesboro, he asked, "That guy back at the factory," Darryl asked. "Do you mind my asking? Is he the one you were avoiding the other night?"

She nodded.

"College guy, right?"

She didn't tell him what Bobby had done, just that it was something she could never forgive.

"He must feel pretty awful if he keeps trying to talk to you. Maybe he wants to be apologize."

"Well," she said. "Some things just can't be forgiven."

Darryl was a real gentleman, not like Bobby, who was smooth and had all the right manners with her parents, but who was a cad at heart.

Darryl took to driving her home every day after work, meeting her a block away from the factory. That was his idea, and she understood. Her parents thought she was taking the bus and didn't question it. She and Darryl talked about the Utica Blue Sox, the new farm team. He'd been to a few games. Had she? No. She was more of a movie fan. She asked if he'd seen *Gaslight* yet. The first time she saw it, she sat through it twice. The twists surprised her each time. He thought it was good, but he preferred where the good guys won.

A lot of the time, they sat in silence, and he'd point out something interesting—a hawk circling overhead, a section of the Erie Canal, the way the light fell on a corn field in the late afternoon, the maple tree on Chenango Street whose leaves would be the first to turn red in August.

One Friday after work, he suggested they celebrate the weekend with some Perillo Lager. Nancy was underage, but she drank beer at home with her parents. It wouldn't do for her to be seen drinking with an employee, a Negro at that. Darryl bought a cold six-pack at a package store, and they drove to a quiet road skirting a farm. He opened the bottles with a church key from his pocket and handed her one. "Best beer in the world," Darryl said as they clinked bottles.

"I don't know," she said. "I think the beer in Europe must be pretty good." She said she'd always wanted to go to Europe and hoped to make it there after the war.

"I don't like Europe," he said.

"The whole continent?"

"Pretty much. I hate the Krauts. Don't much like the Frogs either. I don't mind the Italians I know here, but I hate Mussolini. Terrible things are happening there."

"But the war will be over soon, and we won't have to think of it again."

"You think it's that easy?" He shook his head. "Boy, are you naïve."

She sat back, embarrassed. "Sorry."

He asked, "Have you even lost anyone?"

"A cousin. I didn't really know him though."

"Well," he said, stubbing out his cigarette. "I lost my only brother."

"I'm so sorry," she said, blood rushing to her face. "I didn't know. I didn't mean to say that the war isn't terrible. I worry about the fellows I know who are there now." He was staring straight ahead, and she wasn't sure he was listening to her. "But isn't it good that you're going to be out of danger?"

"You don't understand."

"That's not fair. I can't help it that I haven't been out in the world."

"The world is not a good place to be."

"I still believe it's a good place."

"Well, then, you're lucky." He upended the bottle and drank the rest, tossing the empty behind his seat, then he shook out another cigarette and lit it, inhaling and letting out an angry stream of smoke.

They sat for a minute, and she fought back tears. "I'm really sorry about your brother. I just didn't know."

"That's okay. Let's change the subject." They sat for a moment as she waited for him to talk, knowing she'd just say the wrong thing. "You don't look at all Italian," he said. "How come?"

She said she was adopted and told him that her parents, who'd grown up in big families, had wanted a bunch of children. Her parents had tried for years to have a baby, with no luck. So they'd decided to adopt a baby boy, dark-haired like them. They visited an orphanage in Endicott. As they were touring the orphanage, a strawberry blond toddler, her nose scabbed from a fall, waddled up to them and put her hand out. "My father said I held his hand tight, wouldn't let him go. So they adopted me."

"That's a sweet story. They chose you."

"Well, I'd rather not be reminded of it all the time. I have twenty-one first cousins, and they don't let me forget for a minute that I'm not really a Perillo."

"That's not right. You belong as much as they do."

"No, I don't, but I'm used to it by now."

"I know something about that. Some of the men don't like a Negro as foreman, and I wonder what will happen when the war's over and the men come home." He knew he only had this job because most of the other men were at war. Margaret said he'd earned his position, but he just shrugged. "Does your father want you to run the factory?"

"No, I'm off the hook because I'm a girl. My cousin Richard and his brothers will take over."

She told him that Richard's sister, Anna Marie, was in her class, and they'd been rivals. Nancy was a better student, but Anna Marie did everything else—cheerleading, drama club, class secretary. Anna Marie once said to her, "It must be hard knowing you came from an orphanage, right?" Nancy knew the word "orphan" really stood for "illegitimate." She'd never talked to anyone about this, never said the word "illegitimate" out loud before.

"I never understood that. You're here in the flesh. That's pretty legitimate."

"Tell me more about your brother."

"Clarence. He was the smart one, had a chance of making something of himself." Darryl said Clarence could do figures like no one else. He insisted on enlisting, even though their mother begged him not to go. When he died in the Battle of Dieppe, it nearly killed her. She hadn't been the same since. Two officers came to the house when their mama was home alone. Darryl wished he could have been there when she got the news.

"I couldn't go to the war, and I couldn't be with her then. Always behind the door, I guess." Sometimes his mother even called him Clarence by mistake. He didn't have the heart to correct her.

He turned the ignition key. "It should have been me."

"Don't say that." She put her hand on his arm.

"It's true."

She leaned over and kissed him lightly on the lips. "Don't say that about yourself."

He pulled back, giving her a puzzled look, and put the truck into gear. They didn't talk after that, and she sat next to him, her eyes closed, head spinning, cheeks warm and flushed, her hand itching to reach for his.

After that, they'd meet at the end of the workday and head toward a secluded spot near a field on Route 5 where they'd pull off the road and neck. He always worried that someone would find them and he'd be in deep Dutch, that they'd claim he had taken advantage of a white girl, the daughter of his boss. "No one would think that," she said.

"I wish I could be as trusting as you."

As the end of the summer approached, she realized how much she was going to miss him. It was unfair that he couldn't have gone to college too, that just because she'd been adopted by parents with money, and she was white, she'd had advantages. It might have been different for her as well. Life was a coin toss. Maybe she wasn't really meant to go away to college and become a doctor. What was she supposed to be anyway? What her parents wanted or what was in her blood?

Nancy had often asked her adoptive parents why her natural mother had given her up. They said they didn't know anything, only that Nancy had been at the orphanage since birth, and it was clear that they didn't welcome any questions about her origins. Nancy often imagined that she'd been taken without permission, that her mother had been too poor or too sick to object. When Nancy and her adoptive mother were on the outs, she imagined her natural mother in dire financial straights, caught in a star-crossed love. At other times, she imagined a selfish woman who couldn't be bothered with a child, or a promiscuous one who didn't even know the father's identity.

A couple of weeks before leaving for Smith, as Nancy and Darryl drove to their usual spot, pulled off the road, and started necking. He was quiet, and she kept whispering in his ear, trying to get him to laugh. He sat back. "Why can't you be serious for once?"

"What's wrong? What did I do?"

"Nothing."

"Are you angry at me?" He shook his head. "Is it because I'm leaving? I'll be back."

"No, you won't. You'll meet some college boy. Just you see."

She laced her arms around him and kissed him. "I don't want to meet someone else." She whispered in his ear, "Please. Let me show you." She lay back, taking his hand and guiding it up her skirt. "Please." Was she sure? Yes. He grabbed a blanket from behind the seat and they climbed onto the back of the truck, lying down. He was so sweet, asking her if she was okay. Did she want this? Was he hurting her? It did hurt, but she didn't tell him. Afterwards, she nestled next to him, looking up at the sky, wishing things could be different. She wished she weren't leaving for college, wished she could stay home and work. Why did she have to go away just now?

They met a few more times before she had to leave, and the last night they were together she cried, saying goodbye, knowing he couldn't see her off, couldn't ask her parents how she was doing. She promised she'd find a way to see him at Thanksgiving.

The day her parents drove her to Smith, her mother said, "You'll meet someone new and Bobby will be a distant memory." That made Nancy cry. "I guarantee it. Some nice boy from Amherst or Yale." No, Nancy thought. She'd live the life of a nun. No distractions, just hard work. She didn't want any romantic complications or entanglements. If she couldn't be with Darryl, then she'd buckle down and study, do what was expected of her.

Once on campus, she was drawn into the whirlwind of activities for new freshmen—getting to know her roommate Dot from Scarsdale, choosing her courses, decorating their room, finding her way around campus and town. Although she said she wasn't interested, Dot finally corralled her into going over to Amherst, where she found herself sitting on a sofa at Alpha Delt house with a 4-F named George, who smelled like ashes and collar dirt. "You virgins are all alike," he said, as she brushed off his advances. "You don't know what you're missing."

"I'll just have to live with that," she said, standing up and leaving him on the ratty sofa to catch a ride back to Smith.

Smith had a few Negro students. In her dorm lived Shirley, a senior whose father worked as a lawyer in D.C., and Vonna, a scholarship girl from Philadelphia. But the thought of Darryl in such a place was impossible. Nancy didn't feel she fit in with all these sophisticated girls either. She found the calculus and chemistry courses overwhelming, and the girls from New York City and New-England boarding schools were light years ahead of her and what she'd learned at Utica Catholic Academy. When not in class, she spent most of her time holed up in the library, hunched over a book, taking notes. Did she really want to be a doctor? Wouldn't she be better off staying at home? She was so homesick, missing her parents, her room, but mostly Darryl. She composed letters to him in her head, but she didn't know where to send them and was afraid to put anything on paper that might get him in trouble. The thought of seeing him at Thanksgiving kept her going.

On Mountain Day in October, when the bells rang to cancel classes, Smithies took off for hikes on Mount Tom or boat rides at the Oxbow, but Nancy stayed behind. She wasn't feeling well, and she had a mid-term in chemistry coming up. Maybe she had a stomach bug. When a week went by and she still couldn't keep food down, she went to the infirmary. The doctor asked her if she could be pregnant, and she told him it was impossible. "Either it is, young lady, or it isn't." She counted the days and realized she hadn't yet opened the box of Modess she'd brought from home and had missed two periods.

She staggered back to the dorm, surrounded by girls laughing, clutching books to their chests as they hurried to and from classes. What was she going to do? How would she explain it to her parents? Her biggest worry involved her mother's reaction, particularly if she learned that the father was a Negro. It would confirm her fears that Nancy was destined to repeat the mistakes of her natural mother. Nancy had spent her life trying to be the good girl her parents wanted, getting high marks, going to church, helping out at home, working in the summers when her cousins spent their time at the country club, but it never seemed enough for her mother who feared that bad blood would out. And now this scandal would confirm her worst fears.

Although Nancy barely touched the huge Thanksgiving meal, no one seemed to notice. Her cousin Sam even made a crack about her weight gain. "Hey, Nancy, how's that dormitory food?" and she sank into her seat. Her mother said to go ahead and eat, not to worry about calories on Thanksgiving, but Nancy couldn't eat a bite. She couldn't tell Darryl, couldn't even risk seeing him because it would be dangerous for him if her family found out. Once, she thought she saw his truck drive by their house, but she stayed inside, barely leaving her room. She hated to hurt him like that, but she couldn't tell him she was pregnant. Her life was already ruined; no sense ruining his as well.

During the two weeks between Thanksgiving and Christmas break, Nancy barely got out of bed. Dot would wake her in the morning, but she couldn't make herself go to classes. Her work piled up and she was weeks behind in chemistry. Her exams were going to be a disaster unless she spent the entire vacation catching up.

As soon as she arrived home for Christmas break however, her mother took one look at her and said, "You're in trouble, aren't you?" Nancy burst into tears and admitted it. Her mother was furious, fretting about what people would think, but her father said that Bobby had better step up and do the right thing. Did he know yet? "It's not Bobby's," Nancy said and watched her mother's face turn chalk white.

"Who is it?" her mother asked. "Someone at college?"

Nancy nodded, but refused to tell them the name of the father, just that he was a friend.

"I should have known this would happen," her mother said. "That you'd turn out like that other woman."

"Celia, please," her father pleaded softly. "Not now."

Nancy had made a terrible mess for all of them, and her mother just didn't know how she was going to show her face in public again. "This is not just about you. We have a position in this community." Her parents decided that instead of exposing themselves to the scandal of their unmarried daughter getting pregnant, it would be better for her to spend the rest of her pregnancy in a maternity home and give the baby up for adoption. They'd send for her things from Smith and she'd take the rest of the year off. They'd claim homesickness, that she hadn't been ready for college yet. Nancy felt numb, could barely form words, just wanted to sleep, to blot it all out. She went to bed and stayed there through Christmas, wishing she could die.

The day after Christmas, her parents told her that they'd been in touch with Spangler Maternity Home in Endicott, and she'd be leaving right after the New Year. She asked if it was the same maternity home where she was born, but her mother didn't know, only that they'd found her at an adoption agency in Endicott. She realized her parents would latch onto what they already knew, familiar, but far enough away for anonymity. But it also felt as if they wanted to undo their mistake by sending her back to where she was born.

She crawled into bed, where she spent her time either sleeping or staring at the ceiling, wondering how she'd made such a mess of her life.

The day father drove her from Whitesboro to Endicott, a whiteout blizzard stretched the usual two-hour trip out to four. Her eyes were swollen from crying, and she was shell-shocked and weak from eating only clear soup. She and her father barely spoke as he gripped the steering wheel, and she dug her fingernails into her palms, half wishing they'd skid off the road so the nightmare would end.

As they pulled up in front of Spangler Maternity Home, really just a big house, Nancy fully expected her father to drop her off while the car idled. But he got out and took her suitcase from the trunk of the car, opened the passenger door, and guided her up the snowy path to the entrance. Two girls stood out front, their coats gaping over huge bellies. They stared at Nancy as she entered the home, her father's arm linked in hers. "Be careful now. Can't have you falling." She leaned against him as he helped her up the steps.

Her first evening at Spangler, she went to dinner and found a table flanked by nine other pregnant girls, talking and laughing like fast friends. Unlike the girls at Smith, everyone here wore maternity smocks. When the grey meat and potatoes came out on big platters, most of the girls ate ravenously, but Nancy had no appetite at all. The girl next to her said to eat up while she could because there'd be no kitchen raids in the middle of the night if she got hungry later. Nancy took a bite and forced herself to swallow. Back at Smith, exams were in progress, and every afternoon, the girls would devour the tea and cakes left out by the kitchen staff, as they looked forward to semester break when they could escape to go skiing in Vermont or to see shows in New York City.

She kept composing letters to Darryl in her head. She wouldn't let on about the baby, but would tell him her leaving was for the best. Nancy's mother had forwarded a letter from Dot saying she'd miss her, but Nancy hadn't known what to write, so she'd let it sit. How could she explain to anyone what had brought her to this point?

OVER THE FIVE MONTHS SHE'D been in Endicott, she often wondered how her life would have gone if she'd been raised there by her natural mother. No college, probably. Marriage and a child, maybe. Was her mother poor? Did she work at the shoe factory? Did her mother ever wonder what had happened to her child? Now when Nancy walked around the town, she looked at women who'd be the right age, maybe with reddish hair, wondering if she might somehow recognize her mother in the street. What would her natural mother think to learn that Nancy had let herself get pregnant? Maybe she'd understand. "You weren't raised this way," her adoptive mother had said. But who was to blame? Her parents were strict and secretive about sex, and the message she received was that she'd come into the world with an indelible stain. But with her own pregnancy, she'd come to realize it was more complicated than she ever could have imagined.

NANCY FELT ANOTHER CRAMP, so she rubbed her stomach and sat back to let it pass. After a minute, it waned, but she felt she'd better skip the library and head back to the home. When she stood up, her water broke, drenching her pants. She stood there, her legs spread, feeling her shoes fill with fluid. The home was about a mile away, so she started walking, her damp pant legs sticking to her skin, making it look as if she'd wet herself. Every couple of blocks, she had to stop because of contractions. Cars passed, and she tried to flag one down, but no one stopped to help her. Finally, she arrived at the home and hauled herself up the front steps, screaming for help.

Mrs. Gilbert grabbed a wheelchair and pushed her to the hospital wing. "Why were you so far away?" she asked.

"I felt fine when I left." Another contraction took hold, and Nancy groaned.

"Just hold your breath, Nora," Mrs. Gilbert said. "We'll get you a shot as soon as we can. You're the second one today. Patricia went in last night."

"What did she have?"

"She's fine."

In the hospital wing, a nurse stripped off Nancy's wet clothes, cleaned her up, and helped her into a gown. "Lie down. The doctor will give you a shot and you won't feel a thing."

Nancy was shivering. "Can you call my parents?" Suddenly, she wanted her mother there with her.

"Just try to relax. We'll give them a call."

The doctor examined her. "You're going to have this baby. No doubt about it."

"But I'm not due for another week."

"Tell that to the baby." The nurse inserted an IV attached to a drip. "Off to twilight now."

WHEN SHE WOKE UP, UNSURE where she was, she felt sore between her legs, and her stomach was now a small mound where there'd been a mountain before.

The nurse came in and helped her sit up. "Let's change that gown, and I'll bind your breasts."

"Why does it hurt so much down there?"

"You tore pretty good, so the doctor stitched you up."

"I tore?"

"Oh, it happens. But you'll be good as new. You'll see. Tighter than before. Your husband will love it."

"I don't have a husband."

"I mean when you get married some day."

Laying her hand on her tender stomach, she asked, "Where's the baby?"

"She's in the nursery. A big one. That's why she had such a hard time being born."

"A girl? Is she okay?"

"Uh huh." The nurse was tucking in her sheets, patting them smooth.

"Can I see her?"

"You know that's not a good idea. Best not to get attached since you're releasing her for adoption."

"I want to see her first."

The nurse poured her a glass of water. "You need to get some rest. Maybe later."

"Is there something wrong?"

Fixing her with a stare, the nurse said, "She'll be hard to place. It might take a while to find a family that will take her. You know that, right?"

"No, I don't. What's wrong with her?"

"She's not the kind of baby most couples are looking for. But I'm sure there'll be someone who wants her bad enough."

So it was obvious. "I'm sorry," she said. She'd lied to the intake nurse when asked about the race of the father, again hoping that if she wished hard enough, she could bend the facts. Now everyone would know the truth. Somehow, she'd hoped that her pale skin would offset Darryl's darkness and produce an olive baby, more Mediterranean than Negro. A stupid, naïve wish.

She asked, "Is my mother here?"

"They couldn't get here in time for you to deliver. We called to let them know you're okay, and they'll be here to take you home in a few days."

"They didn't come?"

"You need some time to rest before you see them. This is best."

Nancy lay back. She was so confused. Her brain felt muddy, her body numb. She didn't remember anything about the birth.

She slept for a while and when she woke up, Mrs. Gilbert came to visit her. "How are you feeling? Did you get some rest?"

"I'm pretty groggy."

"Well, you did it. It's over and she's fine. You can go home in a few days."

"I don't know what to do. I want to see her before I decide anything."

"Don't waver now. Just because you made one mistake doesn't mean you have to ruin your whole life. Think of your future. It's still open. And this baby will need two parents to have a shot in life."

"I don't know."

"If I bring her in here, will that help you feel better?"

"Yes, please."

"Okay, but you realize this could stir up emotions. You have to look at the facts. Don't be ruled by your heart. It's just not that simple."

EVEN THOUGH SHE'D AGREED EARLY on to the idea of adoption, she'd secretly been trying to figure out a way to keep her baby, to move to a new town to raise her alone. She'd hardly be the first woman to do it. Maybe she could some day introduce Darryl to his daughter. She hated keeping this secret from him.

She tried to imagine living alone with her baby, but all she could picture was a haze, the baby distant and wailing in the other room and Nancy, in a separate room, all alone, unable to reach her. Her parents would never allow her to live with them and this baby, clearly of mixed race. But she had to see the baby before she made a decision.

Later, the nurse brought in a pink-blanketed bundle. Nancy hoisted herself up in bed and held out her arms to receive the baby. She was tiny, her eyes closed tight, sleeping. Nancy pulled back the blanket to look at her hair. A dusting of dark curls covered her head. Her lips were full, her skin reddish more than brown. Whom did she look like? What color were her eyes? Nancy imagined for a moment that this was the wrong baby. How could she know for sure? The baby opened her eyes, a flash of brown, then scrunched up her face and started to cry. "Ssh, ssh," Nancy said, bouncing her gently, her breasts wrapped with elastic bandages to stop the milk. When Nancy ran her finger along the baby's cheek, the baby turned her open mouth toward Nancy's chest. That made her breasts tingle and Nancy started to cry herself. "No, baby, I can't. Sorry." She wanted to peel off the bandages to nurse her, but she felt defeated, too exhausted to do anything but lie there. When the nurse came to take her, Nancy's arms froze and she couldn't hand her over. The nurse said that this was the danger, that she'd feel things she wasn't meant to feel. Nancy held the baby and whispered to her, saying that she'd always love her. That's why we don't do this. But Nancy couldn't let her go until she'd seen her, felt her, known she was real. Nancy kissed the baby on her forehead, murmuring, "I love you. I'm sorry. I love you. I'm sorry," over and over, before the nurse pried her away, and Nancy, feeling as if her arms had been torn off, fell back onto the bed, rolling into a ball as she wept, willing herself into sleep with no dreams.

When the baby was five days old, before Nancy's stitches were removed and with her bound, bruised-feeling breasts still leaking milk, Nancy signed the papers to relinquish her daughter for adoption. After signing them, she curled up in bed and wept until she fell asleep again.

She woke up thinking of her natural mother. What could have led her to this decision? It must have been something big, something that kept her from being a mother. Otherwise she'd have kept her. No way could this have been a light decision. It must have ripped her apart. Nancy felt for the first time a deep compassion for her natural mother, knowing she'd chosen for her child to have two parents instead of one. Nancy hoped her child would be able to feel this way about her someday.

IN EARLY APRIL, AFTER MONTHS of hearing nothing from her mother, Nancy had started receiving letters where her mother talked about the future. *The only thing to do is put it behind you and start again. You can go back to Smith as a freshman. They're keeping your spot open for you. That'll be the best medicine, getting back to your old life.* But Nancy couldn't go back to her old life. Too many bad memories. Staying home with her parents sounded even worse. She'd thought of getting a job to support herself and the baby, but she knew she couldn't do this alone. Life was going to be hard enough for this child. Not fair to make it even harder.

THE NEXT MORNING, MRS. GILBERT, woke her, and Nancy blinked, unsure of where she was for a moment.

"Your parents are coming to get you today, *Nancy*," she said, the alias no longer necessary. "They've forgiven you. They don't hold this mistake against you."

"What do you mean? What did you tell them?"

"They know this baby could never be part of your family, and they want to put this all behind them."

Nancy's face burned at the thought that Mrs. Gilbert would tell her parents that the baby was half Negro.

Later that morning, her stitches and breast binding removed, Nancy sat on the bed, dressed in a now-loose maternity smock and pants pinned together at the waist, her suitcase packed and ready to go, the yellow booties tucked safely underneath her clothes. She'd allow her parents to take her home for a rest, but after she recuperated, she'd be firm with them, wouldn't let them make any more decisions for her. She would never tell them about Darryl. She couldn't go back to Smith or live at home. Instead, she'd move to Endicott or Johnson City and get a job. She needed to stay close to the place where her baby was born in case, one day, they passed in the street. She had to be there, in case they saw each other in the street. She couldn't let her baby down.

When her father's car pulled up out front, she watched out the window as her father and mother opened the doors and climbed out, stretching. Her father fiddled with the side mirror, adjusting it, but her mother was looking up at the second floor of the home, her eyes traveling across the row of windows, her hand a visor over her forehead. Nancy stood at the window, wondering if her mother would recognize her now.

CHAPTER 8
Chicago, 2007

Andrea's cell phone rang, and the caller ID showed the number from Pearl's school. With Pearl, news from school was rarely good. "Ms. Barton? This is John Kramer." The Assistant Dean. "I'm afraid there's been an incident involving Pearl that we need to discuss."

"What happened?" she asked, sinking into a chair. Her eyes fell on the framed photo over her desk of Pearl bounding off a raft, her arms wide, chubby legs spread-eagled. "Is she okay?"

"She was involved in some inappropriate behavior."

"What kind of behavior?"

"I'd rather discuss this in person. Is there any way you could come to school now? I have Pearl in my office."

"I'm on my way." She grabbed her bag and told Freya there was an emergency with Pearl.

She didn't know when she'd be back. Freya said she'd cover for her.

Andrea sat in the midday traffic on Lincoln, pounding the horn when the light changed. From Lincoln, she turned onto side streets, zigzagging across and down, all the time wondering what it could be this time. Cheating? Stealing? A fight?

Twenty minutes later, she arrived at school and found a parking space, then she ran into the building, hurrying toward the Dean's office as she struggled to catch her breath. The administrative assistant, sipping a Starbucks, pointed to the door behind her. "They're expecting you."

When Mr. Kramer opened the door, Andrea saw Pearl's advisor, Mr. Sykes, and the school psychologist, Dr. Owen, sitting across from Pearl, who was slumped on the sofa, her arms crossed. Andrea rushed over to give Pearl a hug, but Pearl tightened and pulled away. "Mom, stop." She smelled of sweat and gum. Andrea risked smoothing Pearl's tortured hair, brittle and burnt by relaxers, and itched to pull down the hem of Pearl's short skirt, which had inched up to show an expanse of bare, dark thigh. Why had she let Pearl leave home wearing such an outfit, a jean jacket over a tight tank top and too-short skirt? "Are you okay?"

"This is so stupid," Pearl said, hugging herself.

"Pearl," Mr. Kramer said. "It's not stupid. It's quite serious."

"Please tell me what's going on," Andrea said, settling on the sofa next to Pearl, her heart pounding.

"Earlier today, a teacher saw Pearl run out of the boys' locker room. He was suspicious, so he went inside and found three boys laughing. Although they denied it at first, the story came out that Pearl had engaged in sexual activity with them."

"Did those boys hurt you?" Andrea asked Pearl, who shook her head. "Who did this to her?"

"It's more the case of what Pearl did to them," said Dr. Owen, a balding man with readers perched on his head. "It's our understanding that Pearl was a willing participant, that she wasn't forced in any way."

143

"What did they do?"

"They said that Pearl performed oral sex on each of them."

Andrea's eyes blurred. "Could they be lying? Who are these boys?"

He wouldn't reveal the names due to confidentiality but said that they were all in the eighth grade, two years behind Pearl.

"How do you know for sure what happened?" She turned to her daughter. "Pearl, you have to defend yourself, even if it's embarrassing. Otherwise, it's just their word against yours." But Pearl dug in, her mouth clamped shut, heat radiating off her. "You're intimidating her. No wonder she doesn't want to talk."

"Ssh, Mom. You're making it worse."

"No, I want to make sure you're not being railroaded into a confession."

Dr. Owen laced his long fingers over one knee and continued, his voice soft as if talking to a young child. "You understand, don't you Pearl, that this kind of behavior is cause for concern?" Pearl shrugged and re-crossed her legs. "Okay, I'm not sure what that means, but we're concerned. You should know that."

"But what about the boys?" asked Andrea. "Have you brought their parents in too?"

"We're dealing with them," said Mr. Kramer.

"Did they pressure you, Pearl?" asked Andrea.

"God, Mom," Pearl said, curling up as if to hide in her jacket.

"Listen," Mr. Kramer continued, "We don't want to make this more uncomfortable for her, for you, Pearl, than it already is, but I have to act on this. We've decided to deal with this in-house." He took a pen and circled a number on his calendar. "Pearl, I'm giving you a week's suspension. Assuming there are no more incidents, we can erase this from your record. No harm, no foul." Andrea glared at him. Jackass with his sports analogy. "However, any other major infraction, and I'm afraid we won't be able to offer you a contract for next year."

Andrea's head started to throb. "But isn't anyone considering that she may be the victim here?" She looked at the three men sitting in judgment of her daughter. "Are the boys also being suspended?"

"Mom!"

"Again, I can't share that with you," said Mr. Kramer, looking at his watch. "This is about you, Pearl. We want the best for you, but you have to live within our rules. We want you here." The others nodded in agreement. "But you have to want it as well. If you can't live by our rules, then you can't be part of our community." He closed the file to signal that the meeting had ended.

Pearl mumbled something under her breath, and Andrea shot her a warning glance not to make things worse by being rude.

"Pearl and I will talk, but we need to do it privately." She forced herself to thank them for their time, tamping down her fury.

She followed Pearl as she stomped out of the office through the main entrance. Students stared at them, one girl nudging her friend and laughing. Pearl steamed ahead, shrugging off Andrea's arm as she bolted into the street in front of a car, causing it to stop short.

Once in the car, Andrea turned to Pearl. "Now, will you please tell me what happened?" Pearl slumped lower in her seat. "We're not leaving until you talk to me."

Pearl puffed and shook her head, yanking a loose thread from her jacket. "God, Mom, it was just blow jobs. They aren't a big deal."

"Excuse me?" Andrea said, the blood wooshing in her ears.

"Maybe they were a big deal in your day, but they're not now."

"Oh, Pearl. You don't give them to just anybody." Pearl gave her a nasty look. "Well?"

"I know those guys. It's not like they were strangers in an alley."

She imagined Pearl with shards of glass ground into her knees. "But you don't do that to a bunch of boys. It's not how you behave at school. Or anywhere." Her voice sounded shrill. "That's the kind of thing that will get you thrown out."

When she touched Pearl's arm, Pearl yanked it away. "How did the boys get you into the locker room?"

She burst into tears. "I can't talk about this now. I want to go home." And she curled up into a ball, her breath rattling. Andrea was afraid Pearl's asthma would flare, so she said they'd talk more at home.

As she drove, Andrea stole glances at Pearl, past the heavy body and angry face to the little girl peeking out. Always big for her age, Pearl was often mistaken for older. What did it feel like to be a girl in a woman's body? The image of Pearl's mouth welcoming one penis after another kept crowding Andrea's mind before she could shake it off.

Pearl had turned on her iPod, her fingers thrumming on her wide, bare thigh. Although Pearl was overweight, Andrea found her beautiful. Her skin was a sheet of unblemished mahogany, smooth and lustrous, unlike Andrea's pale, freckled skin. Pearl's eyes were large and widely spaced, her full lips soft pillows. Andrea wanted Pearl not to squander her self-worth on some jerks who were obviously using her.

Back home, Pearl hurried ahead of Andrea up the stairs and into the apartment, dropping her backpack on the kitchen floor before grabbing a bottle of juice and a granola bar on her way to her room. Andrea picked up the too-light backpack, wondering if Pearl had brought any of her books home for the week of suspension. Andrea would stop by school to get the books and assignments later.

When she called Mike at work to tell him, he was outraged. "It's a witch hunt," he said. "A racist cabal." She filled Mike in on the basics but left out Pearl's admission, at least for the moment, not quite believing it herself.

Andrea called work to say she wouldn't be in for the rest of the day, microwaved a cup of morning coffee, and sat at the table. She wasn't hungry. Like Pearl, she tended to eat when stressed, but today, she couldn't imagine putting anything into her mouth.

Andrea had always assumed Pearl could confide in her, that Andrea would help her figure out how to deal with boys and sex, not like her own mother, who'd used all the right terms but seemed embarrassed to talk about the personal implications. The news of Pearl giving blow jobs didn't square with what Andrea had thought up to then, that although she'd had crushes on boys, there'd been no dates, no boyfriend yet, so no sex of any kind. She'd talked to Pearl about sex and about making good decisions. Not just about pregnancy, but HPV and HIV, the stakes so much higher these days. For Andrea, oral sex came after intercourse, only when trust was established, not like now, where it seemed a lot more casual.

Andrea opened the folded memo with the name Deirdre Langley-Smith, the psychiatrist recommended by the dean, a requirement for her returning to school in good standing. She called and made an appointment, knowing she'd encounter a fight from Pearl, but she had no choice. When Andrea searched the doctor on-line, she found her to be black and highly credentialed, but wondered if the school only recommended her to minority students.

Pearl holed up in her room for the rest of the day, only emerging to grab food, refusing to look at Andrea, taking a plate and shutting the door behind her.

Mike came home, still furious at the school. He stood at the stove, slapped down the pan, and poured in a stream of olive oil. "I went to a private school. Do you know what it's like for minorities there?" he asked, as if a Jewish kid from the North Shore could begin to understand what Pearl faced. What did he know about being a black girl in a white world? But then again, what did she?

"The truth is," Andrea said, nudging the slimy flesh of the salmon steaks with her finger, "she admitted it to me. She even said it was no big deal. But what does it mean that she's giving blow jobs to three boys at a time?"

He shrugged. "Kids are more sexual these days." He adjusted the flame, then coaxed the salmon into the pan.

"Are you kidding? This is not typical behavior. She was servicing those boys. Who knows what else she's been doing? She could have HPV or herpes. Or worse." And she realized she'd have to take Pearl to a gynecologist, a visit she'd hoped to delay for a couple more years.

Mike said, "It's hard for you to accept that Pearl isn't a little girl anymore."

"If she were doing this with a boyfriend, one kid, it would be different. Can't you see that?"

AT DINNER, PEARL STABBED AT her food, pushing it around her plate, and Andrea studied her face, the broad planes, the coal-black eyebrows, her round cheekbones and widely-spaced eyes. When she looked at Pearl's full-lipped mouth, all she could think of was what that mouth had done. Although she tried blurring the lines to return her to the ten-year-old who loved her mother more than anyone, she couldn't wipe out the sight of this petulant adolescent, her face propped on one hand, inky clouds of anger spilling out toward Andrea.

"Don't you like your fish?" Andrea asked, biting back the urge to point out that Pearl had been snacking all afternoon.

She pushed her plate aside. "Mom, give it a rest. I'm not hungry." But Andrea knew she'd hear her banging around in the kitchen later, and she'd smell cheese frying.

"We need to talk about what happened," Andrea said.

"Mom, haven't I been through enough today? I can't go over it and over it."

"Well, then, when can we talk?"

"It was so embarrassing to have to talk about it with all those people. Why can't I have any privacy?"

"What you did was not private."

"I know, I know, I know."

"Pearl, you can't run away from this. You're taking huge risks with your health. Don't you understand?"

"No, Mom, why don't you explain how babies are made? Do you think I'm stupid?"

Andrea felt the blood rush to her face.

"Pearl, that's enough," said Mike. "The two of you need a break from this topic, okay?"

"Exactly," said Pearl.

"Okay, fine then. Later," said Andrea. "But did you get all your assignments for the week?"

She dropped her knife and threw up her hands. "Jesus, Mom. Did you not hear Mike? Let's drop it."

"Why don't the two of you just take a deep breath and let this settle," said Mike, pouring himself another glass of wine. "You'll have plenty of time to talk about it this week." Andrea glared at

Mike. How dare he treat the two of them like squabbling sisters?

They sat for a few minutes in silence as Pearl continued to mangle her salmon and Andrea felt nauseated and heartsick. "I can't eat," Pearl said, getting up and dumping her food in the garbage disposal, the plate clattering in the sink.

After Pearl left, Mike said, "Maybe she's trying to send a message."

"And what would that be?"

"I don't know. That she's unhappy?"

"But what should we do?"

"We'll figure it out. Now's not the time though. This has to settle so we can get some perspective." He gave her a hug and shooed her into the other room so he could clean up. She sat in front of a re-run of a sitcom about a family with a sassy teenage daughter, knowing it was facile and cheesy, but envying them their closeness and the promise of a solution in half an hour.

THE NEXT DAY, ANDREA FEARED that Pearl would refuse to go to the therapy session, and she dreaded the struggle. But Pearl emerged from her room on time, her hair raked back, wearing a dirty tee-shirt and jeans as if she'd been dragged out of bed. "Ready?" Pearl shrugged.

In the car, Pearl sulked.

"Just tell her what you're thinking," Andrea said. "It's okay." Pearl gave a mocking puff of air. "I know you don't want to do this, and I appreciate your going along with it."

"What choice did I have?" Pearl asked wearily.

"I've been to therapy, and it helped me a lot." Pearl rolled her eyes. "You have to talk to her, even if you won't talk to me."

Pearl shook her head and looked out the window, folding her arms under her pillowy breasts.

THEY DROVE TO THE BRICK office building a few blocks from Pearl's school. The street-level boutique featured the kind of shoes that Andrea coveted and couldn't afford, but which Crofton mothers wore for everyday errands. They rode up the elevator in stony silence. In the waiting room, Andrea sat down, and Pearl walked to a chair on the other side of the room and sat, her legs crossed, one foot wagging furiously. Would she be as angry if Mike had brought her? He had it easy. Involved enough to weigh in but not enough to face the tough stuff. Andrea picked up a *People* magazine she'd read before and nodded at the mother with a young boy who was sitting with a handheld game, snuffling, scraping his untied shoes on the carpet. The mother, dressed in a business suit, sat next to him, texting. When he snuffled once more, his mother grabbed the Kleenex box and plunked it next to him before returning to her Blackberry.

Dr. Langley-Smith, a tall black woman with shoulder-length braids, opened the door and called Pearl's name. Pearl heaved herself out of the seat and pushed past Andrea, disappearing through the door with the doctor before Andrea could introduce herself.

As she sat there, unable to focus on the magazine, Andrea wondered what Pearl and the therapist were talking about, wishing she could be there herself to mention Pearl's moodiness, her unhappiness at school, her failure to latch onto any interest for very long. Would Pearl tell her why she'd gone off with the boys or if she'd done this kind of thing before? Would she open up to this stranger because she was a woman of color? It hurt Andrea to consider that Pearl might need to confide in someone who looked more like her.

Andrea was a firm believer in nurture, having seen what the

lack of a good environment did to children. In her work, she'd seen children from Russia and Romania suffering from PTSD and Attachment Disorders, how they'd been scarred, forever unable to trust or love. Even though she felt sympathy for the children in Third-World orphanages, this was why she'd chosen to adopt domestically.

For years, she and Pearl had been so close, just the two of them, until Pearl was ten and Mike came into their lives. It was a hard age, Andrea knew, for her to accept such a change. At first, Pearl had been wary, and Andrea made sure to introduce Mike slowly into their lives so that Pearl could get used to him, not letting him spend the whole night until he was ready to move in, making sure he'd hung out with Pearl first, planning dinners and outings that included her. She'd explained that Mike was her partner, not quite a husband, not quite a father, but someone who cared about Pearl as much as she did. Andrea had to be sure Pearl accepted him, and that Mike was the kind of man who wouldn't be threatened by her bond with Pearl. Once Pearl overcame her initial fears, she liked him a lot. He helped her with her homework, and they liked the same schlocky horror movies, preferring the sequels, the IIIs and IVs, to the originals. They'd all managed to settle into a fragile, three-legged stability when Pearl started to change, breasts and hips swelling almost overnight, and she became short-tempered and secretive, flinching whenever Andrea touched her. It even seemed as if Mike had replaced her in Pearl's affections, which pained her, even though she was relieved they got along. And was Mike driving a wedge now? Using it to curry favor at Andrea's expense? She wondered how long had this new—was it new? — sexual behavior been going on, when she'd started she started giving blow jobs, if she'd had intercourse yet and with how many boys.

AFTER THE SESSION, THE DOOR opened and a tight-lipped Pearl stalked out, followed by the doctor, who loomed over Andrea, all of her six feet surrounded by a cloud of perfume. "I'll see Pearl alone again next week, and then I'd like to see you, if that's all right." She offered a hand to shake, her bracelets skittering down her arm. "And if you'd like to include your partner, Mike, that's fine." Her long dark fingers felt cool in Andrea's hand.

So Pearl had mentioned Mike, and Andrea wondered if Pearl had portrayed him as the good parent to her bad. "Of course. Whatever you think is right. Since I'm a social worker, I think that's a good plan—"

"Mom?" Pearl, said, half out the door. "Let's *go*."

"Okay, sorry." When she felt nervous, she tended to run on with no exit strategy. "Coming." Pearl groaned and headed into the hall. In the elevator, Andrea asked, "Well, how was it?"

"It was okay." She'd shoved in ear buds and twirled the dial on her iPod. The thrum of rap coated the air. Men with initials for names spewing angry, misogynist rants. Andrea pictured Pearl opening up to the doctor, talking about her fears, her regrets.

In the car, Andrea studied Pearl's profile for a moment, her round cheekbone, the whorl of hair in front of her ear, and wondered what crucial key to Pearl Andrea had missed, allowing her to go so far off the rails.

"Hey, can I ask you something?" She tapped her on the shoulder.

Pearl punched off her iPod. "Mom, Deirdre said I don't have to talk about it if I don't want to."

"O-kay, never mind," Andrea said, gunning the engine.

"God, Mom. You're so passive-aggressive."

Andrea blinked back tears, wondering if she'd just handed the reins over to a stranger.

On the way home, she noticed a woman pulling a metal cart packed with groceries, her son walking by her side. No need to hold his hand; he followed. A woman down on one knee, tying her son's sneakers, his hand poised on her head. A Hispanic woman with two small daughters, each carrying pink purses like their mother. Andrea swallowed back the fear and anguish that clenched her throat. She fought the urge to stop the car and grab Pearl, asking her what the hell was wrong. What did she want? *What?*

When they pulled up in front of their building, Pearl jumped out and slammed the door, running ahead to let herself in. Andrea sat in the car, finally letting herself cry, grabbing a tissue from the floor to blow her nose. She made herself breathe slowly, composing herself before going inside, wishing that she could start the car again and drive as far away as she could, west, into the sunset, the wind ruffling her hair, her eyes trained on the horizon.

That night, as Andrea and Mike sat with a drink before starting dinner, Pearl came into the kitchen and brought up the issue of transferring to another school, a plan which Andrea had previously vetoed.

"Deirdre said that if I hate Crofton, I should be able to decide for myself where I go to school," Pearl said while scarfing down almonds.

"Well," Andrea said, adrenaline zapping an electric current to her fingertips, "Deirdre isn't your mother."

"I'm fifteen."

"My point, exactly."

"God, that's so fucked up. I hate it there. I'd do so much better at the School of the Arts."

"Hey, language. And that's out of the question. I'm not paying for a school that's not even academic." She moved to the counter, grabbing the cutting board.

"It's good. I have a friend who goes there."

"Well, I've heard otherwise. And besides, it's too soon to specialize yet. You might find you like something else other than art. That's what college is for."

Pearl shot her a hateful look. "I don't need college to be an artist."

"Don't start on—"

"Pearl," Mike asked. "What makes you interested in the School of the Arts?"

"It sounds like a cool place. And it's not Crofton," she said, glaring at Andrea, who was channeling her nerves into chopping shallots.

Why was Mike even pretending to consider this? "Yes," Andrea said. "It's cool because they don't make you do any work."

"That's not true!"

"Why not let her look at it?" Mike asked.

Andrea felt the sand beneath her give way. Where was the united front? "Because I have no intention of sending her there. And at this point in the year, there are no options except public school, and that's completely out of the question. Not after all of this." She fought to keep anger out of her voice. "I think you need to stay at Crofton to get the best education."

"I hate it there!"

"Pearl. I'm sorry. You've made a mess of things, and I'm worried about you. At this point, I think it's better to stay with what we know, a good school academically, and one where someone is paying attention to you."

"What if I ask Gram and Grandpa? They're the ones paying for my school."

"But I still make the decisions."

"That's so unfair."

"Pearl, I want to help, but you have to understand." She leaned over and laid her hand next to Pearl's arm, not daring to touch her. "I'm so worried about you."

Pearl slammed her hand on the counter and steamed out of the room, muttering in angry bursts.

After Pearl left, Mike said, "Would it be such an awful thing if she transferred?"

"Yes, it would." And she said he wasn't helping by entertaining the notion as if it were a possibility. She blew her nose and wiped her eyes.

"Do you think she's trying to get your attention?"

"She gave three boys blow jobs. She's in trouble. Letting her run to a school with no rules is not an option. I can't do it."

"But can you imagine what it's like for her at Crofton and how it'll feel to go back there as the BJ girl?"

"Don't you think I worry about how she's going to return there? Give me some credit. There are no good options."

He shut his eyes, sighed and continued, "I'm trying to help. That's all. I don't like to see you and Pearl butt heads."

"I don't want to butt heads with her. I'm worried this is just the beginning. What might she do next? She's practically turning tricks now."

"You're not serious."

But she was and told him nothing would be gained by his being the good cop to her bad, that they needed to stick together in this, and asked him to follow her lead, please. His silence told her he was pissed. But he needed to trust her in this.

"Don't you see she's pitting me against you? It's divide and conquer. And you just love being the good guy. But where does that put me?"

"And you're too angry to see that she's in distress. She's flailing."

"She's playing you. I can't believe you don't see that."

"That's not true and not fair."

She said she had to get dinner ready, and he set the table. But she wasn't hungry and the meal passed with the three of them barely speaking.

ANDREA HADN'T TOLD HER PARENTS about Pearl's suspension. They'd attended every recital and play at Crofton where Pearl sang from the back row of the chorus or acted in a crowd scene, and each time they swore she was the standout performer. Andrea knew that her mother's favoritism toward Pearl rankled her sister Joanne, whose two children had perfect grades and juggled a long list of extra-curricular activities. But Andrea knew there were problems—Blair's anorexia, never acknowledged by Joanne, Gary's anxiety leading him to pluck out hair until he had a bald patch. When he didn't get into M.I.T., and had to settle for Stanford, he'd had a minor breakdown, which Joanne never talked about. Those were two tightly wound kids. Joanne pretended that everything was fine, but Andrea knew that Gary avoided coming home from California for vacations and, since Joanne never mentioned Blair's college grades, Andrea assumed she was just barely scraping by, or worse. She suspected that Joanne would secretly revel in Pearl's crisis, and Andrea's mother was too preoccupied with her husband's glaucoma and Parkinson's to be burdened with Pearl's problems right now. First, Andrea thought her mother had exaggerated his condition, and that he'd retreated into silence to turn out her carping.

Lately, however, Andrea had come to accept her father's decline and saw that her mother was coping the best she could, even trying to spare her daughters more worry. Her mother's nerves frayed easily, for sure, but there was more to it than Andrea had realized.

Andrea wondered why she'd taken the week off since Pearl slept most of the day and avoided her when awake. Andrea itched to get back to work, knowing files had piled up in her absence, wishing for the distraction and predictability that work would provide. She tried to read but couldn't concentrate, so she vacuumed and dusted, moving heavy furniture to reach the hidden corners, then she scoured her copper pots and sewed a new curtain for the kitchen window, anything to keep herself busy.

Pearl took the bus to her next session with Deirdre and came back in a better mood. Andrea allowed herself the hope that the worst of the crisis had passed. She returned to work on Pearl's first day back at Crofton. After school, Pearl told Andrea and Mike that it was no big deal. No one seemed to notice she'd been gone, which made Andrea sad. What was worse—to be stigmatized for a bad decision or to be ignored completely?

Maybe Mike was right. This was a no-win situation and maybe she should consider letting Pearl transfer. Not to the School of the Arts, but maybe to Sandberg High School, where they had an International Baccalaureate program, although she wasn't sure Pearl would qualify or could handle the pressure. Or maybe the art school, but she couldn't start until fall. Andrea decided to broach the subject with the therapist when she and Mike saw her together.

A BLACK EAMES CHAIR WITH matching ottoman dominated Deirdre Langley-Smith's office. Art decorated the walls—a Hmong embroidery of a small village with colorful peasants scurrying around, a geometric African print that Andrea guessed to be Ndebele, and a photograph of a brilliant sunset with giraffes in the foreground. She squinted at Deirdre's framed degrees—Penn undergrad, U. of C. Medical School, Illinois Board Certification.

Deirdre motioned to the couch and sat down in her chair, settling her feet on the ottoman and gathering the flowing material of her duster around her legs. Andrea and Mike sat down, but Andrea felt something hard beneath her, so she stood up and extracted a plastic baby doll from between the cushions.

"Sorry about that," Deirdre said, reaching for the doll.

Andrea looked over at the playhouse in the corner surrounded by plastic figures. On the shelf behind a low table sat a cloth figure with a hollow hole for a mouth and, Andrea knew, additional holes under its clothes. Did Deirdre get down on the floor to play with her patients? Andrea found it hard to imagine the tall, elegant doctor sitting on the floor to watch children poke and probe these dolls, imitating their own violations. Was she the kind of therapist who spent her day expressing sympathy for her patients, always comforting, never judging? Or did she give the same advice as parents but packaged in a way children could stomach? Whose ally was she?

Deirdre folded her arms and asked, "So how's it going with Pearl?"

"You tell us," Andrea said, but Deirdre raised an eyebrow. Of course, she couldn't divulge what Pearl had said. Andrea continued, "We don't know what to do with Pearl." Andrea clenched her hands, then grabbed a pillow, hugging it to her stomach. "I'm, we're, really worried about her. We were worried before we knew about this sexual activity. Now we don't know what to do. And it's not been easy. She and I haven't been getting along at all. Actually, now she can tolerate Mike better than she can me."

"Adolescents often find it hard to be on the outs with two parents at the same time."

Andrea almost added that Mike wasn't a parent but stopped herself. "It had been just Pearl and me for years until I met Mike. I just don't know what's happened between us." She felt the sting of tears, which she blinked back.

Deirdre nodded. What did that mean? Was she agreeing or pointing out that she'd heard this from Pearl?

"I don't have children of my own," Mike said, "but Pearl and I have a good relationship." As he filled Deirdre in on the circumstances of his addition to the family, Andrea's eyes wandered to the bookcase, where she recognized titles: *The Drama of the Gifted Child, Children and Divorce, Borderline Personality Disorders.*

Mike said, "Pearl really hates her school, Crofton. And she seems to be doing everything she can to get kicked—"

"We're in a quandary," Andrea added, "about what to do. Pearl wants to leave Crofton, and I can understand that, given how hard it's going to be to return there. But we can't just yank her out. It's not as if there are other good schools that would take her now. We can't afford a therapeutic school, and the regular public school program is not a suitable option. So we're thinking of exploring a change for next year, hoping she can make the best of a bad situation this year. We don't want Pearl to know anything about this yet." Deirdre nodded. "She really wants to transfer to an arts high school, and I've been completely against it although Mike is more open to the idea. Maybe though, given how unhappy she is and given that she's made a mess for herself at Crofton, it's something we should consider." Mike took her hand and squeezed it.

"This is a big decision," said Deirdre.

"The last thing I want to do is offer something if I'm not willing to follow through, so please don't mention it to her."

"I won't," she said, scribbling notes on a legal pad. "Of course."

"I don't know how much to attribute to her adoption and how much to chalk up to her own particular rocky adolescence.

"Pearl is a very smart, very angry girl."

"No argument there," said Mike. Andrea nodded, wondering what Mike meant by that. Did he think that Andrea had earned the anger or that she was the obvious target for Pearl's acting out?

"I wish I could say that this crisis will resolve itself soon," Deirdre said.

"And I was hoping this was the worst of it," Andrea said.

"Pearl is having a particularly tumultuous adolescence. It might get worse before it gets better."

Her stomach dropped. "Really? How much worse could it get?" Deirdre narrowed her eyes. "No, I can't even think of that. And I know you can't tell us anyway." She stopped, wishing she could speak more clearly, afraid to say what was really on her mind, that Pearl might be servicing men for money or drugs.

"I'm not saying she's at the point of worst case," Deirdre said, "but listen to her. I know you do listen, but make sure she knows you're listening."

Andrea's scalp prickled. "I *do* that. No, this is new. I'm worried about her and I don't think it's just a simple matter of my being nice." She felt her throat constrict and her voice grow thin.

"It's got to be hard," Deirdre said, peering over her readers. "But remember how hard it is for Pearl."

"They really set each other off," said Mike. "They st—"

"You make it sound as if it's mutual," said Andrea.

"To some extent, it is."

She looked to Deirdre. "Don't mothers always get the brunt?"

"You could say that. But they're also pretty powerful figures."

"It feels as if Pearl is in charge."

"She's not. You are."

"I wish."

"You may confuse being in charge with being in control. You can't make it go your way, but you can set down boundaries." Her tone, oh so patient, felt condescending.

"But I *do*," said Andrea. "I just didn't think to warn her not to give three boys blow jobs. Who knew that would happen?" Deirdre knitted her brow. Andrea spent the rest of the session with lips pinched to keep from blurting out her defense, wanting to add that she listened all right. And why didn't Mike support her more? He knew how hard she tried with Pearl. Why wasn't he saying more about that?

On the drive home, Mike said, "She was good," and he looked pleased, as if this session had settled anything.

Andrea said he'd taken her side. "Pearl's?" he asked. No, the doctor's. And how could he be even a little hopeful when she'd said it could get worse?

"It can always get worse." He took his hand off the wheel to stroke hers. "Sorry, but it's true."

"What could that mean? A Pregnancy? An STD? Herpes? HIV? Prostitution? What are we going to do?" He brought her hand to his lips. She lay her head back and closed her eyes and took deep breaths to dispel the frightening images that kept invading her mind.

AT HOME, SHE WAITED UNTIL Mike was busy on his laptop, then she grabbed a trash bag and headed for Pearl's room. She rarely ventured there, choosing instead to drop piles of clean clothes outside the door. The mess was too much to bear, the struggle not worth it.

Cracking open the door, the mixed smells of body dirt, mildew, and incense wafted out. Mounds of clothes cluttered the floor, and she waded through them—jeans and tee-shirts, a pair of velour pants with JUICY printed on the seat, a tee-shirt with SEXY written in glitter. Andrea tripped over a pile of plates and bowls hidden in the mess. She lifted up the mattress and found a pack of cigarettes, which she threw into the trash bag, her temples throbbing. The space under the bed was stuffed with clothes and crumpled paper. She dug a few papers out and crammed them into the bag. Tangled up in the duvet on the bed, Andrea discovered her missing blue cashmere sweater with an explosion of brown staining the front. She hurled it toward the door. Rifling through the dresser drawers, she found nothing incriminating—she wasn't even sure what that might be—just more wadded-up clothes. The closet floor was piled with clothes and shoes, which she tossed aside. Finally, Andrea stood up, her breathing labored, and looked at the bookcase where several half-burnt candles, their wicks withered and stunted, had crowded out the books, which lay on the floor, their spines broken. Stacked on the top shelf, her cloth Zulu dolls with black faces outlined by white beads, their mouths open Os. Her American Girl doll, Addy, naked, her hair a tangle, her arms hanging over the shelf, looking like a crime victim. CDs spilled onto the floor in front of her dusty boom box. Mugs filled with a thick liquid gone mossy and bluish-brown cluttered the desk. She pulled open the drawers and pawed through them, finding only a couple of broken pens, loose change, and a troll doll with green hair, its hands chewed until they were splintered and feathery.

Magazine pages plastered the wall, photos of models, black and Hispanic women with shiny eye makeup, the white girls with smeary panda eyes, all with scowls. Page upon page of slutty-looking women, draped over men with oiled pecs and low-riding pants. Among the magazine pages, Andrea spotted a photo of Pearl taken when she still had braces. Her mouth a gaping cavern, her tongue extended. Next to it was a more recent photo of her in a tank top, hanging onto a tall, black kid with his hand snaked around her waist, fingers splayed lewdly. Her breasts nearly spilled out of the tiny top. The photo had been skewered by a pushpin stuck through the boy's crotch. What kind of world did her daughter live in? What secrets would Andrea never understand? Did she and Pearl have anything in common? Andrea grabbed the sweater and hurried out of the room, her cheeks hot, her lungs stinging.

She found Mike in the living room, working on his laptop.

"I can't let her transfer. I just can't."

He looked up from the screen. "What made you decide that?"

"I was just in her room, and it scared me. She needs to be some place that I'm familiar with, where she can get help if she needs it."

He removed the glasses, sitting back. "What about the fact that she'll always be the girl that gave those blow jobs? Is that the right thing to do?"

"Who knows what's right? I don't have a clue. I feel bad that I haven't searched her room before. I haven't been paying close enough attention."

"You shouldn't have gone into her room. She'll be pissed."

"Why aren't you pissed at her? This goes way beyond her being pissed."

"But why confuse things by invading her privacy? You have to stand back and get a grip on how you're going to handle her."

Every time she imagined Pearl in another school, with the gangs at the public school, the druggies at the art school, she knew that she needed to stay at Crofton. No good solution. She ached for Pearl, knowing how hard it would be to stay at Crofton, but it was the right decision. Mike couldn't really understand. He wasn't her father. She alone would have to bear the burden of the hard decisions and their consequences.

THAT AFTERNOON, PEARL CAME HOME, grabbed a granola bar, and announced that she hated Crofton more than ever, that she just had to transfer. She couldn't stand it anymore.

Andrea was at the open refrigerator, rooting around for leftovers. She closed the refrigerator with her foot and juggled a tower of plastic containers, which she piled onto the counter. "Sorry, Pearl. We've decided that's just not an option."

"What?" she said, her mouth full. "I thought you were thinking of letting me."

"Where did you get that idea?"

She opened a Diet Coke and took a swig, then swallowed. "From Mike." Pearl stood defiantly, chin jutting forward.

Feeling dizzy, her vision pierced by little flickers of light, Andrea continued. "First, Mike shouldn't have said anything about that. I briefly considered it and decided it was a bad idea."

"Why not? *He* thinks it's a good idea."

Did he? "Mike doesn't make these decisions by himself."

"And you're the only one who does? That's so unfair." She slammed the cabinet door shut.

"Hey, easy there. It's not the right place for you. I thought about it, and it's not. I'm sorry."

"No, you're not. You don't care what Mike and I think. I should be able to make my own decisions. I'm fifteen. Why can't I decide where to go?"

"You gave three boys blow jobs. Three! That's seriously reckless behavior."

"Mom, that was only once."

"What are you going to do in a school where there are gangs and drugs?" Pearl sighed and rolled her eyes. "I saw your room and those photos. You're out of control. I need to help you."

"You went in my room and snooped?"

"Do you have something to hide?"

"No, but it's my stuff."

"Not all of it. I found my blue cashmere sweater."

"I was going to return it. Don't go in my room without asking."

Andrea reminded her that it wasn't Pearl's apartment. There were still rules.

"I made one mistake and you're going to keep punishing me forever? That's so unfair!" She threw the half full can at the sink. "I hate you! I can't wait to get out of here!"

"Pearl, you're not ready to leave yet." Pearl stormed out of the kitchen.

Andrea stood for a moment, leaning against the counter, her heart pounding, her face burning, as she tried to catch her breath. She splashed water on her face and wiped it with a towel before heading into the living room, where she knew Mike had heard them argue.

"Did you tell Pearl I might let her transfer?" she asked, struggling to keep her voice from shaking.

He sat back, reading glasses magnifying his eyes. "I didn't say it was a certainty, just that you were considering it."

"Don't you see that now I'm even more the bad guy than before? Where's our united front? You had no right mentioning that to her."

"I only mentioned it after Pearl asked me if I could talk to you. She was crying and I thought it might give her something to aim for, an incentive."

"It's not an incentive if it's not a real option."

"Well, you were thinking about it."

"When did you tell her this?"

"The day before we saw Deirdre."

"We hadn't even talked to the doctor yet?"

"It was a real possibility when she and I talked. How was I to know that you'd change your mind so completely?"

"That was the point of not telling her anything until I'd thought it out." He sat staring, his usual trick of refusing to react. "It wasn't your place to tell her that. Just butt out, okay? You're making it worse."

"Butt out? Really?" He shook his head. "Either I'm part of this or I'm not."

"Honestly, Mike. You haven't raised a kid. You don't just dangle a prize and then whip it away. That's Parenting 101."

"Well, I'd have let her try it."

"She's playing you. Don't you see that? She needs an adult, not a pal."

THE THREE OF THEM BARELY spoke during dinner. Andrea ate

without tasting anything, and Mike drank an extra glass of wine. Pearl wouldn't look at Andrea but she kept her chair turned toward Mike, and Andrea caught her sighing at him as if to say, *What are we going to do with her?* Why didn't Mike stand up for her and say that he went along with her decision? Even if he didn't? After they scraped the half-eaten dinner into the disposal, Pearl retreated to her room, Mike watched TV, and Andrea went to their room and lay awake wondering if Mike really wanted to be a father to Pearl. Would he bail now that the going was tough?

Mike came into their room and sat on the bed. He ruffled her hair, and she put down her book. "What say we take a weekend and go to Door County? We could use a break, huh?"

"It's been ages. I loved that inn where we stayed, the one that had the pool that Pearl loved."

"But just the two of us this time, okay?"

"Do you think it's wise to leave Pearl alone?" she asked.

"We need to get away."

"Maybe. I'll think about it," and she picked up her book again.

THE FOLLOWING DAY, A FRIDAY, Pearl texted from school that she was going out with friends. Andrea called and was tempted to tell her to come straight home, but, afraid of a meltdown, she relented, telling Pearl she needed to be home by ten. Pearl objected, but Andrea reminded her she was lucky to go out at all. She hung up, still worried, but hoped that trusting Pearl would pay off.

She and Mike ate in front of the TV and after dinner, she told him she was going to bed to read until Pearl came home. He took her hand, pulled her in for a kiss, and she headed into their bedroom.

On the table next to their bed sat a framed photo of baby Pearl on Andrea's lap with them in matching flowered dresses. They were nothing alike. Andrea's lame, forced smile, Pearl's stern stare. Andrea hadn't given birth to her own child. What made her think she could raise Pearl? What was she thinking trying to cobble together a family with Mike and Pearl?

Andrea's eyes ran over the same few lines in her book without absorbing anything. Ten o'clock came and no Pearl. When the door opened and shut at ten-fifteen, she heard Mike and Pearl talking and listened to see if they were arguing, but she couldn't tell. She slipped out of bed and walked into the living room, where Pearl sat next to Mike, facing the TV, watching *The Daily Show*, laughing as if nothing had happened. Way to undercut me, Mike.

"Pearl, you're grounded," she said. "We'll talk tomorrow. I don't want to get into it now." Shaking, so angry she wasn't sure if she could get to sleep, she went back to bed, turned off the light and pulled the covers up over her head, taking deep breaths to calm herself down. Around midnight, she felt Mike weigh down his side of the bed, and she pretended to be asleep, steeling herself not to flinch when he touched her, but refusing to talk to him. They hadn't made love since Pearl's trouble, and she wondered if their relationship would survive this crisis intact.

CHAPTER 9
Chicago, 2011

"**M**om!"

It was after 2:00. Andrea sat up. "Pearl?"

She called again. Andrea bolted down the hall toward her room and peeked inside.

"Mom," she said, her voice thick, "I feel awful."

Andrea stepped through the jumbled clothes and sat down on the edge of the bed, touching Pearl's forehead. No fever. Her eyes were muddy with smudged mascara. "What's the matter?" She reeked of cigarettes, but Andrea squelched her impulse to question Pearl about that.

Pearl was tangled up in the sheets, which smelled sour like the bottom of a laundry hamper. Her hair lay across her pillow in ropy snakes. Andrea smoothed the hair and let her fingers linger on Pearl's skin, her smooth cheek, pleased that Pearl didn't flinch, that she needed her mother. Andrea traced the curve of her cheekbone. "What's wrong? Are you sick?"

"No." She shut her eyes and laced her hands over them. "Promise you won't get mad?"

"About what?" Andrea said, bracing herself.

She pinched her lips together, took in a ragged breath, and let it out with a whoosh. "I got a tattoo."

"You what?" Andrea drew back her own hand as if it had been pricked by a needle. "A tattoo? Oh, Pearl, no." Her stomach lurched. "Where is it?" Pearl covered her face with a hand, swiped at her nose with the other, and curled up into a ball.

"On my shoulder. Don't get mad. It's not what I wanted."

"Let me see it."

"You'll get mad."

"I need to know what you're talking about. Come on."

Pearl rolled onto her stomach and hiked up her tee-shirt. On her shoulder an angry welt circled the word HO in crooked letters.

Acid rose in Andrea's throat, but she swallowed it back. Feeling the room tilt, she dropped her head below her waist. "Oh, my God, Pearl. What were you thinking? What's going on with you?"

"Mom, stop. I'm freaking out about this. I wanted a rose."

"A rose? Are you kidding? What were you doing getting a tattoo? Who did this?"

Pearl was wailing.

"Who did this to you?"

Pearl buried her head in the pillow. "Some guy I know."

"Where's he from? School?"

"God, no."

"Who've you been hanging out with? Who are these kids?"

"Some are from Sandberg. Some are from the neighborhood. I don't know."

"Are they in gangs?"

"Oh, yeah, *right*, Mom." Her wet eyes flashed. "All public school kids are in gangs."

"Are they? This is a home-made tattoo."

171

She didn't answer for a moment, then in a tiny voice said, "Some of them are."

"Jesus, Pearl."

"I'm *sorry*, okay?" hitting her like a fist. "I'm sorry I'm not your perfect little girl." She spat out the words as if she wanted to rid her mouth of the taste. She shoved her face so close that Andrea recoiled from her tobacco breath. "You're a shitty mother. I can't believe they let you adopt me."

Tears stung and Andrea's throat squeezed tight. "You know, at times like this, I wonder why I did."

She shrank back, wide-eyed.

"I'm sorry." Andrea reached for her, but Pearl pushed away. "I didn't mean that."

She burst into tears. "God, Mom."

"I didn't mean what I said. Please. I was angry about the tattoo, and I'm so worried about you." Pearl was now weeping in big gulps. "I'm sorry. Come on. Just tell me. What happened?"

"They're…my friends. They're nice to…me."

"This wasn't nice. Friends don't do this kind of thing."

"You don't know what it's like…at school."

"Then you have to tell me."

Pearl boosted herself against the pillows, swabbed at her eyes, sniffed, and rocked as she talked. "I've never been accepted there. If you're not exactly like them, there's no way. I can't go out to lunch because I don't have the money." Andrea handed her a tee-shirt from the floor, and she blew her nose on it. "I've tried like you told me to, but they always ignore me. I eat lunch alone. I sit in class alone. I never get phone calls."

"I'm so sorry." She took Pearl's hand and squeezed it.

"The only people who paid attention to me were those guys

who, you know, and that was such a huge mistake. I thought they were being nice to me, but it was just a joke to them." Her voice tightened into a raspy croak. "But then I met some other kids from Sandberg. They like me the way I am. They don't judge me."

"But, Pearl..." Andrea forced herself to place her hand gently on the swollen skin, as if the screaming, hateful word could be burned into her fingers and erased from Pearl's skin.

"Mama, are you mad?" She rolled onto her side. "Do you forgive me?"

"Yes, but I'm so worried. You're out of control."

"Mama?" She drew Andrea into a hug, quivering, her breath coming in stale hiccups.

"Can I get it removed?"

"Oh, Pearl, of course," she said, running her hand along Pearl's hot, wet face. What else could she say? The little girl she thought she knew, whom she loved but no longer recognized, needed her to tell that lie: that every painful assault could be washed away, every blot on her record wiped clean—even though she didn't believe it herself. "And we can talk about a transfer if that's what you really want." Andrea sat with Pearl until she fell asleep, listening to the reassuring rise and fall of her breathing, knowing that her daughter was home, under their roof, more or less safe, for what was left of the night.

CHAPTER 10
Chicago, January-February, 2011

Andrea walked into her mother's apartment at the Claremont Assisted-Living Facility, and her eyes fell on the sampler that Pearl had cross-stitched when she was eleven, which hung just inside the front door. The alphabet marched stiffly along the bottom row, and two figures in profile heralded a message, "To a Friend's House the Road is Never Long." Andrea wondered how far from home Pearl actually was and what kind of trouble she'd found. Accustomed to shielding her mother from her daughter's problems, Andrea shoved this fear to the back of her mind and steeled herself for this encounter, not sure what she'd find: a self-pitying decline or a ramped-up snit.

Her mother was in the bedroom, sitting in her recliner. A handsome woman, she'd grown into her features as she aged. Her strong nose, which had once made her look plain, now set off her piercing blue eyes and gave her face character. Today, though, her hair looked slept-on and greasy, Nancy wore her favorite blue pants, an oxford cloth shirt with a stain on the front, and shearling slippers on her slender feet. A crooked, lipsticked mouth told Andrea that her mother had groomed herself this morning, no doubt rebuffing the offer of help from Gabriela, the earnest aide who worked at Claremont.

She glared at Andrea. "You're late. Now I'll never get my place at the table."

"Mom, I'm early." She pointed to her watch. "It's only 10:45. I got away from work as soon as I could. You'll find your seat."

"We've got to go down there right now," Nancy said, pushing the handle to lower her footrest and attempting to hoist herself out of the chair. "And we can talk about the restaurant for my birthday dinner with Pearl."

Andrea pulled up a chair and sat, facing her. "Mom, I'm so sorry. Pearl called and said she's got a big project due and won't be able to get away for your birthday."

Pearl, let's talk, okay? I don't want to leave things the way they were. Please call.

"Oh, dear," Nancy said. "Couldn't she just fly in for the day?"

"Mom, it's too expensive. She's very busy."

"Too busy for my birthday? Was that *her* decision?"

Swallowing the dig, Andrea said, "It's just not possible for her to come home now."

"Did you remind her that it's my eighty-fifth? I may not have any more birthdays, you know." Her voice grew thin and teary. "But I should have expected this. No one takes the time to come see me."

"I'm sorry, Mom. It's just too hard for her to leave."

Nancy sat hunched in her chair, her hands folded in her lap like broken birds.

"Mom, you can't expect everyone to drop what they're doing and fly home for one day. She'll be here for Easter."

"That's too far off. I'm all alone."

"Mom, *I'm* here," Andrea said, her throat constricting.

Her mother sniffed angrily and shook her head. "You know what I mean."

With Pearl gone, Andrea found herself the only one left, Joanne having decamped to Connecticut with her husband. Mike was out of the picture as well. Pearl's problems had become a growing source of friction with him. After being Pearl's main cheerleader, Mike had done a 180 when some of his possessions started disappearing. Finally, after $200 went missing from his wallet, Mike and Pearl had had a screaming fight about it, her refusing to admit anything. He said that Andrea was deluding herself about saving Pearl, that she couldn't keep bailing her daughter out. Pearl needed to take the consequences for her actions.

"I can't abandon her."

"Not abandon, force her to grow up."

"But she needs me."

"She needs you to do this."

Andrea suspected he'd finally paid attention when it impinged on him directly. Where had he been through all the other troubles? She said he didn't have the stomach for the hard stuff, and they'd gone back and forth, feeling themselves rip further apart. Finally, they'd broken up, and she'd gone it alone with Pearl, seeing her limp through the rest of her time at the School for the Arts. When she was accepted to the Museum School in Boston, Andrea had been hopeful that Pearl had found her way. Until she ran away. Where was she?

ANDREA WALKED OVER TO THE windowsill, where the crystal dolphin and porcelain horse stood in a face-off. She wiped them with the hem of her skirt, repositioning them to look out at the Chicago skyline and expanse of Lake Michigan. Crouching, she gathered discarded newspapers into a pile and dropped them into the recycling bin and inspected the laundry basket. A wrapped package of linens sat on the bed. Housekeeping had clearly made a recent, if cursory, sweep of the apartment. The family photos on her dresser had been disturbed for dusting. A black-and-white glamour shot of Nancy with pageboy and pearls, her hair tinted strawberry blond, her lips pink; the sisters, Joanne, her mother's clone, and Andrea, who favored their brown-haired father, in matching plaid dresses; Joanne on her wedding day wearing lace and a fierce look; school photos of the grandchildren, Gary, Blair, and Pearl. She picked up Pearl's second-grade school photo. Against Andrea's advice, Pearl had insisted on wearing her favorite sweatshirt that day, purple with a unicorn leaping across the front. Wiry curls escaped from the barrettes, with which Andrea had struggled to tame her hair in a daily pitched battle of wills between them. Pearl's crooked front teeth shone bright against her dark skin. Andrea felt a flush roll up her face, and she sucked in her breath, returning the photo to its place on the dresser.

"Come on," Andrea said. "Let's go down to lunch now." As Andrea leaned over her mother, she caught a whiff of stale urine. "Are the aides helping you bathe?" Graciela could do that for you. It's her job."

"I don't want them touching me. I'm not one of those crazy old women."

"But they have to make sure you're safe in the shower."

"Look what one of them did to me yesterday." She thrust her hands at Andrea. Her pale skin was fragile as a rose petal, and purple splotches bloomed even from gentle touches.

"That's too bad." Andrea took her mother's pinky and rotated her hand gently. The bruises didn't look suspicious. "Well, how are you *today*?"

"I'm in a place where people go to die," she said, shooting Andrea a hateful stare.

"Mom, you know that the doctor said you weren't safe living alone. You've had several falls, remember?" Her mother shrugged. "And I can't help it that Pearl can't come home. You and I will have a nice time, the two of us." Why wasn't her mother angry at Joanne, who could never seem to tear herself away from Connecticut to visit? True, her money, well, her husband's money, had helped provide for this top-tier place on the Gold Coast, but that wasn't the same as showing up in person and dealing with their mother's constant demands. Mitchell and Joanne paid with cash, but Andrea paid with sweat: the doctors' visits, shopping for shampoo, antacids, and tissues, checking to see that her mother was safe, paying her bills, rebuilding goodwill fences with the staff after her mother tore them down by her rudeness. It was never Joanne's fault. Their mother always stuck up for her, accepting her lame excuses for why she couldn't--wouldn't—visit: she had to babysit for Blair's child, Mitchell had a partners' dinner with wives, or there was some Pilates class she just couldn't miss. But most of all, it was Pearl Nancy wanted to see, more than any of her biological family.

Andrea cradled her mother's elbow and helped her stand. They headed down the long hallway, decorated with loveseats, lined with handrails and prints of country scenes, and Andrea slowed her step to match Nancy's as she crept along behind her walker. By the time they reached the elevator, her mother was breathing heavily. Posted inside the elevator was that day's schedule of activities—shopping, crafts, bridge, Happy Hour, a movie, trivia, trip to the Art Institute—all the things Nancy refused to do. She mostly stayed in her apartment and read *The New York Times*, front to back, deigning to go to meals but not making any effort to fit in.

"Why can't Pearl come home?"

"I told you. She's busy at school."

I know you're angry, Pearl, but we have to talk. Come on. I'm so worried.

"YOU DON'T HAVE TO SNAP at me. I can't remember everything."

Right. The woman who could hold her own in any political argument claimed a fuzzy memory. She clearly remembered what she wanted to, and Andrea knew that whatever the truth, Pearl's actions would be Andrea's fault in Nancy's eyes. Because of that, Andrea had carefully shielded her mother from Pearl's worst escapades--the suspension from high school, the bad grades, the cigarette and pot smoking, the low-life boys she hung out with, the obscene tattoo, and now, dropping out of college--knowing that it would crush her mother to see her beloved grandchild go so far off the rails. But it also protected Andrea from her mother's judgments. Permissive parenting, her breakup with Mike, failures her mother warned would come home to roost. Was it true? Despite her best efforts to create a good home for Pearl, had Andrea failed her in some major way? Or had some thread of Pearl's DNA slipped in and cancelled her upbringing?

In the empty dining room, Nancy scuffed over to her chosen place at table sixteen. Andrea scooted her in, snapped the bib around her neck, and laid extra napkins in her lap. Nancy swatted the air around her as if Andrea were a pesky no-see-um. "I can do this myself!" The servers were standing near the kitchen talking, and when they saw the early arrivals, their circle tightened. Andrea crossed the dining room and grabbed a menu from the sideboard along with a pitcher of water and walked back to her mother. Nancy cast the menu aside. "I'm not hungry," she said, sulking.

"You have to eat something."

"Okay, I'll have some chicken broth, if that'll make you happy." She pushed the menu, which crinkled the place mat and made her water glass shudder.

"Come on, Mom. Let's have a nice lunch."

They sat waiting until they could order. The dining room had been decorated for Valentine's Day, a couple of weeks off. Red and pink hearts with silhouetted cupids were taped to the walls, and red garlands stretched along the ceiling.

"Oh," Nancy said. "Did I tell you that Cyd Charisse moved in on the third floor?"

"The dancer?" Andrea asked. "Is she still alive? And why would she live here?"

"I'd know those legs anywhere."

"Sure, Mom."

A woman scuffed into the dining room, her pencil-thin legs covered by sagging support hose, her body hunched over a walker, Graciela guiding her from behind. Everything about her was white–hair, skin, clothes–except for her coal-black eyes and drawn-on eyebrows. She looked like a snowy terrier, all jowls and wheezy mouth. Nancy rolled her eyes as Graciela aimed her toward their table. "Hello, Nancy!" Graciela said in a high, chipper voice. "You're going to be eating with Irene today."

"Oh, wonderful," Nancy grumbled as she grabbed her glass, water sloshing over the top.

Graciela lowered the woman into her seat and whisked away the walker. "I want orange juice!" the woman announced. "Oh, dear, oh dear." One of the servers stole a glance over her shoulder, but didn't approach.

"Oh, be quiet, you old bat," Nancy stage-whispered.

"Mom!"

"She can't hear me. She's deaf."

"I want coffee!" the woman barked, and Andrea jumped up to get it.

Nancy stopped her. "They don't want us helping ourselves to anything hot. Afraid of a lawsuit or something. Ridiculous." She patted Andrea's place. "And don't encourage her. They'll get to her in time." The woman continued to ask for coffee, for orange juice, for coffee.

At a couple of minutes after eleven, a young Asian man walked over with an order pad. "Whatwouldyouliketodayladies?" Nancy ordered broth, Andrea asked for her usual grilled salmon, and the snow-white woman asked about her coffee.

"Irene, I'll get it in a minute. Do you want your usual? Chowder and orange juice?"

"And coffee."

Nancy sighed deeply. Andrea shrugged and rolled her eyes at her mother, who was angrily fishing ice cubes out of her glass.

"Sorry, Mom. I forgot about the ice."

"So you didn't tell me when Pearl *is* coming home."

"Spring break." She cringed, both at the lie and the thought that Pearl might still be at large, even then. The dining room was filling up, and the wait staff maneuvered around tables with trays and pitchers of water, avoiding collisions with the teetering residents. Their server arrived with the food and slid the plates in front of them. "Enjoy."

Nancy turned to the woman in white and bellowed, "My granddaughter is smart as a whip. She goes to art school in Boston. I don't know why she's not doing something she can actually use, like the law or medicine." The woman sat there, crumbling crackers into her chowder, then leaning in, her hand trembling, trying with pursed lips to slurp up a viscous spoonful.

"No, Mom," Andrea said. "*You* wanted her to be a doctor. And, okay, for a while, she kind of liked science, but now, she's studying art. *She* wants to be an artist. It's not about what *we* want."

"I was going to be a doctor," Nancy said.

Andrea knew that claim was a stretch, but it could be one of her mother's many fantasies. She and Cyd Charisse, rooming together and exchanging organic chemistry notes with each other before going out on a double date with Gene Kelly and Paul Newman.

"I hope I don't die before I see her again."

"You won't. She's busy now, but she'll come home when she can."

"I just don't know what kind of test she has in art school that's so important she can't take a day off."

Andrea didn't, in fact, know what Pearl had been asked to do in art school. Crits, foundation, color theory—these were terms she gleaned from what little Pearl had told her, but she didn't really know what Pearl's life had been like since high school.

THE LAST TIME ANDREA TALKED to Pearl a couple of weeks ago, they'd had a huge argument about her quitting college. "It's a done deal, Mom." When Andrea had asked her how she'd live,

Pearl had said that she and her boyfriend, Renny, would get jobs. They'd figure it out.

"Your grandparents didn't set up your college fund for you to run off like this with some boy."

"Great, so now you're going to guilt me about that? I'm not like you, remember?" She accused Andrea of having a grand plan to save and mold her into a success. But it was her life to choose. "I'm not your fucking social science project, okay?"

"You're being very foolish. And selfish."

"I can't talk to you." And she'd hung up. Andrea had resisted the urge to call right back and had forced herself to wait ten minutes. By then, Pearl didn't answer.

NANCY PUSHED ASIDE HER BROTH and motioned for a package of crackers. "The food here has gone steadily down the tubes. You tell me they can't make a simple chicken broth?"

"I've always kind of liked the food here," Andrea said, biting into a forkful of salmon.

"Yeah, well, they put on the Ritz when family come to visit." She fumbled with the cellophane, yanking it open, spilling crumbs on her blouse. "I miss my own cooking."

"I'm sure you do. You're a terrific cook."

"You never really took an interest in cooking, did you?" she asked. "Now that Mike and you are finished, are you back to eating those frozen dinners again?"

"Mom, I cook," she said, although it was mostly a lie.

"Well, you can certainly operate a microwave."

Despite her mother's supposed lack of an appetite, she finished her broth and two packs of crackers, then decided to have coffee and a bowl of strawberry ice cream for dessert. She took her time, adding Sweet and Low and a few drops of milk, stirring her coffee just so.

Andrea checked her watch. She was due back at work but needed to wait for her mother to finish. Finally, they made the excruciatingly long trip back to her mother's apartment, and Andrea was able to leave, her chest tight, her head pounding.

You know, Pearl. Gram keeps asking about you. What am I supposed to tell her? Think of that.

Wonderful, now *she* was laying on the guilt with a trowel. Of course, she knew where she'd learned to do that. Scary.

Her mother took credit for all of Pearl's good qualities, as if, because she'd given birth and Andrea hadn't, she could do a better job. "Sometimes a child just needs a grandmother to teach her some manners," she'd say as she rapped the dinner table sternly, motioning for Pearl to place her napkin in her lap. Yes, of course, table manners really set kids on the straight and narrow path. That's all it takes: use the right fork and you'll meet a prince, chew with your mouth closed and you'll live happily ever after.

Pearl was the only one though who could bring out Nancy's soft side. When she was a young girl, they shared a love of scrapbooks. Nancy would sit next to Pearl, her slender hands guiding Pearl's pudgy ones as she wielded huge, scary scissors, cutting out pictures from old copies of *Ladies' Home Journal* and *Life*. They loved anything that required a needle–sewing, embroidery, knitting–and gave each other home-made gifts. She framed and hung Pearl's art work: a drawing of Pearl standing under a rainbow, Pearl riding a horse, Pearl swimming in a turquoise Lake Michigan. She prominently displayed the lumpy candy dish that

Pearl made for her in school. Couldn't her mother see that this probably spawned Pearl's love for making art? Andrea didn't have the patience or skill for close work. Under her tense hands the threads seized up, buckling the cloth beyond repair. She envied her mother's easy way with Pearl, even after Pearl had become a prickly adolescent, how they managed to slip into a comfortable pattern even after weeks of separation. Pearl had acquired—because she hadn't inherited it--Nancy's withering stare that could render Andrea mute when it was aimed in her direction.

During the long, steady decline of Andrea's father due to Parkinson's, Nancy had coped well enough, taking on the lion's share of her husband's care, even tasks that required strength, balance, and a strong stomach. But after his death, she'd taken several falls and so, a year ago, Andrea and Joanne had forced the decision to move her to the Claremont. Since then, Pearl sent her hand-painted cards for holidays and visited her regularly. They'd sit on the sofa, her mother holding Pearl's hand—a touch Pearl no longer permitted Andrea—as Pearl patiently answered questions about art school, questions that, if Andrea had asked them, would have made Pearl snap at her. What would happen now?

FOR TWO WEEKS, ANDREA'S CALLS to Pearl had gone directly into voice mail with no response, and it worried Andrea that Pearl's phone could either be out of juice or lost. And if so, what did that mean? She didn't know Pearl's roommate's last name or her cell phone number, so she couldn't call her.

Swallowing her pride, Andrea called Mike on the off chance that he'd heard from Pearl.

"Why do you think she'd call me, of all people?" he asked. Andrea said she was covering all her bases.

"You know," he said, "she's yanking you around, hoping you'll cave. What does she want from you now?"

"Mike, I'm really worried."

"Trust me," he said, "she's fine." Then, his tone softer, he added, "Andrea, I'm sure she's okay."

When he asked how Andrea was doing, she started to cry but said she was probably overreacting, as usual.

"She'll call when she's ready," he said. "Try not to worry too much. I know, easy for me to say."

Andrea was worried, of course, but she thought, she was pretty sure, that if Pearl were in trouble, she'd have let her know. Pearl couldn't be that angry. Andrea welcomed anger over the alternative, that Pearl couldn't get in touch with her for any number of horrible reasons. How could she drop out, just like that, in her freshman year, to go off with some boy? Pearl had seemed to straighten out after a very rocky adolescence, and Andrea had hoped this new, more even-keeled existence would last. But she knew that was naïve, that there were more bumps to come.

Andrea called the Museum School to see if she could locate the R.A. in Pearl's dorm.

"It says here that Pearl Barton is on a leave of absence," the woman in the Registrar's office reported. "So she's not registered. The address in Chicago is the only one of record."

"Of course, that's her home."

"Have you tried calling her and leaving a message?"

"Well, I've obviously done that or I wouldn't be asking you," Andrea said, clicking off the phone, blood roaring in her ears. She set up a new anonymous email account in the hope that Pearl would open the message, thinking it was a friend. She even tried to text, but couldn't make it work, her fingers cramping as she fumbled with the tiny buttons, then either did or didn't send the message.

The following day, Andrea met Freya for their weekly lunch and frustration vent away from the workplace. They drove separately because they both had afternoon appointments off-site, and had chosen a café that served good salads, which allowed them to justify wine and dessert. After the muzak and fluorescent lighting in the Claremont dining room, Andrea welcomed this dark place where the lines were softened and no one shouted to be heard or wore a bib.

Andrea hugged Freya. They settled at a booth and ordered their food. "I really need that big glass of wine today," said Andrea. "We won't tell anyone at work."

"No word yet?" Freya asked, unwinding a long striped shawl from her neck, her curly hair a staticky halo around her cold-flushed cheeks. A dab of lipstick smudged one of her front teeth.

"No, and I'm just so worried," she said, setting her cell phone on the table next to her and giving it a pat as if to coax out a ring. "I just can't imagine why she won't at least send me a message."

"You're imagining the worst, and that's understandable, but I'm sure she's fine and she's holding out until she feels able to get in touch. Kids don't have any idea how much we worry."

"You'd be worried, right?"

"Hysterical. But it doesn't do any good. You have to slow down and keep your wits about you." Andrea started to cry, and Freya took her hand. "Pearl will get in touch. She's off on some lark, and she's afraid to tell you where she is."

"What if she can't get in touch?"

"She will."

"What if she's strung out somewhere? Or turning tricks?"

"Don't even think that. She's with a boyfriend, right?"

"Who knows? She said she was, but I don't trust her about anything anymore. Doesn't she know how worried I am?"

"She may not see it that way. If she's fine, she might not realize you're a wreck. I remember Claudio snuck off to be with a girl and had what he thought was an ironclad alibi of spending the night at a friend's house. However, I called his friend's house and he wasn't there. I was a wreck."

"And when he came home, you weren't mad?"

"I was furious. But the stakes were lower. He was in town. I knew that much. And he's a boy. If it had been Rosa, I'd have felt just like you."

The food arrived on huge plates. Andrea picked out the olives and took a bite of lettuce. "I've called everyone I can think of, even Mike, if you can believe that." Freya winced sympathetically. "At this point, my mother and Joanne are the only ones who don't know." She ripped apart a roll and crumbled it. "And to think I went along with art school against my better judgment and now she's thrown that away too."

"You'd feel better if she were blowing off Yale?"

"Of course not." Suddenly full, she pushed aside her half-eaten salad and took a deep gulp of her wine.

Freya ordered a piece of chocolate cake with two forks. "You may need to let her go for a while in order to come back of her own accord."

"I just can't imagine her running away like this. Did I cause this? Or is this about the adoption? Is this a birth-mother-roots thing?"

"I don't know," Freya said, thinking a moment. "Could be."

"I've tried to let her be herself."

"It may not matter what you did or didn't do. This is Pearl's thing. She may not finish college. She may not do what you want her to do."

"But some things are non-negotiable. Like college." Andrea heard her tone grow angry and shrill. "I just want her to aim higher than where she came from."

"That's why you adopted her?"

"No, of course not."

"Andrea, you have to sort out your feelings. It's hard not to feel hurt by this. I suspect she's just trying to find herself and needs to do it away from you."

"She *was* away from me."

"At a college you approved of."

"Yes, I forced her to try to have a better life," she said, feeling tears push their way to the surface.

"Andrea…"

The server arrived with the cake and removed their salad plates as Freya rubbed Andrea's arm, and Andrea fought not to break down.

"How can you be so certain she'll come back?"

"You have to believe she will."

"What am I going to tell my mother?"

"How is she, by the way?" Freya took a bite of cake and edged the plate toward Andrea.

"Pissed at me because Pearl isn't coming home for one day for her eighty-fifth birthday. I mean, even if she were still in school, I wouldn't pay for a one-day trip."

"I understand your mother is driving you crazy, but she doesn't even know Pearl is missing."

"Well, I can't tell her. I keep hoping Pearl will show up and I won't have to." She wiped chocolate from her mouth. "If I tell her, it'll be my fault."

"Isn't that what you're worried about anyway?"

Andrea felt her scalp contract. "Oh, God, *is* this my fault?"

"Andrea, I didn't say that. It's more complicated, of course. One advantage your mother has is that she can reshape the world to fit her needs. You don't have that luxury."

"But this would just kill her."

"Do you think you need to keep up a fantasy for your mother?"

"I cushion my mother from the harsher realities, but I don't make stuff up. Mom's in another league from me on that."

"Nancy has always been a fabulist."

Andrea had always hated her mother's stories and wondered why she needed to embellish life, to exaggerate Andrea and Joanne's accomplishments to her friends. "Wasn't I enough for her as I was?" Andrea asked as she motioned for the cake and ate another bite. "Someone had to decipher Mom's fantasies for Pearl. I promised I wouldn't inflict the same skewed view of the world on her."

"We all inflict something on our kids. And maybe Pearl wouldn't have minded a dose of fantasy."

"No, adoptees especially need their parents to give them a firm grounding in fact. I've always tried to tell Pearl the truth. If only Pearl would get in touch, I could stop worrying."

"Kids have a state of grace that takes them through hard times. Maybe she's holed up in Chicago, blocks away, afraid to come home, afraid you'll be angry at her. Just take her back without a lecture. There'll be time for that later."

"What if she's trying to find her birth mother?"

"How would she do a search? Her mother vanished. Besides, *you're* her mother."

"I wish I could be as optimistic as you," she said, her voice thin, her eyes stinging. She swiped at her face. "At this point, I'd be happy to have her here, pissed as hell, than off doing who knows what."

At the end of the meal, Freya led Andrea out to the car and tied Andrea's scarf for her as if she were a child. She gave her a big hug and made her promise to call "any time of night" with news.

As ANDREA WAS DRIVING NORTH on Ashland on her way to her appointment, she saw a young black woman with curly hair tied into a brush on top of her head, like Pearl's. She even walked like her, with long strides, her body bent forward as if struggling against a strong wind. Like Pearl, she was solid, her hips swelling from underneath a short jean jacket. Andrea kept her eye on the woman while she negotiated traffic, cursing at the red light. The woman turned onto Wrightwood. When she got the green, Andrea sped to the corner, turned right, and headed down the street, her breath coming in short gasps. A taxi sat in the middle of the street, idling, as a woman climbed out and reached back in for shopping bags. Andrea honked then squeezed past, shooting the cabdriver a dirty look before continuing down the street. When she saw the young woman up ahead stop to light a cigarette, she slowed down the car, careful not to alarm her in case Pearl made a run for it. Andrea edged up alongside her, bracing for the encounter, willing her to turn around. She lowered the passenger window and leaned over. "Pearl?" The woman spun around, and it was a stranger, who frowned, shrugged her backpack higher onto her shoulder, quickening her pace as she ducked into an alley.

Now I'm losing my mind. I thought I saw you on the street today. It made me so sad when I realized it wasn't you. Sorry if that makes you feel bad, but you need to know that this is not just about you.

THAT NIGHT, TO DISTRACT HERSELF, Andrea tried cleaning up the apartment and ended up in the hall closet digging through the box of Pearl's baby clothes--overalls, sleepers, corduroy tie-on shoes, all shabby and stained. At the bottom of the pile, she found the quilt, which had been Pearl's constant companion until the age of four when Andrea convinced her that big girls didn't take blankets to Pre-K. Pearl bravely gave it up, but continued to suck her thumb at school. Now she wished she'd let Pearl hang onto it. What harm would a blanket have done anyway? A baby-block quilt of gingham squares, its reds and blues were faded now, and tufts of batting poked through the tattered fabric. A rust-colored stain in the corner came from a nosebleed Pearl had one night. Barely hanging together now, it was the ghost of a quilt. Andrea held it to her nose and inhaled deeply, but it had been washed and packed away, smelling of dust and old cotton. All traces of Pearl, gone.

Pearl, I'm sorry I've been so harsh on the phone. I'm just worried. I love you. I don't care where you are or what you've done. Just get in touch. Let me know you're okay. Please.

THREE WEEKS AFTER PEARL'S DISAPPEARANCE, Andrea's cell phone rang and she jumped on it. Deflated, she saw that it was her mother's number and nearly let it go to voice mail, but she braced herself and answered. Instead of her mother, the accented voice of Graciela reported that her mother had fallen and was going to the hospital.

"How did she fall? Can I talk to her?"

"The paramedics just left with her."

Andrea raced to Northwestern Hospital and headed right to the expensive parking garage instead of looking for a metered spot. Arriving at the Emergency Room, she asked where they'd taken her mother. A woman in fuchsia-colored scrubs led her to a curtained area where she found her mother in bed, wearing a hospital gown, her hair wispy and thin, her skin ghostly. Andrea gingerly laid a hand on Nancy's bare arm. "Mom, how are you? I'm sorry you fell."

"Damn desk," she said, licking her dry lips, pale without lipstick. "It got in the way. I brushed by it, and the next thing I knew, I was on the floor. I couldn't move."

"Did you get out of bed by yourself?"

She looked around as if someone else had asked the question.

"Mom? Why didn't you call the aide to help you?"

"I had to go. I'm almost eighty-five. I should be able to go to the toilet without company."

"I wish you could, but you see what happened. Now you've really hurt yourself." Nancy's head was bowed. "Mom, look at me." Nancy raised pitiful, watery eyes. No, she wouldn't give in to her mother's games.

Andrea ran through the scenario in her head. Nancy's hip would be broken, and she wouldn't be able to walk, so Andrea wouldn't be able to take her out because she couldn't lift her mother, and she'd have to call a Medicar every time Nancy had a doctor's appointment, even though the hospital was just a few blocks away. And there'd be no birthday dinner.

When they took Nancy into X-ray, Andrea stepped outside the hospital and dialed Pearl's number. As usual, it went right to her throaty-voiced message: "Hey there. This is Pearl."

Pearl, Gram fell and is in the hospital. At Northwestern. They're doing X-rays now, and we hope it's not a hip break. It's her birthday in three days, and she keeps asking for you. Please call her. Even if you don't call me, just... Her voice cracked, so she hung up.

ANDREA REMEMBERED THE EXCRUCIATING PAIN when she dislocated her kneecap during a performance of a high-school play. She lay on stage helpless until the paramedics arrived, screaming when they lifted her, embarrassed that dozens of people still sat in their seats, staring. Andrea remembered Nancy sitting in the ambulance and how she'd tried not to cry anymore so her mother wouldn't be angry at her. What would happen to Andrea when she herself was old if Pearl never came home?

She dialed Joanne's number.

"How did this happen?" Joanne asked, annoyed. "Aren't they supposed to keep an eye on her?" Meaning, Andrea supposed, how did Andrea fail to protect her?

"They can't watch her every second, and she won't let them help her anyway."

"Well, you have to make her see that she needs help."

"Yeah, that'll be easy." Her head throbbed, making it hard to think straight. "I really could use your help right now. Can you come? Maybe for Mom's birthday?"

"But if she's being taken care of, wouldn't it make more sense to wait a while? I can come when she's out of the hospital and help out. I mean, what would I do except sit in the hospital?"

"Which is what I'm doing now."

"And I appreciate it, Andrea. You know that."

Couldn't Joanne see that Andrea needed her even more than their mother did?

Joanne continued, "How are you holding up?"

Her throat tight, Andrea said, "I'm just worried about what this means." She hadn't told Joanne about Pearl and couldn't now. How much more could she take?

"Keep me posted. I want to help."

"Do I have that option? Just to *help*?"

"Andrea..."

"This. Is. Hard."

"You think I don't know that? But as you said, she's in there for a while. I'll come in a couple of weeks."

Andrea struggled to keep her composure. "I guess that'll have to do. Bye." She hung up, face burning, head aching, as she massaged her stiff neck, smoothed her skirt. When she pushed the revolving door back into the stale air of the E.R., she felt a vice clamp over her chest, squeezing tight.

Luckily, the hip, although broken, would heal, but the doctor said Nancy needed to use a wheel chair until her strength came back, and she'd have to be a regular visitor to the physical therapy room at the Claremont or she wouldn't walk again.

The day after the fall, Andrea visited her mother in the hospital, but she looked odd, distant, as if she were looking through Andrea at someone on the other side of the room. She kept peeling off the elastic stockings the nurses had put on her legs to prevent clots from extended bed rest.

"Get these things off me!"

Andrea pulled them up, but her mother kicked her feet. "Mom, stop it." They struggled. "Now!" Nancy looked startled, then gave another kick.

After Andrea finally calmed her mother down, Nancy said, "The woman next to me has Ebola. I'm going to be contaminated. Get me another room."

"Mom, I think you mean *E. coli*."

"I know what I heard," she said, her eyes flashing.

Andrea turned on the TV as a buffer, then placed the untouched tray of food in the hall and poured her mother a glass of water, making sure to strain out the ice cubes.

"Andrea, what's that dog doing in here?"

"What?" She looked up at the TV, which was showing *The View*, but no animals appeared on the screen.

"A dog, under my bed." She teetered on her side, swiping at the air beneath her bed. "Here, puppy."

"Mom, be careful." Grabbing Nancy's bony shoulder, Andrea lowered her back onto the pillows. "There's no dog here." Could her mother have hit her head in the fall? "Mom? Are you okay? Do you know where you are?"

"Of course I do," she said, craning her neck to look out the window.

"Listen, I'll be back in a minute. Don't move. Hear me?" Andrea ran down the hall to the nurses' station and found the young doctor, sipping a coffee, chatting with another doctor.

"She's sun-downing," he said. "It's a very common disorientation for older people when they're in the hospital, particularly at night. It should subside."

"But this is morning."

"Well, she's at an age where some dementia could be setting in."

"Dementia? No, she has a razor-sharp mind. She molds the world to fit her fantasies, but she knows what's real."

"That may be so." He stood, staring at a computer screen. Did he even know what patient she was talking about? "You'll just have to wait." He dropped his cup into the trash and headed down the hall away from her mother's room.

AT HOME THAT EVENING, ANDREA called Joanne to report on their mother's confusion. Joanne thought it must have been trauma from the fall. "You had to see it, Joanne. It was scary. Her eyes were vacant."

"Okay, if you really need me, I'll try to shift some things around and come for a few days."

"Thank you. I just can't do this alone." She hated admitting this to Joanne, who had Mitchell and her children. "Call me when you get a ticket."

After hanging up, it occurred to her that Joanne would need a place to stay and that Andrea didn't want Joanne at her place. She'd have to clean up Pearl's room and even then, Joanne's unspoken displeasure would be deafening. Maybe Joanne could stay at their mother's apartment. At least there was housekeeping and food.

And what would she tell Joanne about Pearl? She could pretend to her mother that Pearl was too busy to visit, but what would she do if her mother died? What excuse would she make for Pearl's absence, for no contact whatsoever?

She called Freya who didn't answer her cell phone, so she left a message. Sitting at the window in the dark, she looked out at traffic along Sheridan, then walked through the apartment, lit only by the light from street, waiting for hearing to kick in and guide her by sonar.

Pearl. I'm worried that something awful has happened, and I can't face that right now. Just leave a message. I won't even pick up. Please.

The open freezer gleamed bright, and she took a pint of chocolate ice cream, dug in with a spoon, and stared at the cell phone photo of Pearl taken at her high-school graduation. One bite turned into the whole carton as she counted out fifteen more minutes. She dumped the empty into the trash and sat down, her head aching, her stomach bloated, then dialed again.

Pearl. Gram's dying. Come home.

From the refrigerator, she grabbed a cold chicken leg, gnawed on it, swigged some milk with an Ambien, and staggered off to bed.

The phone woke her up, and she answered it, breathless, "Pearl?"

"No, Freya. You sounded awful in your message. What's happening with your mother?"

Andrea's mouth was sticky, and she found it hard to string words together.

"Do you want me to come over?" Freya asked.

"No, I just need to get some sleep. Thanks."

JOANNE ARRIVED AND THEY HAD a meeting with the doctor, who said their mother's mental status was tenuous, that she hadn't been compliant with the physical therapist who'd come to assess her case. "We'll hire a private therapist," Joanne said.

"But if Mom won't do what he says, what's the point?"

"She can't help it, Andrea. She's in pain."

"Her being difficult doesn't help, for sure."

Andrea wondered why Joanne cared suddenly about the details when up to then, she'd been content to leave everything to Andrea.

The doctor asked if their mother had an Advanced Directive. Andrea knew her mother didn't want heroic measures, but Joanne balked at the idea of a DNR. "How can you decide ahead of time not to resuscitate?"

"But it's better to decide before there's a crisis."

"She broke her hip. She's not dying."

"And you're going back to Connecticut, and I'll have to make these decisions on my own."

"So it's just easier for you to decide now that she's a lost cause."

Not fair of Joanne to put it in those terms, as if Andrea were waiting to pull the plug on their mother. Did she think any of this was easy for her?

That night, they ate take-out salads at their mother's place in front of the TV. The reality show provided a buffer zone, even allowing them to agree on how stupid those housewives were. "Just how much would you have to drink to go on that show?" Joanne wondered.

"There's not enough Pinot Grigio in the world," Andrea said. "Not that they'd want me. But people love this kind of blood sport."

"Mitchell hates it when I watch junk TV. Does he think I sit around all day, melting my brain on soap operas? It's really about my not catering to him at every moment. Hey, I've raised my kids. I've catered to him for years. Let him get his own damn beer."

199

"Mike would always wait until I was in the middle of a good book to try to have a serious talk. 'Go away and let me read, please.' Where was he when I actually wanted to talk? He was like a cat, only paying attention when I wasn't."

"Well, they're not here now, are they?" Joanne said as she leaned her head against the pillows and put her feet up.

THE MORNING OF HER MOTHER's birthday marked a month since Pearl's disappearance. Andrea and Joanne showed up at the hospital with gifts–a sky-blue pashmina from Joanne, lemon verbena shower gel and a Jade plant from Andrea. As they walked into the shared room, they saw their mother's roommate lying in bed, snoring raggedly. Joanne again mentioned that they should have insisted on a private room.

Beyond the dividing curtain, an aide was rubbing lotion into Nancy's feet. Andrea expected to see Nancy push her away, but clearly, she enjoyed it. Her eyes closed, she was almost cooing. A pile of diapers sat on the windowsill next to a large bouquet of freesia sent by Joanne.

"Happy Birthday, Mom," said Joanne as she gave their mother a kiss.

Andrea slid into the narrow space on the other side of the bed, lifting a pile of blue absorbent pads and placing them on the floor. She kissed the air near her mother's ear. "We brought your gifts."

"Mom, are you comfortable here?" asked Joanne. "Would you prefer a private room?"

"This is fine. I don't much care."

"Let me show you the newest picture of Blair's baby, Ruby. Can you believe she's four months already?" Joanne held her phone in front of Nancy, flipping through the photos, talking about Blair and her family and how Gary was doing just great. Nancy blinked at the screen.

After a minute or so of photo sharing, Andrea asked, "So, how are you today, Mom?"

Nancy's face brightened. "I had the most wonderful thing happen last night."

"Tell us," said Joanne.

Nancy's hands drew a dramatic arc above her head. She still wore her rings, despite Andrea's offer to take them back to her apartment for safekeeping. "Pearl came to see me."

Andrea's vision blurred. "What?"

"Oh, yes. She came and we sat and talked."

"Pearl's in town?" Joanne asked, looking at Andrea. "Where is she? Why didn't you tell me?"

Andrea's fingers started to tingle. "Mom, that's not possible."

"Now, why would you question me on that?"

"Pearl called you on the phone?" asked Joanne.

"No, of course not. She was right here." She pointed to the foot of her bed. Andrea looked in that direction, seeing only the plastic box for used syringes.

Andrea wondered if it could be true. "Mom, she must have called."

Nancy turned her steely-eyed gaze on Andrea. "Are you telling me I don't know when my Pearl is here?"

Andrea's heart leapt in her throat. "Mom, I know for a fact that Pearl isn't in town. I told you. She's at school."

"She was here!" Nancy jabbed her finger toward the foot of the bed. "I saw her, right in front of me." Ruddy patches had sprung up on her cheeks.

Was it possible that Pearl slipped into town without telling

Andrea? That she'd been here all along? Would she go to that much trouble to avoid Andrea? "Mom, you know I can check with the nurses to see if she did come. I'm going to do that." As she stood, a wave of dizziness forced her back against the windowsill.

"She told me she's working and has an apartment."

"Here? No, that can't be. Come on, Mom. I don't want your stories now." This had to be a fantasy. "Please, I need you to be truthful."

"What's going on? What about art school?" Joanne asked.

"Well," continued their mother, "we mostly reminisced. She told me about her school play, when she played the lead in *South Pacific*. She did that dance while washing her hair." Nancy's fingers wagged at the sides of her head.

Andrea glanced at Joanne, who looked alarmed. "Okay, Mom," Andrea said, hearing her voice thin and grow weak. "Clearly, you're confused. That was *me*. *I* was in that play. You remember that." Of course, she'd think that anything good had been Pearl's doing. Couldn't her mother give Andrea credit for once? "You're not making any sense."

"Well, it was Pearl this time. Last night. I was there. She's so talented." Nancy shut her eyes. "I can see her now, wearing that towel on her head, belting out a tune. And that night she hurt her knee on stage. I raced backstage because I knew she needed me and held her hand all the way to the hospital."

"Sure, Mom," Andrea said, although this wasn't the way she remembered it at all, more that her mother was tense and irritated. "Whatever." But what did happen? She wasn't sure of anything anymore.

"Pearl was just fine though. Bounced back by the next performance with an ace bandage on her knee. What a trouper."

"That she is."

"You'd have been proud of her."

Andrea fixed Nancy with a dead-on stare. "*I* was there too."

"Then you know what I mean, how proud a mother can feel about her daughter." Nancy smiled at Andrea, who felt her eyes well up.

"Mom," Joanne said, "Blair wishes she could have come to see you, but she's so busy with the baby."

Nancy stared at Joanne as if she didn't remember Blair. Or Joanne, for that matter.

Andrea sighed. "Mom, can we talk about something else? I know you want Pearl to be here. I want her to be here. But she isn't. I can't help that." Andrea stood and cleared the bean-shaped plastic bowl and tissue box from her table. "But it's your birthday, so why don't you open your gifts?" She forced herself to breathe slowly as she watched Joanne help her mother tear off the paper, running the soft pashmina along her mother's cheek. Andrea opened the gel bottle so Nancy could smell it. She placed the Jade plant on the windowsill, moving Joanne's bouquet just out of her mother's sight line.

Nancy's hands stroked the cloth as she laid her head back on the pillow. "I told her I was sorry to have let her down. I wish I could have raised her, but they wouldn't let me." She was shaking her head, her eyes watery.

"Mom, you didn't let her down," said Andrea. "And what's that supposed to mean, raise her?"

"I was just too young, and I let them tell me what to do."

"What are you talking about?" asked Joanne.

"I never should have let her go."

"But she wanted to go to college."

203

"No, it was my fault. I buckled under. I always do that."

"Mom," said Joanne, patting her arm. "You're a terrific grandmother."

"I think about her every day."

"Remember, Mom?" said Joanne. "You have three grandchildren."

"Do you know how hard it's been? But you have to understand. I had no choice. I had to let her go."

"Mom, you're tired," said Andrea. "Take a rest."

"I'm going to go find the doctor," said Joanne, and she left the room.

Andrea could see the effort her mother was expending to cling to scraps of memory and re-form them into whole cloth, but none of this made sense. She'd try to find out if this was, indeed, sun-downing or something more serious, wondering what was ahead for all of them.

"There are legal papers in my desk from the lawyer."

"Don't worry about such things now. You're getting upset."

"I need you to understand. So many secrets."

"It's your birthday. You're bound to have lots of thoughts."

"I didn't know my real mother either. I didn't want that for her."

"Mom, I'm Pearl's real mother. And I'm doing the best I can."

"Be sure to look for the papers. Mine and hers. Don't mix them up."

"Of course, Mom. I'll take care of it." But she had no idea what that meant.

Nancy's cuticles were dry and cracked, her knuckles red. Andrea was afraid the rough skin would snag the strands of the scarf so she reached for her mother's hands, which were surprisingly cool. She studied the blue veins and the valleys of ruined skin, which lay slack between the raised hills of bone. Picking up the tube of lotion, she squirted some into her palm. "Here, Mom. Let me," and started rubbing the lotion into the papery skin. "Okay, so what else did Pearl tell you?"

Nancy worked her hands over and over as if she were scrubbing for surgery while she continued to spin out her fantasies, and for once, Andrea let her, content to lend her own life to Nancy's version of Pearl, whatever her mother wanted, knowing that all they could have was this moment together. And for the time being, that was enough.

CHAPTER 11
Paris, February 2011

Renny had warned Pearl not to take the Métro through Châtelet, reminding her that pickpockets stream in from the housing projects outside Paris to converge on that most-traveled station, to fan out and work in pairs. Pearl was distracted though because Renny had left her in the middle of the night, taking off with all their pooled money. She still had a paltry amount in her checking account back home, but she'd hoped to save it for an emergency. More furious than worried, she set out to ride around on the Métro, protected from the February cold, so that she could figure out what to do next.

In the train, she sat on a fold-down seat, studying a travel advertisement on the wall featuring two couples, the white man and woman on the beach in Ibiza and two blacks in the Seychelles. At Châtelet, the doors hiccupped open and a swarm of passengers wooshed in, forcing her to stand up. She wove an arm between two people to grab the pole and planted her feet to steady herself. Two of the male passengers with skin several shades darker than hers, stared as if to judge her own diluted African blood. She wished she knew how to say *Fuck off* in French, but turned instead to look at a Middle-Eastern man and a white woman, their fronts plastered together as they made out. Pearl gulped back angry tears as the train shuddered and swayed.

Looking back on it, she remembered a bump but had thought nothing of it until she'd reached for her wallet and realized it was missing. Passport, debit card, gone. All she had left was her cell phone, which wouldn't work in France and was, by now, out of juice because she'd lost the charger.

At St. Michel, she pushed her way out of the car and climbed the stairs, tottering on the sidewalk, buffeted by people rushing to work in the gray, sooty morning. Stumbling across the street to the bank of the Seine, she leaned against a stone parapet and looked down at the brown, oily water. On the greasy cobblestones below, a homeless man lay asleep, passed out, or maybe dead. Pearl shivered, blew her nose, and pocketed the grey-smudged tissue. How had she ended up in this cold, dirty city where she didn't really speak the language? She heard her mother bitch at her for not making more of an effort in French class, for not practicing it with the African refugees at her mother's workplace: "The perfect chance to learn French from native speakers." As if it were that easy. French speakers were all around her now, but none of them slowed down enough so she could understand.

Pearl looked at the island beyond the bridge where she could just make out Notre Dame through a scrim of haze. A scaffold covered the façade as if, left without support, the building would crumble. But nothing in Paris had met her expectations since she and Renny had arrived a couple of weeks earlier. The days were drearily short, and the sun never burned through the pollution that hung like smoke in a crowded café. The damp air settled in her lungs, making her wheeze and gasp for breath. Paris was beautiful enough if you could peel off the depressing layers of grime. She and Renny had hoped to stake out a place in front of Notre Dame to draw charcoal portraits, but because of the weather it hadn't panned out. They'd run through their money more quickly than anticipated. Tired and grouchy, they were starting to piss each other off. Despite the cold, she'd hoped to walk around to get a sense of the city, but Renny had taken to sleeping until late afternoon, and they would emerge only as the sun was setting, going out to jazz clubs where they couldn't afford the cover charge, in neighborhoods where the signs were written in Arabic more than in French, places so far away from tourist attractions that she even wondered if they were in Paris at all. They hadn't been to a single museum yet. Wasn't that the point of artists traveling to Paris? At these clubs, she usually drifted off to sleep on Renny's shoulder as he smoked *Gauloises* and spoke to men with nicotine-stained teeth in loud French, punctuated by wild gesticulations. French cigarettes had made her asthma flare, and she only had one inhaler left, so she'd pretty much stopped smoking. Renny had also bought a lot of weed, which he shared with her, but she suspected he was into more serious drugs. A couple of times, he'd slipped out in the middle of the night, and she'd awakened to find him gone. He came back a couple of hours later, claiming he'd been out walking, but he'd looked high. She began to fear his temper. He never hit her, but he'd taken his anger out on objects around him--a bottle he smashed against a brick wall, a children's discarded plastic car he stomped under his heel. No sense provoking him. In fact, when she'd first awakened this morning, she'd assumed he had gone on one of his walk-abouts, but then she'd seen that his duffel and books were gone, with only a butt-filled ashtray and a crumpled-up Gauloises package left behind. She checked her wallet and found he'd taken her money as well, leaving only her debit card. But now that was gone too.

How would she pay for the hotel and food? She couldn't wire home; her mother didn't even know where she was, just that she'd left school. She didn't want to admit that she'd screwed up, that she might even want to come home. Maybe she could ask her grandmother to give her some money to tide her over. Gram would approve of Pearl going to Paris and seeing the world, but she didn't want her grandmother to have to keep such a secret. Gram was old and tended to get frantic over small things. Pearl even considered asking her mother's ex for money but knew that Mike was probably still pissed at her for stealing from him. She'd planned to return the money before he found out and felt bad that he didn't trust her anymore. When she was little, they used to do these drawings where he'd start by sketching a few lines, then she'd add some, and he'd continue until they had these weird figures. Maybe she and Mike could have patched things up if her mother hadn't broken up with him. She considered asking her cousin Blair for a loan, but worried her mother would find out where she was. So Pearl would have to earn the rest drawing on the street. First though, she'd need a new passport.

At least she'd thought to tell her mother she was taking a leave in time to avoid paying the next semester's tuition. But her mother had gone completely batshit, screaming about how selfish and wasteful she was. Of course, her mother really meant how dare she mess with The Plan of turning a poor black kid and raising her into a model citizen? "I'm not your social science project, okay?" Pearl had said before hanging up. She hadn't answered any of her mother's calls after that. It was too late now anyway.

She looked up the address of the American Embassy and found

it down the river and across a bridge from where she stood. She'd have to walk. Heading west, she clung to the sidewalk nearest the river, but after a car barreled past, splashing her feet with foul-smelling water, she veered into a blackened alley and staggered toward a sliver of light. When the street opened up, she discovered the crowded wooden stands of a market.

Overpowering smells assaulted her–pungent wedges of Roquefort with varicose veins of blue and Brie that smelled like old shoes. The wave of a stinky fish stand forced its way into her nose, and the oysters, looking all snotty, made her gag.

The street bustled with people carrying string bags, pushing their way toward the counters. Determined housewives barked their orders to the merchants. The fish seller, a cigarette clamped between his teeth, plunged his raw, red hands into ice chips to retrieve two filets. Tormented by the smells of bread and pastries at another stand, Pearl looked in vain for free samples. She only had a handful of Euro coins and knew that she'd need what little she had for replacement photos.

On the curb sat a homeless North-African woman with two children, one a baby, its head hidden in the folds of her coat, nursing. Her free hand formed a bowl, jutting toward Pearl aggressively. The woman's dirty feet spilled out of sandals, and a young girl lay by her side, playing with some pebbles in the wet street. An apple rolled off a pyramid fruit display into the street, and Pearl snatched it, ducked between two stands, wiped and gnawed at it. She roamed up and down the back of the stalls and stole a couple of apples and a bruised pear from a crate, eating one piece of fruit and stashing the rest in her bag.

Following the flow of people on the narrow street, she emerged onto Boulevard Saint Germain, where trucks and cars idled, belching exhaust. Commuters on mopeds wove between the choked lines of vehicles. The boutique windows along the boulevard displayed designer clothes, the sleeves and hems of dresses stretched and skewered by pins. A chic-looking woman in a suit waited for her dog to add more globs of crap to the already littered sidewalk. She shot Pearl a nasty look, as if Pearl had crapped on the sidewalk, then took off at a fast clip, dragging her dog behind. Pearl stepped around the pile.

Arriving at the river again, Pearl walked onto the Pont de la Concorde. She doubled over coughing, taking long, wheezy breaths before straightening up. She shivered, a mask of mist covering her face. In front of her stood the obelisk, fountains, and beyond them, the American Embassy. Cars and buses raced around the square, six deep. She screwed up her courage to follow a middle-aged man who wove among cars and buses so that they emerged at the curb safely. Breathless, she wanted to thank him, a kind stranger, but he strode off before she could.

At the photo booth, she stared at herself in the mirror and noticed one of her braids had come undone, and a spray of wiry hair had fluffed up into a cloud. She'd tried patting it down, but it wouldn't stay put. Her hair, her eyes, the corners of her mouth–everything appeared to unravel at the edges, as if she were made of some fragile, disintegrating cloth. Would she fall apart and blow away?

When she arrived at the Embassy, a sandstone block behind an iron fence, she was dismayed to find a long line snaking around the corner, but the guard told her they were foreigners awaiting American visas. Pearl produced a Xerox of her passport, creased and damp, tucked in the toe of her shoe, a trick she'd learned from her mother, and was allowed to bypass the line. A couple of the people in line protested, pointing at her, and for a moment, she felt like an imposter.

At security, a blond, stony-faced guard motioned her toward the metal detector, but when she walked through it, the buzzer sounded. She froze, backed up, walked through the frame, and the alarm sounded again. "I already emptied my pockets," she said to the guard, dabbing at her nose with a tissue and fishing around for a stray Euro cent. The guard motioned for her to look again. Just sodden tissues. She'd spent her last change on the new passport photos. Finally, she unearthed a foil gum wrapper from the linty folds of her pockets and held it up to the guard, who frowned and took it from her with a sniff of disdain. This time, she passed the barrier without a sound, retrieved her shoulder bag from the bin, and proceeded through the courtyard of the Embassy, taking deep breaths to keep from tumbling into total panic.

A sign with the eagle seal pointed to the passport office on the second floor, and she climbed the stairs, her fingers curled around the cardboard housing the new photos. At the top of the stairs, another uniformed guard standing under an American flag gave her a paper to sign. He looked at her Xerox, frowned, looked at her again. She told the man, "My hair is different, but it's me. See?" She was asked to raise her hand and swear to her true identity. Could she even answer that question truthfully? Who was she? The abandoned baby with a made-up name and substitute family.

"Just pass to the next room," he said, grabbing her sheet and shoving a form at her. She headed toward the line of people facing a windowed counter under large photos of President Obama and another man, a white guy, probably the Ambassador. She stood behind a man who turned and stared at her fixedly. She stiffened under his gaze and ducked her head to avoid eye contact.

Olive-skinned, early middle-aged, with black hair and large, off-kilter eyes, he wore maroon pants and a tan jacket. He rocked from one foot to the other, as if his legs were of different lengths. He studied her for a moment so she turned her back. *Fuck off, perv*, she wanted to say. Behind her stood a young couple with a squirmy toddler, who struggled to free himself from his mother's grip while shrieking, "*Non!*" The parents' conversation shifted back and forth between French and English, and they didn't seem bothered by his cries. Pearl wished they'd make their brat shut up.

She could tell that the man wanted to talk to her, but she busied herself by looking in her shoulder bag. Inside, she found the beaded necklace that Renny had bought her, and sadness hit her like a chilling wave. She shook her head and took a few shallow breaths.

When the man was called to the window, Pearl listened as he gave an account of losing his passport, realizing only this morning as he was packing to leave that it had disappeared. It was urgent that he get a new one. The Embassy employee asked him identity questions. He'd been born in Syria and was a naturalized American citizen. However he couldn't remember the year he'd been sworn in and couldn't answer a question about the three branches of government. At that, the employee eyed him and said, "You know, sir, this is the second passport you've lost in three months. That is not a good pattern."

"I know," he said, shifting from one leg to the other. "I realize that this is not good at all. I am so sorry."

"And if you were to lose your passport again, we'd have to classify you as a frequent loser."

Why was he wasting time on this moron? Hurry up! The employee said the man hadn't done himself any favors, a naturalized

213

citizen of Arab origin, particularly in the present environment, not to have things in order. They had to be careful after all.

"Are you calling me a terrorist?" The employee didn't answer, just told him to move aside, waving Pearl to the window. The man stormed away, muttering in Arabic.

Pearl feared she'd blank on the most basic questions. Would the pasty-faced guy give her a hard time because she was black? Forcing herself to smile, she struggled to keep her voice from quavering. The man didn't look up from the form and asked her, "Where was President Obama born?"

That was it? "Hawaii," she said.

He stamped her form and slipped it under the grate. "The computers are down. Come back tomorrow."

"Tomorrow? But I need it today."

"Sorry. Please step aside." He waved her away and turned his attention to the couple with the child. Pearl couldn't move; her feet lead weights, her mind a blur. Afraid she might faint, she staggered over to a seat by the window and sat down. She pulled the pear from her bag and took a bite, but the guard shook his finger and pointed to the door.

She stumbled down the stairs and out onto the street, pulling her coat around her and retying her scarf, wishing she had a hat. She headed back east on the Rue de Rivoli, passing stores selling hats and scarves, perfume, souvenir shops selling plastic Eiffel towers in various sizes, University of Paris sweat shirts, prints with big-eyed street kids, schlocky crap for tourists. She passed a tea salon and inhaled the buttery smells of croissants. She kept walking, hoping to find another market where she could steal some bread. The exhaust fumes from buses had given her a headache, and her legs felt wobbly.

She came to a square across from the Louvre and saw a street musician, a man, maybe African, singing and playing a one-stringed instrument. A space heater sat next to a café awning, and she stopped there to watch him, hugging herself against the cold. The man was tall and husky, with a crocheted cap on his head. He sang a bouncy song in a language she didn't recognize. His instrument case lay open on the ground and inside he'd pasted a green, yellow, and red flag sticker. Pearl remembered the flags-of-the-world poster her mother had hanging in the kitchen when she was a girl, and how Pearl liked to draw copies of them with Craypas in bright colors and her mother would hang them up around the poster. Thinking of her mother made her sad for a moment, then she banished that thought and focused on the throaty burr of the man's voice. He sang with his eyes closed, tapping on the wood of his instrument between strums, managing to get a lot of sound from the single string. Pearl wondered how he could make his fingers work on this cold day. He wore gloves with the fingertips cut off, a bright yellow scarf tied in the French slip-knot way and a battered olive drab jacket. His high tan work boots had scuffed toes. During the time she watched him, no one else stopped to listen, instead, they steered around him, intent on their paths. When he ended the song, Pearl clapped. He blew on his fingertips and checked his case to count what he'd accumulated. She made a gesture of empty pockets, shrugging, and said, guessing at the French. "*Pardon, pas de, um, monnaie.*"

"*D'où viens-tu?*"

She shook her head. "*Je ne parle pas bien français.*"

"You are American?"

"How did you know?" she asked.

"Because you do not know French." He shook his head and smiled.

"How do you know English?"

"Everyone knows English now." He bowed and said, "I am Ousmane Bagayoko. I am from Mali. You know it?" She did. "And I visited New York once. Crazy drivers. But Paris is worse." He shook a cigarette out of his pack and offered her one. She refused, and he lit his, taking a deep drag.

"I wish I could give you something, but I lost all my money."

"What happened to your money?"

"Stolen."

"Oh," he said, his voice gentle. "That is horrible. What will you do?"

"I don't know." To her surprise, she burst into tears. "I'll make some, I guess."

"How?"

"I wanted to draw portraits, but I don't have money to buy paper. I was going to draw outside, but it's too cold and wet, so I thought I'd go sit in the Métro. Why don't you sing there?"

"You need a license. I tried, but they ejected me. You need a license to do anything here. Fucking bureaucracy." He hawked and spat on the sidewalk, then leaned over and gathered up the coins in his hand, letting them fall back into the case, shaking his head.

A license would cost money. She saw her options dwindle further.

Picking up his instrument again, he asked, "What is your name?"

Pearl hesitated, then decided to try on a new identity. "Rayann."

"Well, Rayann, do you sing?" he asked.

"Not that well."

"Tell you what. I will play a little longer and if you direct people over to me, I will give you some of my money." The cigarette between his lips bobbed as he talked. "We will be a team, yes?"

"Oh, no, I couldn't take your money."

"You will help me. You would earn it."

"What should I say?"

Repeat this: "*Venez écouter la musique malienne*. And smile." He pointed to his own grinning mouth, which made her smile. "There you go."

"I can do that." And she repeated it to him.

"*C'est ça*. But," he said, wincing, "your accent is horrible. No mistaking you for French."

"I'm sorry," she said, embarrassed.

"No, that is good. Better that they not think you are African. You are too light to be an African anyway. No, This is better." He tossed his cigarette and took up his instrument. "Yes, Miss Josephine Baker, let's go."

"Who's that?"

"An American singer who lived in Paris long ago. She wore a skirt of bananas."

"Okay, whatever."

He started playing again and she walked around, trying to engage people on the streets, to get them to stop and listen, but they steered around her, hugging themselves against the cold. She knew that lots of Africans, both black and Arab, lived in Paris. What did the French think of American blacks?

He played and she waved people down, gesturing for them to listen and to pay up. Occasionally, someone would toss in a coin; mostly they walked by without looking. She stamped her booted feet, wiggling her cold fingers inside her gloves.

After about half an hour, he asked, "Are you hungry?" He lifted his instrument and laid it in the case.

"Remember? I don't have any money."

He counted the coins. "You will be my guest," he said. She shook her head. "I insist. Not around here though. Too expensive."

"That's okay," she said, struggling to keep her voice from shaking. "I'll manage."

"And how will you manage without money?"

"I don't know." At that moment, the hopelessness of her situation nailed her to the ground, making her utterly unable to act or think for herself.

"You need to eat. I know a place in my neighborhood that is very good and not expensive. Come, Rayann."

Before she could refuse, she found herself following Ousmane. Along the edge of the square, a young rollerblader was executing a serpentine through a line of plastic cups set on the ground. Ousmane pointed to him. "Every Friday night skaters gather here and are ten thousand strong, rolling all over the city. It's genius." She looked at the young man in a stocking cap and baggy jeans and wished she had the nerve to cruise Paris like this, one in a crowd of strangers, traveling together. As Ousmane entered a side street, she looked back longingly at the Louvre, which she hadn't yet visited.

He led her to a beat-up white car and opened the creaky door for her. She climbed in. The ashes and incense smell of the car gave her a headache, so she lowered the window a crack. He shoved the car into gear and they took off, weaving in and out of traffic. Since there was no seat belt, Pearl gripped the side of the seat, taking shallow breaths. His hand rested on the gearshift, the skin dry, his fingernails long and yellow. They whizzed past monuments she'd seen in books—the Opera, the Pompidou Center with its blue, green, and red pipes, an ornate train station, buff-colored buildings of stone plastered over by posters, covered in turn with graffiti. He'd turned on the radio, which emitted loud, scratchy French rap. The words came so fast she couldn't make out more than a few of them: *heure, du, faire, terre*. They seemed to be heading up a hill, and she caught a glimpse of the white church, Sacré Coeur, in the narrow space between two streets. Finally, he pulled over and yanked back the emergency brake. "*Voilà*. Goutte d'Or. Drop of gold? My quarter. The real Paris." He grabbed his cigarettes. "Time to eat." Pearl was starving.

On the median strip, she followed Ousmane as they zigzagged through a street market selling tooled leather goods, jewelry, and scarves. African women, their bodies and heads wrapped in brightly colored cloth, browsed as they strolled along, children cinched to their backs. The air was filled with the smell of roasting nuts and incense, which managed to lend a smell of summer to the air despite the winter's damp cold. She stopped to look at some carved wood animals and a woven coin purse and was tempted to pocket it, when two men closed in on her from both sides, and a hand snaked up her front, squeezing her breast. She batted the hand away, shrieking, "Get the fuck off me!" The men backed off as she stood, breath coming in ragged wheezes, her body buzzing with adrenaline.

She stumbled onto the sidewalk as she reached into her bag for her inhaler, taking a puff. Looking up, she saw Ousmane up ahead, talking to a man. He waved for her to follow and she did, her head muddled, as he turned onto a narrow side street.

They entered a tiny café with lettering written backwards on the window to be read from the inside. A man in a white apron was sweeping the floor. He greeted Ousmane in a language she didn't recognize, and they shook hands as he glanced at Pearl, then looked back at Ousmane and smiled. Warm smells wafted in from the kitchen. Pearl's legs buckled beneath her, and she sank into the first seat she found. Ousmane gestured to another table near the back, mimicking smoking, and she dragged herself over to a table under the sign *Espace Fumeurs*. Her head was swimming, but the café was warm and she'd get a meal, so she could ride it out for a while until she figured out how to get some money. Three African-looking men wearing blue coveralls sat at a corner table, smoking and drinking. The café owner approached the table, and Ousmane said something in French, and she recognized the words for lamb and potatoes as the man wrote on his pad. "But I can't pay you back," Pearl insisted. He stopped her with an upraised palm.

When Ousmane ordered wine, she asked for water instead.

"Are you a teetotaler?" he asked, as he tipped an imaginary glass to his mouth.

"No, I just don't drink that much before dinner." She eyed the full glass he'd poured for himself.

"Yes, I am Muslim and yes, I drink. Some of us do, you know. It's a myth that we don't." He took a pack of cigarettes from his shirt pocket and offered her one. She took it and he lit both of them. The first drag made her woozy, so she placed it in the ashtray. "You have been through something very trying," he said. "You must calm down." He grabbed a bottle and two glasses from the bar and poured something yellow into them.

She sniffed at it, the smell weaving up into her brain. "Okay, but just a tiny bit, I guess." He clinked glasses with her, and she sipped. The liqueur burned her lips, mouth, and throat, but it also took the chill off. "Whoa, what is this?"

"You don't like it?"

"It's just kind of strong." She looked around the café and saw she was the only woman. Above the bar, a huge landscape of an African village with baobab trees dominated the room. The paint was darkened by layers of grease and smoke, and it took a moment to distinguish a tiny figure peeking through the branches of a tree as if imprisoned in the painting, and Pearl was almost certain she saw an eye blink. She shuddered. "How about some wine instead?" Ousmane asked.

"Okay."

The waiter appeared with a glass of red wine, and she took a big sip. She sat back and began to relax.

"Tell me about Mali." She asked, her eyes smarting from her smoldering cigarette. "Why did you leave?"

"No money. No life for me there."

"Was there a war?"

"No," he said, as if she should know that.

"My mother works with refugees from Africa."

"I am *not* a refugee," he said, his tone suddenly cold.

"I didn't mean that. I just said that I know there are a lot of African refugees."

"Yes, they come to suck on the teat of America," he said, eyes flashing.

"Not exactly."

He poured her another drink. She was very hungry and wanted some bread to soak up the alcohol. When she asked for it, he waved her off. After she took a couple of sips, he filled her glass again. He'd turned away from her and had started a conversation with the man behind him. Was he angry at her? She looked around the room, her sight obscured by clouds of smoke, the edges fuzzy and indistinct.

221

When he turned back to her, he lit another cigarette and blew smoke in her face.

"So what are you doing alone in Paris?" Ousmane asked, leaning back in his chair, taking another puff and letting smoke trail out of his nose. "It is dangerous for a woman to travel alone. You American women take too many chances."

"I was with someone." She sipped the wine and closed her eyes, wondering if Renny was eating lunch in Paris or if he'd already left town for who knew where.

"Oh, a friend?"

"Sort of. My boyfriend." She shrugged and shook her head. "But we broke up."

He sucked at his cigarette before crushing it in the ashtray. "Well then, that's what you get for living in sin."

The skin on Pearl's skin scalp tightened. She looked around and realized she had no sense where she was or any sense of what he expected from her.

"I don't have to answer to you for my actions," she said.

"Are you ashamed of what you've done? To sleep with a man before marriage? To travel with him openly? In my country, women are pure before marriage." His lips lingered on the word "pure."

Pearl flushed. "It's not your business what I do in my own life."

"But here you are with me, and where is your man?"

"He had to leave." Renny's absence ached like pain from a phantom limb.

"If you were my woman, I wouldn't abandon you. I'd make sure of that."

"It wasn't like that." But of course it was.

"You Americans. You want your independence, but then when something goes wrong, you make excuses and you want to be taken care of. You don't take responsibility for your actions." He refilled his glass and downed it in one swallow.

"I didn't ask you to take care of me. You insisted."

"And you put up a real struggle." He had a strange look, between a smile and a sneer.

"I think I should go," she said, her head swimming.

"No, I am not through. You American women, kissing in public, throwing away husbands like garbage. Women shaking their sinful bodies on stage with few clothes on. They are whores."

Her ears were buzzing. "I've got to go." She stood up.

"Sit," he said, and she did. "Now where are you going to go with no money?"

"I don't know," she said weakly, determined not to cry as she leaned back in her chair.

He poured wine for both of them. "Listen. I am sorry. I have the opinions of my culture."

He took off his hat, and his wooly hair was matted, the hairline receding. With his scarf off, she could see a necklace of cowries strung on rawhide. His knuckles were nicked and calloused and his long yellowed fingernails made her feel sick. Her wine glass sat on a paper coaster, a red ring bleeding onto the crest of the German logo. She felt incredibly tired, her thoughts jumbled. It took all her strength to keep her head up. The room spun, and she shut her eyes to stop the whirling. Laying her head back against the wall to wait until the food came, she felt herself melt back into the chair. Warmth pushing her eyelids down. Just rest, she told herself. Rest.

SHE WOKE UP IN THE dark, naked, lying on sheets that smelled dirty. Her breasts felt bruised. Her gut cramped, and she felt something leaking between her legs. Maybe she'd gotten her period. But it wasn't blood. She sat up for a moment, but zigzaggy lights in her head forced her back down again. Lying on her back, she tried to remember where she was and how she'd gotten there. She could make out the sound of dishes clattering and the smell of food, the taste of wine and cigarettes. Scraps of memory about drinking and a man, smoke, ashes, sour wine. Her stomach lurched and she feared she'd throw up so she pulled her legs up and hugged herself. Next to the bed, she could make out a guitar case and the red, yellow, and green flag. Ousmane. Another cramp clenched her gut, so she tipped onto her side and vomited on the floor. Wiping her mouth, she heard a shower running in the next room, a sliver of light showing under the door. She groped for her clothes on the floor, her head pounding, her arms and legs like bags of sand. As her eyes adjusted to the light, she made out a chair, next to which lay a crocheted hat and scuffed boots. Ousmane. Another wave of nausea hit her and she lay on her back until it passed. She lifted her butt to tug on her underwear and tried to straighten her tights, but they twisted, so she threw them into her bag. Ousmane's pants hung from a chair, his wallet on the table. She grabbed her coat and wound the scarf around her neck.

Before she slipped out the door, she reached into the guitar case and grabbed the sack with the coins from the street singing. She took his wallet from the table and emptied it, stuffing the Euros into her bag, and she stumbled out of the room, past the café owner sitting with a cup of coffee, out the door, keeping her head down as she wove through the chairs of the café and out into the street.

She trudged up the street to look for the Métro sign, wondering what her mother was doing now. Sleeping? Or had she lain awake, unable to sleep, deciding instead to make a pot of tea and sit at the kitchen table, doing the crossword puzzle, making a list of things to do that day? Did she think about Pearl, worry about her, hoping she'd call? Or had she written her off, a fragment of a distant memory, a lost and forgotten part of her past?

CHAPTER 12

Chicago, April 2011

Andrea's cell phone rang, and she pounced on it without looking at the Caller I.D.. "Pearl, where are you?"

But it was Franck Ngoga, one of her Rwandan clients to whom, in a moment of unguarded generosity, she'd given her cell phone number.

"Franck, it's late."

"The man come. He take the children."

"What man?"

"From DCFS."

"Protective services? Why? What happened?" She fumbled in the drawer for some paper and a pen, her fingers tingling with adrenaline.

"Marie, she pee blood, and we take her to the clinic."

"Okay. What did the doctor say?"

"Marie come home from school and is in the bathroom too long. Aurélie call her, 'Marie, come out.' But she do not come out. She call me and we go in and see that Marie is blooding."

"But what did the doctor say?"

"The doctor only say she need to pee in a cup, but she say it hurt to pee. Tonight, the man say nothing. Just give him the children."

"Wait. Did he give reasons why he took Marie? And Félix too? He must have given you papers and a reason for taking both children."

"Some papers, but no reason. Just give him the children."

"Franck, that's awful."

"He say we can visit the children at the shelter tomorrow."

"Did you get his name?" He spelled it for her—Robert Ventnor—no one she'd worked with before. "You should have asked for more explanation. Are you sure he didn't explain to you why he was there?"

"He ask me, 'Franck, do you hurt your daughter? Do a friend hurt her?' I say 'No! I never hurt her.'"

"I know that." She could hear wailing in the background, and, at first, thought it was three-year-old Félix, but then she remembered that both children were gone. Aurélie, Franck's wife, was the one crying. Since her English was limited and Andrea only knew a few words in Kinyarwanda, Franck usually talked for her, either in English or in French.

"I'm so sorry about this. It doesn't make any sense to me." She scribbled down notes as she talked. "Listen, I'll make some calls, but nothing can be done until tomorrow and maybe not for a few days."

"Oh," he said, his voice small.

"Where are the children?"

"Granny's Shelter," and he gave an address on the South Side.

"Are you sure he said you could visit tomorrow?" Franck assured her that Ventnor had said so.

"Franck, can you possibly get some sleep? You'll both need your rest." She rubbed her eyes.

"No sleep. Aurélie, she is too sad. She is praying now."

"Try to calm her down so she can rest. I'll call you tomorrow morning. We'll figure this out."

She put down the phone, massaging her neck and arching her back, knowing now that she wouldn't get back to sleep either. Those poor children. How scared they must be. Something didn't add up though. Either Ventnor hadn't followed protocol, or Franck had mangled it in his account. What really didn't make sense was how quickly DCFS had intervened. Andrea had often been in the position of begging them to act when she'd been certain of parental violence or flagrant neglect. Usually, it took several pleas for them to budge. With the recession, DCFS was stretched tight, all the caseworkers overloaded and stressed, so this quick action seemed particularly strange.

Franck and Aurélie had faced so much already—war, hunger, displacement, relocation. And now this. Who knew how this might have happened? Why wasn't DCFS investigating the school, where this most likely had happened?

Another thing didn't make sense. Why would DCFS take both children without trying to find a family member as a temporary replacement? This was a total breach of procedure. But why, also, hadn't Franck called her when the DCFS officer was still in their apartment? Why hadn't he fought it more? If they'd been white and middle-class, this probably wouldn't have happened. Andrea had spent her career dealing with racist attitudes, but not until she'd adopted Pearl had she seen how deeply ingrained were the assumptions that came with race. For all her scrapes with authority, Andrea knew that Pearl had been given more than one pass because Andrea was white. And if Pearl had also been white, she might have escaped any suspicion at all. She'd seen too much to believe in the fantasy of a post-racial America.

ANDREA PICKED UP A BOOK but couldn't concentrate, thinking instead of Marie, her sweet face—large eyes, shy smile, widely spaced teeth. And her skin. The thought of anyone touching that child made Andrea ill. Marie was in kindergarten at a Chicago public school, and she loved her teacher, loved books, loved her friends. School had opened up the world for her. When Andrea visited their home, Marie would come and sit next to her and rub her smooth brown hand over Andrea's freckled white one, just as Pearl used to do at the same age. It was all Andrea could do not to scoop Marie up and hug her fiercely. Marie had newly pierced ears and was proud of her little zirconium studs. Marie was delicate, but Félix was sturdy. Cooped up in their small apartment all day, he ran around banging things with a mop, a stick, a plunger, anything he could find. The only English he heard regularly came from the TV. He loved music though, and danced and bounced when a song came on. Marie was quiet and placid. Maybe too trusting?

ANDREA CLIMBED INTO BED AROUND midnight, hoping to read, but she couldn't concentrate. When Pearl was in her worst stage of acting out—the smoking and drinking, the promiscuity and drugs—Andrea spent many sleepless, anxious nights. In the three months since Pearl had disappeared, the hours between two and five had been the worst—the longest, loneliest, most desperate hours, the time when Andrea's mind recycled horrible fears about what Pearl might be doing or what might have happened to her. Andrea was just now starting to sleep through the night, finding a way to divide her mind into two halves, a functional one for work and the other that focused on Pearl. Otherwise, she wouldn't have survived, and she needed to for when, if, Pearl returned. Work helped, and Freya had folded Andrea into her family, not letting her spend too much time alone. Andrea didn't know what she'd have done without them, their closeness, the sheer physical contact they provided. Hugging Freya's children, inhaling the warm yeasty smell of hair, the silky feel of skin. Her heart needed that.

By two-twenty, it was clear she couldn't fall asleep, so she got up and walked down the hall to Pearl's room, which, since she'd left for college, had become the spillover space for Andrea's papers. A layer of papers and files covered Pearl's bed like scabs over a wound. Since Pearl's disappearance, Andrea played a game with herself, that if she pretended the room wasn't Pearl's anymore, Pearl would return home, indignant that her space had been usurped.

Andrea pulled a box from under the bed. When she opened it up, a mixture of Pearl smells—lotion, spice, tobacco—drifted up from the box. Andrea sat back on her heels, tears springing to her eyes, fluttery images winking at her. In the box, she found crumpled, half-finished math homework papers, a CD of some rapper with gold teeth, a crocheted potholder, a bent copy of *Hamlet* with the HA scratched out and O in its place—OMLET, barrettes in the shape of a bow, the arm from a plastic Japanese cat, a cootie catcher made from notebook paper with boys' names scrawled on it, a lighter, and Mike's Boy Scout pocket knife with his initials scratched into the metal. He'd accused Pearl of taking it and they'd gotten into a huge fight about it, her shrieking that he was crazy, that she hadn't even seen the fucking knife. At the time, Andrea had believed her daughter, accusing Mike of always thinking the worst of Pearl. Andrea palmed the knife and decided she'd send it to him with a note saying she'd found it behind the sofa, knowing that he'd probably see through her lie. Had Mike been right? Had she hobbled Pearl by cleaning up her messes, tanking her own relationship with Mike in the process?

Finally, Andrea found an envelope addressed to Pearl in her mother's handwriting. Andrea pulled the folded sheet from the envelope. It was a chatty note, saying how proud she was of Pearl going off to art school. In her loopy handwriting, Andrea's mother had written, *You just go out there and knock 'em dead!*

Pearl didn't even know about her grandmother's broken hip or the series of strokes that had made her more confused, angry, and difficult. Now she had several pressure wounds that weren't responding to treatment. Worry upon worry.

Andrea hadn't told her mother that Pearl had run away, and when her mother continued to ask for Pearl, why she hadn't come to see her, Andrea lied, making excuses. Now her mother was too far gone to understand. How could Pearl, the favorite grandchild, be so cruel to her grandmother?

She brought the letter back to bed with her and lay there, holding pages that both Pearl and her mother had touched, trying to see if she could separate their mingled smells, envious of their closeness, their easy give and take. Then she put the letter on her bedside table and pulled up the covers.

THE ALARM CLOCK WRENCHED HER out of a deep sleep at six. Every morning when she'd wake up, the fact of Pearl's absence would drop like a rock in her stomach.

She opened the blinds and stared at the sliver of the sun breaking through wispy gray and yellow clouds. She put on the CD and started her Tai Chi form, wincing when her knee twinged, but slowing her breathing, all her movements, to a slow, continuous flow. Since she'd started practicing Tai Chi, she was calmer, less distractible, more patient. For the Cloud Hands move, she circled her hands, one arm up, one arm down, staring at each palm as it passed in front of her face, pushing it out and away from her as she stepped to the left. Breathe in the good, out the bad. Her Tai Chi master had told her to visualize something she wanted as she looked at each palm, and usually, it was Pearl in the center of her palm, a little girl with big eyes and a smile of crooked, oversized teeth. Today, she visualized Marie in one palm, Félix in the other. Get them home, get them home.

Since Pearl's disappearance, she'd blamed herself, Pearl, herself again, whipping herself into a state where her chest tightened and she could barely breathe. Andrea would give anything just to know that Pearl was okay. At this point, Andrea would settle for alive and not okay. She hoped she could accept Pearl back, no matter what, that she could face whatever challenge Pearl brought home with her.

Raising Pearl had humbled Andrea, making her a less judgmental caseworker and more empathic advocate. But with Pearl missing, Andrea had found it hard to deal with some of her client families—the good ones because she envied them, the bad ones because she resented their having children they didn't deserve. Recently, she'd lost it with a Somali father who'd slapped his six-year old son in front of her. "Don't you know how lucky you are?" saying she was *this* close to reporting him for abuse. Her temples throbbing, she'd apologized and explained to him that laws existed in this country to protect children.

Franck and Aurélie seemed like good parents. Too much TV, not enough green vegetables, but they loved their children and kept them clean. Had some creep spotted sweet, compliant Marie and preyed on her?

Andrea dressed and drove to work so she could answer emails and then devote the rest of the day to helping Franck and Aurélie get in touch with Robert Ventnor at DCFS. She wondered how the children were faring at the shelter, how scared and confused they must be, particularly Marie, who'd need medical care. At nine, she dialed Ventnor's number and listened to his voicemail. He sounded black. She left a message: "Mr. Ventnor, this is Andrea Barton from Breadbasket. I'm the caseworker for Franck Ngoga and his family. I understand that you were the DCFS officer who took their children Marie and Félix Monday night. It's now Tuesday, and I have some questions. I'd appreciate a prompt return call." She fought to keep her voice calm. During the next hour, she tried several more times, with no luck.

She drifted down the hall to Freya's office, where she found her, reading files.

"Do you have a minute?"

She looked up over her readers. "Just about."

Andrea told her about Franck's children and Freya agreed that it was strange, that something didn't add up.

"It's driving me crazy. I can't concentrate on anything else." She sat down next to Freya's desk. "I brought a sandwich, but I need to get out of here. Can you do lunch?"

"I can't. I have a doctor's appointment."

"Didn't you just have one? Are you okay?"

"It's just my gyne. I have to race out between meetings. Maybe tomorrow?"

Because of government cutbacks, Breadbasket was operating with a skeleton crew. Dale had been furloughed along with some of the newer hires, and the support staff had been slashed. And although there were fewer refugees to resettle, Freya and Andrea each had more work than before. They'd taken to eating lunch at their desks instead of going out, and they rarely had time to sit and talk during the day.

Andrea returned to her office and, although it was only ten-thirty, took out her sandwich and ate it in a few bites before dialing DCFS again.

She reached a woman, who told her that Mr. Ventnor wouldn't be in until two-thirty. Andrea left a message with her and then called Granny's Shelter. Since she wasn't a family member, it took some cajoling to be connected to the director, but finally, she reached a Ms. Fitch.

"The children are fine," said Ms. Fitch. "Playing happily." Oh sure, thought Andrea. "But the parents can't just show up. They have to be approved for visitation. Then you can call back and they can get an appointment twenty-four hours after that."

"But I'm talking to you now," Andrea said, scribbling down notes, trying hard not to sound too impatient, knowing she had to win this woman over. "Listen, I'm a social worker. I know you have to be careful. Why don't we make the appointment for tomorrow, and if you find any reason why they shouldn't visit, and I'm sure you won't, you can cancel, okay?"

She agreed to let them have an hour with the children on Wednesday at eleven. Andrea agreed, knowing this tiny toehold was the best they were going to get for now. She didn't have time to take the morning off, but this had to come first. At least now she'd have something to tell Franck and Aurélie.

But when they showed up at Breadbasket an hour later, Andrea was dismayed to see them carrying bags and a cooler. Aurélie's face was wet from crying, her eyes puffy. Franck looked drawn, his cheekbones sharp, the skin around them sunken.

"Aurélie, she make food for the children," he said. "She is afraid they are not eating."

"Oh, dear," said Andrea, clearing files off two chairs so they could both sit down. "I wish you'd called first. You can't just show up at the shelter. The man shouldn't have told you that. I got through to the director, and she said that you have to be approved before you see the children."

They looked at her blankly. Clearly, they didn't understand. She explained that the shelter had to ensure the children's safety.

"We are good parents," he said, his eyes flashing.

"Of course you are, but when a child has been…um…hurt like that, they have to be very careful."

"We will be careful."

"I know. It's just one of their rules. Sometimes, children are hurt by their parents, and the shelter protects them."

"We do not hurt our children."

"Of course not, but the agency doesn't know that, and they want to find out who might have done this to Marie."

When Franck translated for Aurélie that they couldn't go to the shelter until the next day, she spat out a string of words in Kinyarwanda, followed by "No good, no good," as she shook her head.

"Aurélie, she is worried that the children are scared."

"I know," she said, touching Aurélie's arm. I'm so sorry. You can see them at eleven tomorrow. You have to hold on until then. At least you know where they are." She asked if Franck could get off work for the meeting, and he said he was working the night shift. "So you haven't slept at all."

"No, we are not sleeping."

"I'm so sorry. Can I get you some tea or coffee? Or some cookies?" Franck said no and added that Aurélie planned to fast until the children returned. "I wish I could make it easier for you," she said. "It's awful, I know, having to wait." But she also knew not to promise a speedy return of the children. It wouldn't be fair to raise their hopes.

Andrea noticed Aurélie studying a photo of her with Pearl taken at the Taste of Chicago when she was about nine. Pearl stood holding a barbecued turkey leg and wore a sauce-stained tee-shirt, her tummy bulging out, her hair braided with ball-topped elastics. A sun visor shaded Andrea's face.

"That's my daughter," she said. They looked puzzled. "Yes, I'm her mama. Her mother couldn't raise her, so I adopted her." Fearing they might see her cry, she tidied a pile of papers on her desk. "I worry about her too. She's big now, but I worry." She closed her eyes for a moment and swallowed.

Reaching for the bag of clothes, she asked, "Do you want to leave that here, and I'll bring it tomorrow?"

Aurélie hugged the bag to her chest.

"I hope at least that you can eat the food tonight." But Franck reminded her that Aurélie was fasting.

Franck offered a hand to Aurélie, who took it and raised herself on unsteady legs. Andrea knew that DCFS could keep the children for up to sixty days before making a judgment, but she didn't tell them that. "You need to eat something. To keep your strength up." She put her hand on Aurélie's shoulder, wishing she could say, I know what you're feeling. My child is missing. I don't even know where she is. She wondered if hiding the truth from them was the right thing to do since they might get their hopes up, only to be crushed later by reality.

She walked them to the elevator and watched as the door closed. Aurélie put her head on Franck's shoulder, and he pulled her close.

At two-thirty, she called Robert Ventnor again but got no answer. She wrote an email to one of her contacts at DCFS and tried Ventnor again. This time, she left a terse message, asking him to call immediately.

WEDNESDAY MORNING, DURING HER TAI Chi, she repeated her familiar mantra--get them home, get them home—as she breathed in and out, punching the air as she imagined Robert Ventnor's face receiving her fist, then breathing in, summoning all their children back home again with her palms. By the end, she felt lightheaded, and her hands tingled.

She arrived at Franck and Aurélie's apartment building at ten-fifteen to pick them up. Because the buzzer didn't work, she'd asked them to meet her out front, but they weren't at the curb. Franck didn't answer his cell, so she double-parked and waited. Just as she decided to look for a space, they appeared at the front door, carrying the same bag and cooler. Andrea clicked on her hazards and jumped out to get them settled in the car. Aurélie accepted Andrea's hug, but her arms hung at her sides. A sheen of sweat covered her face, and she smelled of flowery lotion. Franck helped her into the car, placing the bags next to her in the back seat, and he climbed into the front. Andrea headed toward Lake Shore Drive.

Since the Drive wasn't crowded, they made good time to the South Side, exiting at Hyde Park and heading west along 57th Street, past the University of Chicago toward a neighborhood with abandoned buildings amidst liquor stores and fried chicken shacks with men loitering out front. Andrea kept an eye out for Pearl, as she always did now while driving. She tried to make conversation with Franck and Aurélie, but the words died in her throat. What could she say?

When they pulled up in front of the shelter, a square, red-brick building with a long wheelchair ramp and attached, fenced playground, Franck helped Aurélie climb out of the car. Andrea grabbed the bag of clothes as Franck took the cooler, one arm around Aurélie's waist. They walked up the ramp into the lobby, which was lit by a dim light that gave off an eerie glow, lending their faces a greenish tinge. They signed in and Aurélie reached for the bag, clutching it as she would a child.

"I can't go in with you," Andrea said. "Parents only. But I'll be back in an hour." She gave Aurélie's arm a tentative squeeze. "Call me if there's a problem, okay?" The young black woman who worked the desk was wearing tight jeans and boots, her hair hidden beneath a crocheted cap. She opened the glass door for Franck and Aurélie, closing it quickly behind them.

Andrea drove to a nearby McDonald's, where she was the only white person, and ordered coffee, taking a seat near a window. At a neighboring table, a bored-looking woman fed her toddler French fries while the child played with the plastic give-away figure, a pink, white-haired pixie. Two old men in suits sat across from each other, talking and laughing. She hoped the visit was going well, trying to imagine how it would be for Marie to see her parents after what she'd been through. Would she be too scared to tell them or even have the language to do so?

Just before noon, she drove back to the shelter and waited for Franck and Aurélie in the lobby. At ten past, Félix darted across the hall, followed by Marie, wearing shorts and a tee-shirt, her hair pulled back with a headband. Andrea waved, and Marie stopped to look, but didn't wave back. Then Franck appeared and opened the door for Aurélie, who rushed out, crying.

"How did it go?" Andrea asked.

"They do not let us give the children any food," he said.

"I should have realized that. Sorry."

"And Marie. She say she do not live with us anymore."

"Oh, I'm sure she's just confused," Andrea said, uncertain herself whether Marie was confused or was protecting herself.

On the trip back north, Aurélie cried the whole way, sniffing with little catches in her throat. Franck sat stony-faced. The only thing he said was, "It is too hard in this country. Maybe we make a mistake to come here." He leaned forward, his hands clasped between his knees.

"Oh, Franck, you can't say that. You've gone through so much just to get here. It'll get better." But she hated herself for spouting a platitude that she didn't believe herself. Things didn't always turn out. Look at her and Pearl. Look at any number of families who couldn't catch a break, who had bad things happen to them. As for Marie, who knew if she'd ever be able to trust anyone again? At least Franck and Aurélie knew where their children were.

Andrea dropped them off at home, giving them both a hug, and then drove back to work. She tried several more times to reach Robert Ventnor. Finally, she left an angry message: "I assume you're retrieving your messages, and I can only assume that you've chosen not to answer mine. I'm going to call your supervisor to make a formal complaint. In all my years as a social worker, I've never seen a case handled worse. I advise you to make clear the specific, justifiable charges to the family or return the children immediately." She hung up, her head pounding, and burst into tears. The next thing she knew, Freya was standing next to her desk, wearing her coat, a hand on Andrea's shoulder.

"Have you heard something about Pearl?"

"No, the idiot from DCFS has gone missing and the children are stuck there and the parents don't understand."

"You're on it."

"And that means absolutely nothing. I'm crying down a hole here."

"It'll work out."

"You don't know that," she said. "Sorry. I'm frustrated." She laid her hand on Freya's arm. She looked tired. "Are you okay?"

"I'm fine. I'll call you later."

She tried to focus on the files and emails that had piled up over the past couple of days, but she wasn't able to shake her despair over what had been done to that family and her own failure to help them out, even though she knew they were up against an intractable system.

Finally, she reached Robert Ventnor, but he seemed distracted and didn't remember the details of the case. She had to remind him of everyone's names.

"You know, Ma'am," he said, "if the parents are guilty, it's going to be very hard for them to regain custody."

"How do you even know for sure what happened? It could have been someone at school. You're jumping to conclusions. I've never seen them act inappropriately with the children."

"But you don't live with them. These things go on behind closed doors."

"I know them better than you."

Andrea complained about sloppy procedure, but Mr. Ventnor cut her off, saying, "Let's take this one step at a time." He asked

Andrea about her relationship to the family, what she knew about their friends, how often she saw them, if she had any reason to question their fitness as parents.

"No, nothing whatsoever. I've known them for two years and I can honestly say there have been no red flags at all."

"Still, they—"

"I don't understand why you felt you needed to take the children like that."

"Ma'am, please, let me talk."

"Sorry. Go ahead," Andrea said, forcing herself to slow down and not interrupt.

"Apparently, the doctor at the clinic had some concerns during her examination of the child."

Andrea told her what Franck had reported about the doctor making him go out to buy juice for Marie when she hadn't been able to produce a urine sample. "She's been traumatized. Both of them have."

"I am trying to follow protocol here."

"I've worked with DCFS for years. I know how it's supposed to be done," she said, then told herself to tone it down, not to antagonize him. "Why isn't anyone investigating the school?"

"I can't answer that. My job is to make sure the children are safe."

Too late for that, thought Andrea as she hung up.

Later that afternoon, Mr. Ventnor called her back. "Do they have family in Chicago?" Andrea thought not. "Do they trust you?"

"Yes."

"Would you be willing to take them temporarily while the case is being investigated?"

She felt a flip of excitement in her stomach. "I *am* a licensed foster mother." Could she? There was room. Why not?

"It would be less confusing for the children to stay with someone they knew. It might be for several days, even weeks. Are you willing to do that?"

"Of course," she said as she mentally cleaned up Pearl's room and prepared a futon for Félix on the floor, something she'd done a few times when Willa had spent the night. "I could manage."

Mr. Ventnor kept referring to them as Mr. and Mrs. Ngoga, and Andrea explained, again, that there were no family names in Rwanda and that everyone had two given names. She spelled each one out—Aurélie Akimana, Marie Keza, Félix Nkunda—afraid that a misspelling could bury the children's cases further in the morass of red tape. She arranged to meet them later than afternoon at her apartment.

She called Franck to tell him about the temporary placement. He answered, sounding sleepy. He must have worked the night before.

"They are not coming home yet?"

"No, but I hope it'll be soon. This would be better than having them stay with a stranger. And they'd be out of the shelter."

"I have to tell Aurélie." He put down the phone and was gone for a couple of minutes. She heard both their voices and worried that Aurélie wouldn't understand.

Finally, when he returned, Andrea said she'd take good care of them. "Until they come home, of course." Andrea worried that if Mr. Ventnor knew about Pearl's disappearance, it would disqualify her as a temporary guardian. But he clearly didn't, so Andrea arranged to take some vacation time so she could stay with Félix and drive Marie to school or even home school her if DCFS wanted to investigate the school.

She left work early to go home and get the room ready for the children. Franck called her to ask if the children had arrived yet. He again mentioned Aurélie's fast. What a futile gesture, Andrea thought, but then again, how was that different from praying or crossing one's fingers or offering puja? When stressed, Andrea ate junk. Since Pearl had disappeared, she'd gained six pounds. Would it have been different if she'd fasted like Aurélie? Would Pearl come home now if she made the same sacrifice?

On the way home, she stopped at Target to buy Nighttime Pull-ups for Félix, kid-friendly food, books, a cartoon DVD, a comfortable quilt. She tackled Pearl's room, throwing most of the papers into boxes to be filed later, and separating out clothes to donate to the Vietnam Veterans, stuffing a few of Mike's socks and a pair of shorts into a bag. She washed the sheets along with some of Pearl's child-sized clothes salvaged from the basement storage locker. She also found toys and books that smelled musty, but would air out. Having two children would be more work than one, but the kids could keep each other company. She could do this.

She called Freya to tell her that she'd be taking some personal days to stay with the children.

"Andrea. Do you think that's a good idea? Did you tell him about Pearl?"

"Why would I do that?"

"Because it might just be relevant to whether you're able to take on two children. You're worried sick about Pearl, and you decide it's time to foster two kids?"

"Why? Don't you think I can do it?"

"I think you're at your wits' end, and it's going to stir up emotions."

"You think I'll screw them up? I won't have them that long, if that's what you're worried about."

"Andrea, this is as much about you as about those children. What if Pearl shows up while the kids are staying with you?"

"Then I'd be thrilled and relieved. Can't you see this is a good thing for me? A distraction?"

"They're children, not a distraction. Just be careful."

"I know how to take care of kids."

"I mean for yourself."

"Well, I thought you'd get it, but I've got things to do now, so I'll talk to you later."

She said goodbye and hung up, squeezing Pearl's stained and frayed stuffed rabbit, holding it up to her nose and inhaling deeply.

Andrea opened the door at five to Mr. Ventnor, a tall, big-bellied, middle-aged man with dark skin and a shaved head. He held the children's hands stiffly. Félix had gone limp and dangled from his arm, and Mr. Ventnor gave it a sharp yank. Marie stood frozen at his side. He nodded at Andrea, clearly surprised and displeased to see that she was white. Didn't he know that already? But he wasn't about to throw up roadblocks to make his own job harder. He nodded curtly and entered, leaving the children behind in the hallway.

"Hey, Marie, Félix. Come on in," Andrea said, careful not to overwhelm them. Andrea waited to see a sign of recognition from Marie, afraid that she might balk and then where would they be? A flicker of a smile crossed her face, but so briefly Andrea wasn't sure what to make of it. The kids were dressed in shorts and teeshirts. Mr. Ventnor held a plastic bag with the rest of their things.

"I had a hard time getting them to come here," he said.

"Do you blame them?"

Andrea directed the kids to the sofa in front of the TV where *Dora the Explorer* was playing, and sliced fruit was laid out on a tray.

Even though he seemed out of breath, she'd already decided not to offer him coffee and a seat. Instead, they stood near the door to fill out the paper work. Again, she had to correct the spelling of their names, which he'd botched. Andrea reminded him that she'd taken in a foster child before. "My daughter, before I adopted her, was my foster child." He nodded, frowning at a photo of Pearl as a toddler, sitting on Andrea's lap.

"You know this is just until the parents are cleared, right?" he said as he stuffed the papers into an accordion file.

"Of course," Andrea said, and added, "And I hope that's as soon as possible." But she knew that could take up to two months and had already in her mind spun out days and weeks of things to do with both kids—trips to the zoo and to the Children's Museum, books, art projects, wholesome meals. They'd need that kind of attention and regular routine, particularly Marie. No sense rushing her. She'd been traumatized and would need time to trust again. Marie stood by the sofa, staring across the room at the TV. Andrea told her she could sit down and play with the bin of toys if she wanted. Félix sat on the floor, eyes glued to the TV. "Go ahead, Marie. You can play with anything there." Marie picked up a doll from the pile and put a dress on her, then started scissoring her legs. Reaching into the bin she grabbed Pearl's old My Little Pony and dropped the doll.

When she showed him to the door, he said, "You just never know with these refugees, what they're used to doing in their countries."

"Well, they can't have a good impression of us at the moment."

He shrugged, hitched his pants and walked toward the stairs.

Andrea sat down next to Marie, saying she could have the My Little Pony if she wanted it. Marie said she'd like that. Did she want a snack? She shook her head. Andrea sat for a moment, then said she'd be out in the kitchen. Did they like spaghetti?

"I do, but Felix doesn't like tomato sauce."

"Then I'll make some for him with butter. Do you want to come into the kitchen with me?" Marie followed her, and Andrea reached over to put her hand on Marie's forehead. "You're hot. Do you feel okay?" Marie shrugged.

"Let me take your temperature. Do you mind?" She didn't. Andrea wondered if she were getting sick. Marie didn't talk, but she stuck tight beside her. Andrea didn't have any children's Tylenol, but she broke an adult pill in half and crushed it, stirring it into applesauce. She wet a dishtowel and had Marie sit at the table as she held the cool cloth to the child's forehead. "Does that help?" Marie said it did. "You can go back and watch TV until dinner if you want." Marie didn't move. "Or you can sit here and keep me company, okay?"

Andrea gave her paper and some markers to use at the table as she cooked. She noticed that Marie gripped her crayon just like Pearl, high up in the crook of her thumb and index finger. Pearl had gone through a phase of drawing a mash-up, girl-bird kind of creature with human legs and head with multi-colored wings. Marie drew a house and was filling in the background in dark blue.

During dinner, the kids picked at their food. Andrea didn't know if they weren't used to her cooking or if they were too buffeted about, and Marie too sick, to have an appetite. They rubbed their eyes, so Andrea got them ready for bed right after dinner. "Do you want a story?" she asked. Félix lay on his futon, and Marie got up next to her and ran her hand, cooler now, up and down Andrea's arm lightly, a phantom touch that reminded her of Pearl. She had to take a few breaths before continuing. Was Freya right? Had she gotten in over her head?

By the end of the book, Félix was asleep and Marie was nodding off. Andrea suggested that she go use the bathroom and knew not to intrude on her, so Marie went and returned, smelling like toothpaste. Andrea tucked her in and hesitated before giving her a hug. But she'd hugged her before, so why not? "Do you want me to leave a light on?" Marie did. "I'm right down the hall in the room I showed you. Okay?"

AT AROUND MIDNIGHT, SHE WOKE up to find Marie standing by the side of her bed. "Marie, are you all right? Do you feel crummy again?" The child sniffled. "Marie?"

"I peed in bed." She started to cry.

"That's okay. Don't worry about it. I'll get you something to wear."

She gave Marie one of her tee-shirts and sent her into the bathroom. "You can wear this tonight, and I'll do the laundry tomorrow." She'd have to deal with the mattress in the morning and put plastic bags under the sheet for the following night.

When Marie came back, Andrea asked, "Does it hurt down there?"

"No," she said, but Andrea guessed she was too shy to say yes.

"I can lay down blankets in the room with Félix, and you can camp out there." But something in Marie's face made her ask, "Would it help if you slept in this bed? Just for tonight, okay?" Marie nodded. "You have to get used to your room, but with the bed all wet, it'll be okay just this once." She knew that DCFS wouldn't approve of her doing this, but she had to go with her instincts.

Marie crawled into bed and curled up fetally. Andrea rubbed her back for a minute, then heard her breathing and knew that she was asleep. Her little ribcage, rising and falling, her mouth breathing, nose whistling, so much like Pearl at that age. As a young child, Pearl's middle-of-the-night asthma attacks had sent them to the hospital more than once. As a result, Andrea became keenly attuned to the rhythm of her breathing and developed the routine of slipping into the room and feeling Pearl's cheek before going to bed herself. Now, Andrea resisted the urge to wrap her arms around Marie and cuddle her. Instead, she rolled over and felt herself start to drift off to sleep herself.

The next morning, she woke up to the sound of the TV from the living room. Félix sat on the floor and Marie lay on the couch, dangling one leg over the side as they watched a cartoon.

"Hey, you guys. How are you?" They stared at the program. "You know, you can't watch TV all the time. It's a beautiful day. Let's go out and do something fun." They kept their eyes on the screen. "I'm going to fix some breakfast. Do you both like cereal?" Marie said they did.

She watched them eat as she drank her first cup of tea. The sun was streaming through the windows, and she wondered if it would be a good day to go to the park. Or a museum. She figured they'd probably never been to the Field Museum before. Or the zoo. How she missed planning fun outings. When they finished eating, she got them clean clothes, helping Félix into his. Marie seemed content to wear what Andrea had laid out for her, a welcome change from the pitched battles she'd endured with Pearl over the years.

She'd unearthed the old car booster seat from her storage locker for Félix and buckled both children into the back. "How about the zoo?" she asked, looking in the rear view mirror. Marie and Félix were whispering to each other. "Have you ever been before?" They hadn't.

At the zoo, she planned to take them to Pearl's favorite

places—the ape house, the penguins, the polar bear tank. Not the snake house, which both she and Pearl found creepy, or the big cat house, which smelled bad, its close, dusty air aggravating Pearl's asthma.

Inside the ape house, the sun shone through the tall windows. Three adult gorillas sat close to the glass, pulling apart bananas and eating stringy roots. Andrea stood face to face with a mother gorilla, whose limp breasts lay flat against her chest. She cuddled her baby, licking its face and head. Andrea remembered seeing the report on TV of the female gorilla at a suburban zoo, who, when a child fell ten feet into the pit, picked him up and cradled him, unconscious, while horrified humans watched from above until the zoo workers came and gathered the boy from her arms, safe and not seriously harmed. The gorilla's maternal instinct intact.

Andrea noticed that the children weren't standing next to her and, seized by panic, she whipped around to find them across the room, staring up at two TV screens playing videos of gorillas. "Hey, you two," she said, her heart fluttering, "Don't wander off, please." She cupped the backs of their heads. "Why don't you look at the real gorillas?" On screen or behind glass? Was it all the same to them? She steered Félix over to the window so he could watch the gorillas eating and held his hand so he wouldn't pound on the glass.

Outside, she asked them which animals they'd like to see next. Giraffes? Elephants? Penguins? Félix took off running toward the building with a penguin drawing out front. Andrea took Marie's hand and they ran after him. Andrea had given Marie some more Tylenol this morning, and she checked her forehead. "You okay?" Marie said she was. Félix had disappeared into the building ahead of them.

Inside, while Félix stood at eye level with the penguins treading water, Andrea sat on the bench with Marie.

"I'll bet you miss your parents." She nodded. "And school too, huh?" She looked up at Andrea. "If something happened at school that made you feel bad, would you tell your teacher?"

She studied her feet. "Something did happen."

"What, sweetie?" She asked, her heart pounding, as she put her arm around Marie.

"I peed in my pants at school. Like last night."

"I'm sure that embarrassed you. But it happens sometimes. Try not to feel too bad."

They sat for a while in front of the penguins until Andrea noticed Marie fidgeting, her hand wedged between her legs, so Andrea said they needed to go find a bathroom. Félix pitched a fit, making Andrea carry him out, kicking his feet, wailing. This is what it felt like to have two kids.

After making it to the bathroom on time, then eating hotdogs bought at a cart, Andrea said they needed to go back to her place for a rest. Although clearly tired, Félix protested by pulling on Andrea's hand. Andrea steered them out the gate and toward her car, asking Marie and Félix if they'd had a good time. "Oh, yes," Marie said. "I'd never seen those animals before." What was her favorite? The giraffes. At that age, Pearl had also loved flamingoes, which she called fingingoes, and she'd imitate them by standing on one leg, teetering to balance herself.

Back at her place, she lay down with Félix and read to him, unsure how much English he understood, but pointing at the pictures, until he fell asleep and then she played a board game with Marie. One child was easier than two, for sure, but she was getting the hang of it. The key was to aim for the middle, to do things that they both liked. She thought of calling Freya to report on how well it was going, but then decided that she'd had enough of Freya's misgivings.

While she fixed a snack, the phone rang. Mr. Ventnor told her that the charges had been dropped.

"What?" Andrea said, her eyes following a swirl of dust motes in the air. The sun reflected harshly on a silver dish, and she shut her eyes, grasping the back of a chair. "How come?"

He wouldn't elaborate. Clearly, there'd been some dust-up at DCFS and he'd been overruled. "I'm out front with the parents. Can you buzz us up?"

She opened the door to the three of them, and when Marie saw her mother, her face brightened, and she ran to her. "Mama!" Aurélie lifted her up and hugged her, sobbing. Félix wandered in from the bedroom and started to run around in a circle, squealing. Franck pushed past Andrea and grabbed Félix under the arms on one of his laps around the room.

This time, Andrea invited him to the sofa, and Mr. Ventnor, loaded down with a heavy briefcase, sat, avoiding eye contact.

"You need to explain to this family what happened," she said, fighting to steady her voice.

"Marie has a urinary tract infection."

The parents were hugging both children, weeping. The children had started to cry as well.

"That's all?" Andrea asked. No wonder Marie had felt feverish and had wet the bed. "Why did the doctor report to DCFS that there might be molestation?"

"That's standard practice."

"But she's a doctor. Surely, she could see the difference. Wouldn't it be basic anatomy?"

251

"Ma'am, that's all I know." Andrea could hear Aurélie praying, her hands raised, thanking Jesus.

Franck shook hands with Mr. Ventnor, thanking him for bringing back their children, and Andrea wished instead that he could curse him out, but that wasn't in his nature, having been schooled in compliance and gratitude. Aurélie sat on the sofa, braiding a strand of Marie's hair that had come undone at the zoo. Marie had tilted her head back, smiling, her eyes closed. Andrea found herself whiplashed, trembling.

At the door, she hugged Franck and Aurélie and the children, handing over the bags of clothes and toys, asking Mr. Ventnor to stay behind a moment.

"I hope you are sorry for the extreme injustice you've done to this family."

"Just doing my job," he said.

"I hope I never have to deal with you again."

"No argument there," he said over his shoulder.

She listened to their voices as they headed down the stairwell. When she returned to the living room, she saw that Marie had forgotten the pony. She lay on the sofa, trying to catch her breath, clutching the blanket to her face to catch Marie's lingering smell. Of course, she was relieved that Marie hadn't been molested, and that the family had been reunited. But she hadn't been prepared for her own disappointment, the emptiness she felt knowing that she'd be alone in her apartment and that Pearl was still far from home.

She grabbed her purse and drove to McDonald's and got herself a large order of fries, which she stuffed into her mouth, barely tasting them, then forced them down with a drink, her nose stuffed, her fingers greasy. She couldn't go back to her empty apartment, so she headed to her favorite spot near Montrose

Harbor and sat on a bench, watching gulls chase after bits of food. A vendor cycled by with his *paletas* cart, bags of cotton candy trailing behind him like pastel clouds. A mother with a jogging stroller ran past a man with a bucket of bait and a fishing pole. Andrea tried to read a book she'd brought along, but instead stared out at the blue of the lake with the turquoise stripe near the horizon. Her hair whipped around her head, and she found it too hard to read with the pages fluttering, so she left and drove far west, through Korean, Hispanic, and Polish neighborhoods, farther from the lake than she'd ever driven before, where the buildings were newer and lower and housed people whose lives never brought them to the Loop or the lake. Finally, she turned around and drove back home.

At around five o'clock, Franck called her cell to report that everyone was doing well.

"Aurélie, she is smiling all the time."

Andrea said she was very happy for them.

"In my country," he said, "When you lose something, and you find it, you have a party." He invited her to their apartment the following Monday. "God, he hear us. He return our children."

"I'm just glad it worked out," she said, barely able to speak through her tight throat. Off the phone, she reminded herself that it was her job, nothing more. It was stupid of her to take them into her home and to become so attached since she was just going to lose them. Why had she set herself up for such a letdown? She called Freya, admitted she'd gotten in over her head, and Freya told her it had come from a good place, wanting to help people. She'd just been concerned about Andrea's feelings. Freya told Andrea that Rosa had just arrived to make plans for her upcoming wedding in the fall. "So many decisions. And Ramón is freaking out about the cost." Andrea told her to go, that they'd talk in a day or so.

The weekend went by slowly, Andrea trying to busy herself with errands, visiting her mother in the nursing home, doing Tai Chi in the morning with a group in the park, staying away from her apartment, too full of reminders of children--Pearl and her stand-ins, Marie and Félix. None of them hers.

Monday, the morning of the party, she woke up sluggish and she couldn't lose herself in her Tai Chi movements. Then, inexplicably, a memory: *You fucking bitch,* Pearl's breath spraying Andrea's face. A slap. Shrieks. *I'm so sorry.* Tears. *I hate you*! The sound of Pearl's door slamming. Andrea's still-stinging hand absorbing the vibrations of the music through Pearl's door. Giving up and going to bed, hearing Pearl late that night in the kitchen. A day of not talking, then, finally, a grudging truce.

Andrea crumpled to the rug and wept in big, wrenching sobs, rolling onto her back, hugging herself, wailing until her voice grew hoarse. Then she dragged herself and dressed in a skirt and nice top so she could go directly to the party from work and put in a quick appearance.

She didn't want to go, wasn't sure she had it in her to face them, feeling this raw and wrung out. It'd been nice of Franck and Aurélie to invite her, but she knew it was a courtesy and that this was a party for family and friends. It was over. Marie was safe, and no permanent harm had been done. The children would forget, and the parents would, she hoped, put it behind them.

After work, she drove to their apartment in Rogers Park, arriving to find the place packed with guests, some of the women in brightly patterned African dresses with matching head scarves, the rest in shiny cocktail shifts. The men wore suits or sweater vests with pleated pants, and the children in their Sunday best—flouncy dresses with hair bows for the girls, miniature suits for the boys. With all those people, the apartment was sweltering.

Aurélie and a friend were in the kitchen cooking, and Andrea offered to help, but they said no; she was a guest. Back in the living room, Marie, the recovered treasure, the center of attention, sat in a big red chair, her hair tied into two poufs, and she wore a frilly white dress with a purple sash, white sandals, and new dangly earrings. She hopped off her chair and opened her stickers and Dora the Explorer book that Andrea had brought her. Félix tore into his package of Matchbox car and knelt, running the cars over the table, dropping each one on the floor, making crashing sounds as they hit the rug. Marie thanked Andrea and crawled up onto her lap. Andrea hugged her close, breathing in kitchen smells and shea butter, as she blinked back tears. "How are you feeling?" she asked, touching the girl's forehead with her wrist.

"I'm fine." Gap-toothed grin, head tucked.

"You don't feel like you have a fever anymore. Did your mama give you your medicine?"

Marie nodded.

"Have you gone back to school yet?"

"I went back today."

"And you know you're safe, right?"

"Yes," she said, turning to Andrea. "Would you tie my belt for me?" She slid to her feet and turned her back and delicate stalk neck to Andrea. A part ran up the back of her head, tiny curls escaping from her tightly bound hair. Andrea re-knotted the sash and commented on her dress and earrings. Marie said they were new.

"Would you get your new book and read some of it to me?"

Marie jumped down and grabbed her book, then came back and scooted up next to Andrea, showing off her pink-painted fingernails. She leaned against Andrea, who wrapped her arm around her and gave her a hug. "You're where you belong, sweetie."

Marie started to read, knowing some of the words by sight, sounding out the rest, her voice a sweet drone as she slowly made her way through each word. Andrea stroked her shoulder, leaning her cheek on the top of Marie's head, giving her a squeeze.

When Marie finished the last page, Andrea said, "That was beautiful. You're such a good reader! How did you learn to do it so well, and you're just in kindergarten?"

"I don't know."

"Well, I'm so proud of you."

"This is my favorite book," she said, hugging it to her, and Andrea wondered if she owned any others. She could give her some of Pearl's old books and maybe take her to the public library.

Before she could suggest her plan, two little girls whisked Marie away, leaving Andrea behind with the book. Andrea accepted a cup of grape juice, wishing she'd had more time to talk to Marie. Next to her sat a woman in a heavily draped floral print and a matching hat. Andrea said hello to the woman, who nodded, but didn't speak. For the most part, everyone spoke Kinyarwanda, and they couldn't, or wouldn't, have a conversation with her.

Aurélie's friend brought a large plastic basin of water and a bottle of Palmolive. Each adult in turn washed hands and tore off a square of paper towel. Aurélie was drenched with sweat, but her smile had returned. She'd braided her hair and wore an African print skirt and a white blouse, a crucifix shining from her cleavage.

The first platter of food arrived—big cubes of meat on wooden skewers—and each child was given one. Next, came more platters—a big bowl of starchy fufu, white beans in an orange sauce, more meat on skewers.

Andrea nursed her warm grape juice as she balanced a paper plate on her lap. After the meal, when all the plates had been removed and hands wiped, Andrea stood up to make her exit. "No, you cannot go yet," Franck said. "It's early."

"Well, okay," she said. "I guess I could stay a while longer." She returned to her seat, wiping her brow and fanning herself.

Franck called the group's attention to an old man, a wraith with yellowed eyes and a piercing gaze. He wore a suit and cradled a Bible, and Andrea realized she was stuck there for a while. He launched into a rousing talk in Kinyarwanda, punctuated by gestures in which he slapped his hand on the Bible, pounded his chest, and pointed to the sky. Agile for his age, he bobbed and clapped, the others chanting in a call and response. Franck hunched over and did a side-to-side dance, his eyes fixed on the man, mirroring his moves. Andrea chimed in when she could, but the only word she recognized was *Jésus*. Suddenly, the man stopped, sweat runneling down his face and neck, and everyone shouted, "Amen!" The room was thick with the smells of charred meat and sweat and dish soap. Andrea sat back, fanning herself. Now she could slip away quietly, writing a note to Franck and Aurélie later, thanking them. She wouldn't be missed.

But before she could leave, Franck and another man walked over and stood facing her. Franck spoke in Kinyarwanda, and the man translated. "We are here today because we found what was lost. Our children." Everyone nodded and whispered. "Andrea here was willing to help us, even late at night, no matter what. She was always a friend." All eyes were on her, and she felt herself

257

flush, but she forced herself to look straight at Franck and the man. "We are not rich, but we are rich in family. And with friends like Andrea. So we have a gift for you from Rwanda. Thank you, Andrea. You are part of our family." Marie and Félix walked out of the bedroom carrying a tall basket with a conical top. They handed it to Andrea, who hugged the children, her throat tight. She knew enough not to give a speech; that was a man's job. But she nodded her thanks to the group. They applauded. She ran her hands over the basket, knowing it had taken many hours to complete, hoping they hadn't spent too much money on this gift. "Franck, Aurélie, this is beautiful. You didn't need to do this."

"You are a very good friend. You bring us our children."

"You got your children back because you're good parents. This shouldn't have happened in the first place." And she found herself crying and letting Franck and Aurélie hug her. But they didn't know that she was crying because they had their children and she had no one. She'd wanted those children for herself, had wished for more time with them away from their parents. What kind of person did that make her? What did that say about her as a mother? But she shook off her tears and hugged them back, telling herself that the world was, to a small extent, restored to order, and that this was her job. That much she could do.

CHAPTER 13

Paris, Chicago, February-May 2011

THE MONEY THAT PEARL HAD stolen from Ousmane would help get her a ticket home to Chicago, but she needed more, so to bridge the gap, she drew portraits on the street, setting up a pad of paper near Notre Dame or the Luxembourg Gardens. Even though she wore gloves, her hands cramped from the cold, and she had to take breaks inside the entrance to the Métro to warm them. Most of the artists on the streets were caricaturists, but she could do decent realistic portraits, and she also sold drawings of Notre Dame to tourists. Paper and pencils were expensive though, and barely allowed her a profit. Reluctantly, she moved out of the hotel where she'd been staying and looked for a place to squat. Along the Canal St. Martin, she came upon a colony of homeless living together. She met a young woman, Bérénice, who could speak some English. Bérénice offered a spot for Pearl in her tent, but it was freezing, and Pearl kept imagining she heard Ousmane's voice outside, so she didn't sleep at all and left early the next morning, vowing to go it alone. She couldn't take any more chances with her safety.

She avoided Palais Royal, where Ousmane played his music, and Goutte d'Or, where he'd taken her. Once, she thought she saw him near the Cité Métro stop and grabbed her pad and ran across the cobblestones, twisting her ankle, limping over to a group of tourists. She stood next to them, her breathing ragged, the blood pumping in her ears, as the guide pointed to the prison where Marie Antoinette had been housed prior to her execution.

Bérénice had mentioned that Shakespeare and Company, the English-language book store near Notre Dame, let people in the arts crash for free, so Pearl took her sketch pad and walked across the river to the green and yellow painted store with tables out front displaying dog-eared books, their covers curling from the dampness. Inside, she approached an ancient man sitting behind the front desk. He was missing several teeth, his hair was dirty and wild, but he wore a natty red velvet jacket as he sat hunched over a pad, a pen gripped in his cramped claw. He looked up and scowled. "Yes?"

"I heard that artists can stay here. For free?"

"What kind of writer are you?" His eyes were watery and rimmed with red.

"Not a writer, an artist." She held up a sketch she'd done of an old woman she'd seen coming out of Notre Dame after mass.

He studied it, then waved her off. "We're full up."

Outside again, she looked up at the second floor and saw a young man wearing a tee-shirt and neck scarf, sitting on the window ledge, smoking, his hair an enormous puffed bush. Squinting as if he'd just dragged himself from bed, he saluted her and flicked ashes from his cigarette into the air.

Back across the river, she headed toward a youth hostel, figuring that if it took longer for her to make the money, at least she'd be safe. Even so, she slept every night clutching her purse, boots on her feet, drawing pad under the mattress, waking from dreams of Ousmane pinning her down, his winey breath gagging her as he called her a dirty whore.

For days, she'd been feeling sick and couldn't keep anything down except bread, and she wondered if she'd eaten some bad food. When she realized her period was late, and her breasts had become tender, she started to worry. A week later, she was terrified she might be pregnant. And with Ousmane's baby. It had to be his; she and Renny had used condoms. How stupid she'd been to go off with a stranger. But she was desperate, and he'd seemed nice at first. How could she have known he'd slip something into her drink?

She needed to get back to Chicago. Leave this cold city, go home. Limiting herself to one baguette a day, she hoarded every Euro, forcing herself to sit outside from dawn until dark, every Euro bringing her closer to home. But to what? What would her mother say now especially if she was pregnant? That she'd gotten herself into this mess by taking risks?

By mid-March, after a month of eating bread and scavenged scraps, she bought a plane ticket, took the train to the airport, hugging herself against contact with other people, closing her eyes and remembering smells, tastes, and sounds of home.

At the airport, Africans in robes and sandals stood in line for planes to Dakar and Abidjan. Asian tourists with real Louis Vuitton suitcases, shopping bags stuffed with duty free, were returning to Singapore and Hong Kong. Waiting to board her flight was an American tour group with two tired-looking teachers and their charges, high-school students, laughing raucously, sporting their Hard Rock Paris sweatshirts, souvenir scarves slung around their necks. Kids like that had made Pearl hate high school. She sat with her few possessions in a small duffle, her stomach in a twist, feeling desperate to leave but scared of what she'd find back home. Chicago was a big city; she'd find a place to hide. Where else would she go?

On the plane, she couldn't sleep, and thoughts kept rattling around in her head. What would Andrea say now? Before Pearl's phone had died, she'd received a number of messages from her mother, demanding to know where Pearl had gone. She'd sounded so angry. Pearl just couldn't answer. She'd briefly thought of leaving her a message telling her she was fine, but then she and Renny had left the country and by then, it was too late. She had no idea if her mother was still leaving messages, thinking Pearl was ignoring them. Had she given Pearl up for dead?

Taking the El in toward Chicago from the airport, she felt a bubble of excitement when she caught sight of the skyline in the distance. She gravitated to Uptown, where she knew the rents were cheap and she could hide, even though she worried that she'd run into her mother visiting one of her refugee clients or a neighbor who'd recognize her.

A Single-Room-Occupancy hotel in Uptown had a vacancy, but after her first night, she woke up with bites along her left side. Bedbugs. Horrified, she knew she needed to move out but didn't know where, so she put down plastic bags under the sheet. That worked, sort of, but it was so hot she could barely sleep. Between the bites and jet lag, she woke up in the middle of the night, scratching until she bled. Part of her wanted to call home but feared what Andrea would say after all this time, mostly that she wouldn't want Pearl back, especially if she was pregnant. She couldn't show up, broke and pathetic. First, she needed to find a job and get the money for an abortion before it was too late. When she could show her mother she wasn't a complete fuck-up, she'd call her. Maybe.

She set out on foot to scour the neighborhood for places that would hire someone without any work experience, preferably a small store where Andrea wouldn't shop—that shouldn't be hard—and where Pearl could remain more or less anonymous. Walking up Broadway, Pearl stopped at an Asian market, a Subway, an ice cream shop, a car parts dealership, a hair salon that did locs, coils, and braids. Several places had gone out of business, and the other ones weren't hiring. Finally, she came upon an African clothing store and froze at the sight of dashikis, wooden carvings, and cloth dolls, reminding her of the outdoor market in Paris where she'd gone with Ousmane. She nearly passed it by, but she was running out of places to look, so she steeled herself to walk in and ask for a job. The owner, a Nigerian woman, didn't care that she wasn't African, just that she'd be willing to wear one of the outfits when at work and accept payment in cash under the table. Could she start the next day? It didn't look like there'd be many customers, so Pearl figured it would be an easy job, and she could hide out, biding her time while earning some money.

After her first payday, she moved to the Aragon Arms on Kenmore. Although the smell of roach spray and cooking grease made her queasy, there were no bedbugs, and it was right near St. Thomas of Canterbury and its soup kitchen, where she ate one meal a day. She needed to fly under the radar and didn't want to run into anyone her mother knew from work. On her worst days, she nearly called Andrea to come pick her up, but then she found the strength to tough it out.

AT A CLINIC ON WILSON, Pearl sat in a chair with her hood pulled up over her head, surrounded by mothers with their snuffling, coughing children and old men who reeked of tobacco and alcohol. Afraid that the sour smells would make her puke, she scouted out a wastebasket, just in case. The doctor, a woman with a Polish name, gave her a pelvic exam and asked her the date of her last period. Pearl remembered that it had been right as she and Renny arrived in Paris, back in late January. A couple of days before the trip, Renny had told her to stop acting like a bitch, and she said it was PMS, so shut up. Her period started on the plane ride over.

"You appear to be about nine to ten weeks along," the doctor said, motioning for Pearl to sit up on the table. She pulled off her gloves. "Do you intend to continue with the pregnancy?"

"I can't!" Pearl said, and the doctor studied her for a moment, then asked if someone in her family had done this to her. No, Pearl told her. It wasn't that. The doctor asked if she'd considered adoption.

"No," said Pearl, her heart fluttering in her throat. "I know all about adoption. I'd never do that to a baby." The doctor looked surprised. "I just want the abortion, okay? I don't need to be counseled or anything. I know what I'm doing." The sooner she got that baby out of her, the sooner she'd feel normal.

"You need to schedule the D & C," the doctor said, scribbling a note. "Don't wait too long," she said, looking up, reminding her she only had a couple of weeks to decide. "Just make sure that whatever you decide, it's what you really want."

Pearl took the sample of prenatal vitamins, which the doctor urged on her in case she changed her mind. But that wasn't going to happen. That woman didn't know her, didn't have any business trying to influence her. She made an appointment for the following week, worrying that the abortion would wipe out the tiny cushion of money she'd built up.

On her way back to the Aragon Arms, she felt determined. She couldn't handle a baby now; she could barely survive herself. Fuck that doctor. This was the right decision. Twelve days remained to have the abortion.

She divided her week between the African store and the public library, where she waited to grab a chair vacated by one of the homeless men and women who hung out all day, taking advantage of the heat and the free Internet. One time, the police came and removed a crazy, swearing man. A sign posted by the stacks read: NO CHANGING CLOTHES IN THIS AREA. In the bathroom, she ran into a woman who brushed her teeth and sponged her armpits with wet paper towels. Since Pearl's nose and stomach had become sensitive, she avoided bad-smelling clouds. Despite the weird people, Pearl preferred the library to her small, cramped room. At least the library had the Internet, where she looked up people she knew on Facebook. She also wrote an email to Willa using her account from high school.

Hey, Willa. Did this go through? How's Yale? I'm back in Chicago for a while. Write if you want. Pearl

A few minutes later, she got a response:

Pearl? Oh my God. What a surprise! How are you? What are you doing in Chicago? Will you be there this summer? I'll be home for a few days before my internship in D.C. Maybe we can see each other then. Wish me luck on my exams!
W

At the soup kitchen, many of the people shook or talked to

themselves, so Pearl tended to keep a distance, eating her meal—her appetite had returned big time--and then leaving. However, she did get to know a woman about her age named Maxine, who had a son in kindergarten. She was trying to find work so she could get a place for them to live. Maxine had been beaten by her boyfriend, who'd blinded her in one eye. It watered, and the lid drooped. She and her son had been living in various shelters since then. "I got my baby. We don't need no man." It could always be worse, Pearl knew.

Spending time in that neighborhood again made Pearl think about her birth mother, wondering what she must be doing now, if she'd ever gotten married and had other children. Maybe she was homeless, maybe she and Pearl had even eaten together at the soup kitchen. Most often, Pearl wondered why she hadn't had an abortion and why, since she hadn't gotten rid of her, she'd decided to give Pearl up the way she had, dumping her at a church. Had she ever planned to keep her? Pearl wished she knew what had been on her birth mother's mind the day before Pearl was born, the day she was born, and every day since. Did her mother think about her or had she forgotten her, a mistake she'd put in the past? Did she wish she'd kept Pearl? What would Pearl's name be if she had? Did her birth mother feel guilty or was she relieved? And what would Pearl think about this not-to-be baby every day in the future? Stop it, she told herself. There was no way she could have a baby. Not now. Not like this.

On the day she'd chosen to have the abortion, five days short of the deadline, Pearl woke up exhausted and bleary-eyed after a night of looping dreams with mothers stepping on their babies by accident, dropping them in the bath, losing them in the store, on the street, searching for them frantically. She dressed in her loosest clothes and set out to walk, trying not to focus on mothers with children, just looking down, putting one foot in front of the other. By the time she arrived at the clinic, she was sweating, her chest hurt, and she could barely breathe. It'd been months since her last full-blown asthma attack, so she hadn't bought an expensive new inhaler. Now she wished she'd asked the doctor for one. She stood outside, leaning against the window, trying to deepen her raspy breaths, to get some air. Afraid she'd black out right there, she stumbled over to a bench and sat down, her head between her knees, heaving, stars before her eyes, willing herself not to pass out. Finally, her head pounding, her back sweaty, she managed to calm down enough to take in more air. Keeping her eyes shut, she sat for several minutes until she felt strong enough to stand up. She took the El the two stops back to her room, dragged herself upstairs, took the bottle of prenatal vitamins out of the drawer and swallowed one. Then she lay down, rubbing her belly, and closed her eyes.

SHE WOKE UP THINKING OF her mother. Not her birth mother, but Andrea. Okay, she had to admit, her real mother. Until then, Pearl hadn't thought much about whether her mother was worried. She'd only focused on how angry she'd be that Pearl had blown off school. Pearl kept hearing her mother rag on her about the money and the irresponsibility and the wasted opportunities. Would she try to force Pearl to get the abortion in the few days that were left? She couldn't risk that now that her decision had been made.

What would Andrea say to her about the baby? That Pearl had gotten herself into another mess, a big one this time? Pearl could hear her mother, *What am I going to do with you, Pearl? What makes you act like this?* as if she'd been waiting for Pearl to screw up since she was little, had never expected her to be anything but a total fuck-up. But what if it *was* in her blood? What if nothing her mother did made any difference? It wasn't this baby's fault that Pearl had been raped. She just couldn't get rid of it, and she couldn't give it up. Maybe this was her chance to get things right. If she had to, she'd do this alone. When she closed her eyes to imagine herself as a mother to a small dark child, she kept seeing herself instead as the little girl, sitting on the sofa next to her mother, listening to her read *The Giving Tree*, Andrea's white fingers turning the pages, Pearl sucking her thumb, the other hand tucked in next to her mother's side, close and warm.

*** ***

ANDREA HAD TAKEN A PERSONAL day to accompany Freya to her chemo session. A couple of weeks earlier, Andrea had called Freya at home, but she'd sounded distracted.

"Hey," Andrea said, hurt. "I'll call you tomorrow. You're busy."

Freya apologized and asked her how she was doing, but Andrea didn't feel like talking anymore. After Andrea hung up, she'd regretted her whininess, chalked it up to worn nerves, and swore she'd try harder not to let her worries over Pearl color everything around her.

When she called back the next day, Ramón answered and said that Freya had just come back from the doctor and was lying down, which surprised Andrea. It wasn't like her to nap.

"She's putting up a good front for me and the kids," he said, "but I know she's worried."

"About what?"

"She didn't tell you?"

"No."

"The MRI showed a mass and she just got the results of the biopsy. It's ovarian cancer."

"What? Why didn't she tell me?"

"She didn't want to worry you just now," Ramón said. Clearly he knew about Pearl.

"But I could be there with her."

"I know she'd like that. She hates to ask for help, but this has been so hard."

"Why? What did the doctors say?"

"It's not operable." His voice broke. "They're going to do chemo, but it doesn't look good."

"No," Andrea said, feeling faint. "That can't be. She was fine."

He asked Andrea to promise not to let on he'd told her how serious it was. She'd made him promise. Freya had even considered delaying treatment until after Rosa's wedding, but Ramón had insisted. Andrea agreed not to let on that she knew. Ramón said he'd check to see if she was awake, and Andrea heard muffled voices. Finally, Freya came on the line, sounding groggy.

Andrea forced calm into her voice and asked how she was feeling. Why hadn't Freya said anything earlier? Freya said she was going to be fine, that she hadn't wanted to add more to Andrea's stress.

"Freya. Please. I dump everything on you. You have to do the same with me."

"I'd have told you before my hair started falling out." She said her doctor was optimistic. She'd be *fine,* she said again, a catch in her voice. Andrea insisted on going with her to chemo, and would do anything else she needed. She fought to keep the worry out of her voice, telling herself that it wasn't the time to show anything but strength for Freya.

"Thanks. Ramón is trying to help, but he's hovering. It's driving me crazy. I don't want to think about it all the time. I find him staring at me, and I want to tell him to stop, that I'm not going to disappear. His worry is contagious. I have to be strong to help Rosa with the wedding. That's keeping me going."

"Please, let me help you." She held on until she hung up, then she burst into tears. Whom could she tell about her fears for Freya? That was Freya's job.

A WEEK LATER, THEY SAT together in the recliners while Freya was hooked up to the IV. The nurse had put Freya's feet and hands into ice gloves and a cooling cap on her head to protect her hair follicles and nail beds. The nurses gave her popsicles and asked about whether she felt cold. She was packed with ice until she shivered, even under a blanket. Despite this, Freya treated the nurses so sweetly, learning all their names, asking them all about their husbands, boyfriends and kids. That was Freya, always putting others first.

Freya said that Rosa wanted to move in until the wedding, but Freya had refused. "I want her to enjoy this time of her life, not to be nursemaid to her mother."

Andrea lectured her about letting people help, not pushing them away. But Andrea knew that Freya also didn't want her daughter to see how sick she was, that Freya would deny herself this closeness to avoid that. Freya was amazing, so strong. Hearing her talk about Rosa made Andrea think of Pearl and how, if Andrea were sick, Pearl wouldn't even know. She dabbed at her eyes.

"Oh, Andrea, don't cry. I'm going to beat this thing."

"Of course, you are. You just *are*," Andrea said, forcing a smile, hating herself for thinking of own problems instead of Freya's.

"And Pearl is going to come home and everything will be fine. You'll see." She said she was sorry to burden Andrea at a time when she had enough on her mind—Pearl's disappearance and Andrea's mother's recent death.

"I want to be here with you." She ran her hand along the arm not connected to the I.V. and laced her fingers in Freya's.

After the procedure, Andrea drove them to Freya's home to sit with her until Ramón returned from work. Freya lay on her sofa and let Andrea tuck a blanket around her feet and make a mug of ginger tea. Freya didn't want Andrea to see her throw up, but Andrea insisted on sticking close. Freya had tied back her hair with an elastic and wore yoga pants and a ratty tee-shirt. Chemo Fatigues, she called them. Andrea felt good to be able to do this for Freya and was ashamed to admit how much it helped to be needed.

"Some people say it's easier to cut all your hair off before it starts to fall out," Freya said, "but I just can't do that." She tightened her pony tail. "I know. It's just hair."

"It's your *hair*. No small thing."

"I just wish I didn't have to wear a wig at the wedding."

"We'll see to it that you look beautiful."

"I wonder how my hair will look when it grows back."

"Blond and straight, I'm sure," Andrea said, attempting a joke.

"As long as it isn't *all* gray," she said, making a face.

It was touching to see this touch of vanity in Freya. Of course, who wouldn't be upset about losing one's hair? And hers was particularly thick and beautiful.

When the nausea hit, Freya stumbled to the bathroom. Andrea stayed until Freya shooed her off, saying that Ramón would be home in an hour. "He can't do this with anyone else around, afraid he'll cry and you'll see him. Big man, you know? I'll just hang out here in the bathroom. Can you bring me that stack of magazines, please?" Andrea brought them to her and ran her hand over the top of Freya's head, and Freya reached up and held her hand, squeezing with cold, trembling fingers.

"You go, I'm fine. I promise." Her face was ashen, dark circles under her eyes. For the first time, she looked fragile and vulnerable. She lowered the cover and sat on the seat, flipping through the magazine. "Oh, good. An article on best and worst beach bodies. I have some reading to do." Andrea gave her a kiss and said she'd be back the next day.

Andrea drove home, blunted, barely able to focus on the road. When she reached the landing of her apartment, she smelled tomatoes and cheese cooking and knew that Mike had come over to make dinner for them. Since Pearl had left for college, she'd given up on cooking almost entirely, living on salads and grocery store chicken. As a child, she'd loved coming home to a warm house, smelling of dinner. The image of her mother, young and vital, cooking dinner, saddened Andrea. Just one of the many times a day she missed her mother now.

Mike sat at the kitchen table, a glass of wine in front of him, a bag of pita chips opened, NPR on the radio. When he asked about Freya, Andrea walked into a big hug. He told her that she had to believe that Freya was going to be fine, and he poured her a glass of wine and made her sit while he finished dinner.

When her mother died in April, she'd called Mike as a courtesy—was it just that?—and he'd offered to help. He'd been great, helping her sort through her mother's stuff, advising her on legal matters involving the estate. Joanne was useless, as always. And so she and

Mike had drifted back together, or whatever this precarious thing could be called. After all, they'd only spent a few nights together. She didn't want to blow it with him this time.

But even with Mike there, when she woke up at night, she found herself going down the deepest rabbit holes of worry about losing both Pearl and Freya. How would she survive those losses? Mike always said the right things about Freya, but that didn't threaten his place in Andrea's life. With Pearl, it had been a lot more complicated. She couldn't help wondering if the only reason he was back had to do with Pearl being gone. And had she called him only out of loneliness?

*** ***

BY THE BEGINNING OF MAY, too late now for the abortion, Pearl was glad not to have a decision, just take care of herself and earn enough money to put aside for her and the baby. Her baby. Pearl's body was changing, her belly growing round and hard, her breasts full and tender. She ate enough at the soup kitchen to get by, and everything now went to the baby. She continued to take the prenatal vitamins and opted for milk instead of coffee. Every day, she walked to and from work and her legs felt strong, even as she got heavier.

Being pregnant like this made her think of her grandmother's birth mother who hadn't been married either when Gram was born. Little things reminded her of Gram: a hand-knitted sweater worn by a woman in the street, a whiff of lavender picked up while riding the El, the smell of almond cookies from a bakery on Argyle. Pearl wondered if she knew that Pearl had left school, and if so, was she angry? Her money had paid for college, and Pearl felt awful for wasting it. Would her mother shield Gram from the facts or had she been angry enough to tell her? Pearl didn't want to disappoint her grandmother, who loved her so much. Of all people, her grandmother would understand why it would be wrong to abandon this baby.

She could buy a cheap prepaid phone and call Gram. And even if Pearl told her grandmother where she was, she thought she could trust Gram not to tell Andrea they'd been in touch. Maybe her grandmother would help make peace or at least keep her mother from acting too crazy.

However, her grandmother's number was disconnected. When she got through to the receptionist at the assisted living home, the woman said, "Oh, Mrs. Barton died. About three weeks ago."

"What?"

"I'm sorry. Are you a relative or something?"

"Why did you just say it like that, bitch?" Pearl hung up and fell back on her bed, hugging herself, remembering Gram's smell, her voice, the feel of her hands, the pale fingers wrinkled, but strong. Those fingers taught Pearl to knit and crochet. Gram always had pads of paper and markers at her house and she didn't make Pearl finish the drawing before she started another one the way Pearl's mother did. Gram put the finished ones up on her refrigerator, and they fluttered when she opened and closed the door. And she'd say, "Another original from Pearl, a true original."

Now Pearl would never see her again. Worse was the fact that she'd been in town before her grandmother died and could have seen her one last time. Gram would have wanted a religious funeral, but Pearl couldn't see Andrea doing that. What was it like for her mother to go through her grandmother's stuff without Pearl? She cried, rocking herself, saying goodbye to her grandmother, telling her how sorry she was. Maybe she could write to Andrea, to tell her she was sorry about Gram, not to see her, but to let her know she was all right. Pearl curled up and closed her eyes. After a short nap, she woke up with a start. "Mama."

She got up and took the bus to the library. At the desk, Pearl signed up for one of the computers, and, seeing that they were all in use, sat waiting, flipping through an issue of *Cosmopolitan* with an article on loving your body at any size, checking the clock, worried that she'd lose her nerve before she got the chance to write. One man had dozed off in front of his computer, and Pearl coughed loudly to wake him up. Finally, she asked when he'd be done and he stood up and walked away, leaving behind a stinky trail. Once on the Internet, she opened a new Gmail account with a fake name, just to give herself a cushion, and sat down to write, panic clutching her throat.

ABARTON@BREADBASKET.ORG
Rayann@Gmail.com
Hey, it's me. I'm okay. Sorry. Pearl

Her finger hovered over the keyboard for a moment, then she plunked SEND and the message was off, out of her hands, which tingled and shook. It was done. Her heart was pounding, and she felt lightheaded. Quickly logging off, she hurried toward the door on rubbery legs. Outside, she stopped to catch her breath. What had she done? Maybe she could just send another email telling Andrea not to write back, that she just wanted to let her know she was okay. She had to be in control, wouldn't let her mother find her until she wanted to be found. If she ever did.

*** ***

THE DAY AFTER THE CHEMO session, Andrea arrived at work, having grabbed an Egg McMuffin at a McDonald's drive-through. Freya had taken the day off to recover, so Andrea and she wouldn't be having their usual shared breakfast in the break room—coffees provided by Andrea, pastries by Freya—*pan dulce, conchas*, whatever she'd baked or bought at her neighborhood shop. They liked being the first people at work before the others arrived and the day got busy.

Andrea turned on the lights, watered her ficus plant, tidied Dale's desk that, since he'd been furloughed, had given space for her clutter to spread. She logged on to her computer, a sluggish old PC that Breadbasket couldn't afford to replace due to the cutbacks. The place was too quiet. She planned to email Freya rather than call so as not to wake her. First, she opened her work email to start on the backlog of messages from the previous day. Scrolling down, she recognized most of them and decided to parcel out her responses over the course of the day. There were memos about meetings and reports to be filed and a reminder of an interview with new clients, a family from Syria. She worried about their youngest child, who'd arrived with a wicked case of head lice. Had they gone to the clinic and followed through with the treatment? With more clients and less time for them, she found it hard to keep track of all their needs.

She deleted an email from someone she didn't recognize, Rayann@gmail.com, but then she retrieved it from her trash bin. Before opening it, she tried to see if she could remember who Rayann was. A former client? Hoping it wasn't a Trojan Horse, she clicked on the message.

To: ABARTON@BREADBASKET.ORG
From: Rayann@gmail.com
Subject: Hi
Hey. It's me. I'm sorry. Pearl

She shrieked and pushed back from the desk, her hands tingling. Rolling her chair back up to the desk, she read the message again. What? Where had this come from? Her fingers shaking, she pushed reply and wrote:

Pearl, where are you? Are you okay? I've been so worried. Please call me. I love you, Mama

She sent it and sat staring at the screen for several minutes, refreshing her inbox button, waiting for a response. Nothing. Then she saw that the message had been sent the previous day. What if Pearl had given up when she hadn't gotten an immediate response and was now back underground, who knew where? She re-sent her message, heart in her throat, begging Pearl to get in touch again. What if Pearl had disappeared again when she hadn't heard from Andrea right away? What if she'd missed her only chance?

Despite the early hour, she called Freya at home, figuring Ramón would pick up. Freya answered, half asleep. Andrea apologized and told her about the email. Andrea was crying, gulping, trying to catch her breath. Freya told her to slow down and asked her to repeat what it said. Andrea said she didn't know much, didn't even know where Pearl was. Could if be a prank? "Why is she emailing me? I need to hear her voice." She apologized for bothering Freya when she felt so rotten.

"Stop it. This is great news. She's fine."

"I don't know that she's fine. She's alive."

"She made contact. That's huge."

"Why didn't she call?"

Freya said it was probably really scary for her to make the first move, that she'd be afraid to get in touch after so long.

Andrea opened her desk and rifled through it until she found the laminated bookmark that Pearl had given her for Mother's Day in second grade. It was a self-portrait of Pearl, her skin rendered in brown crayon, wearing her favorite purple hoodie and a long arm snaking around a drawing of Andrea, her skin pink, her hair tan and straight. Both of them had large red slices for smiles. And the sky above them was filled with birds and a spiky yellow sun. Andrea ran her finger over the slippery plastic, sad that the bookmark had been folded, the cracked plastic cutting them across the middle.

She sat down to work, but couldn't concentrate and she kept returning to her email, staring at the screen, refreshing the inbox button, the bookmark propped up behind the keyboard. She wrote again to Pearl, asking her to write back, saying she needed to hear from her.

Later than morning, she got another message from Pearl, saying that she was fine and living in Chicago. She apologized for taking so long to reach her.

Chicago? Where was she? Andrea asked in her next message. Pearl wouldn't tell her, but said she had a job and was eating well. Please, Andrea, said. She needed to see her to make sure this was real. Pearl said she couldn't talk face to face yet. Andrea apologized for getting so angry and said she wasn't mad anymore. She just needed to see her. Please. Pearl wrote that she'd heard about Gram dying and was sad. How did she know that? Pearl said she'd tried to call Gram. Andrea swallowed back the hurt that Pearl hadn't called her and said she really needed to see Pearl. Finally, Pearl agreed to meet her the following day at Metropolis, a café near Loyola. Andrea wanted to see her that day, but Pearl told her not to push it. That sounded like Pearl. Andrea said she wouldn't be able to sleep that night, but she agreed to the meeting.

After she logged off, Andrea's hands felt ice cold, and her head throbbed. She stood up but her legs buckled and she flopped back into her chair. Weeping, she called Freya back, the story spilling out of her in gulps and sobs. Freya offered to drive over to the office, but Andrea told her no, she'd be fine. She was just reacting to the shock. At least Pearl was back in Chicago and she'd made the effort, Freya reminded her. It must have meant she was ready. Andrea hoped she wouldn't change her mind and not show up. Freya offered to go with her, but Andrea knew she had to do it alone. She also decided not to tell Mike anything until she knew more, until she'd actually seen Pearl in the flesh.

*** ***

AFTER RECEIVING HER MOTHER'S EMAILS, Pearl couldn't stop shaking. She hadn't counted on feeling so nervous. She wished she'd thought of email earlier. Now, Pearl worried about how her mother would react to seeing her pregnant, whether she'd refuse to have anything more to do with her because of the baby. She weighed how much she'd reveal, to calm her mother down without pissing her off. No way would she mention Ousmane. Maybe she'd wait to tell her about the baby, because her mother would be mad that she hadn't had the abortion. She'd keep the facts to a minimum. When she knew that her mother could accept her back, then she'd tell her about the baby. One big thing at a time.

And if need be, she'd have this baby alone. Women did it alone all the time. Maxine was doing it. Andrea had raised Pearl alone. She remembered her mother reading to her when she was little, Pearl tucked in under her mother's arm, their feet wrapped up in a quilt. Books always came before TV, and Pearl appreciated that now, even though she hadn't at the time. Her mother would sing to her and make up stories late at night as Pearl was trying to go to sleep. She wished she still had her baby quilt and wondered if her mother had kept it. Why would she though? After Pearl left, she feared that her mother had been too angry to keep any reminders of her. Pearl often wondered if she'd wished for a different child, if she'd ever wanted to return Pearl. She herself had often wished for a different mother and wondered if biological children felt the same thing, if being related by blood meant that you were more likely to get along. She and her mother were so different. Would it have been easier if she'd been raised by her birth mother? It might have been a whole lot harder.

Maybe Andrea could help with the baby. That way, Pearl could go back to college and work to put herself through. Maybe she could teach art to kids. Or do art therapy. The city colleges weren't that expensive. And if she had state aid, she could manage. Then she'd worry that it was all too hard and she couldn't handle it and she'd make a mess of things, that her mother would refuse to help her, saying that she had to learn responsibility on her own. She wasn't sure at all how her mother would react to the pregnancy, so she decided not to tell her. Not until she was sure what to do.

*** ***

ANDREA HAD MADE THE DECISION not to tell Mike about Pearl's emails. She wasn't sure what this contact with Pearl meant, or if he'd discourage her from going, so there was no point bringing Mike into it yet. Besides, a lot could still go wrong. Pearl might not show up at Metropolis, or it could go very badly, or Pearl could be addicted and in trouble. And Mike's predictions about Pearl would be proved right. She'd tell him once she'd seen Pearl, but she worried about what Pearl's return would mean for them.

After he made dinner, they sat together on the sofa to watch an episode of a British police procedural he'd recorded, but all she could think of was Pearl. When Mike saw that she was distracted, he hit the pause button and slung his arm around her. "You're not in the mood?"

"Sorry." She closed her eyes and settled into his shoulder.

They sat there for a moment as he stroked her hair. "Freya's very lucky to have you as a friend."

"No," she said. "I'm the lucky one."

"You're the strongest woman I know."

"Not true," she said, her voice thin and weak. "I'm not strong."

"You have so much on your mind these days."

"It's been really hard," she said, pressing the pads of her hands into her eyes.

He sat back, took her hands, and looked her in the eye. "I'm not going anywhere. You won't go through this alone."

"Promise?"

THE FOLLOWING MORNING, ANDREA ARRIVED early at Metropolis and got a coffee and two pastries, one for her and one for Pearl. For their reunion. Their confrontation? Would Pearl come in, guns drawn, or would she be contrite and nervous herself? She checked her phone every minute or so for messages in case Pearl had changed her mind. Fifteen minutes later, she'd eaten both pastries, shredded the napkin, trying to put on the best, most accepting face. Not too emotional, or demanding or anything to scare Pearl off. Should she run over to Pearl or let her come to her? She vowed to accept Pearl no matter what shape she was in, addicted, sick, in trouble. They'd face it together.

*** ***

PEARL GOT OFF THE EL at Granville a few minutes before nine and stood out on the sidewalk, not wanting to arrive early. Keeping her eye peeled for her mother so she wouldn't be surprised by her in the street, she walked the block to the café, fighting the urge to run away. At Metropolis, she glanced in the window and saw her mother sitting with a cup of coffee, glancing at her phone. An electric shock ran down her arms and legs. Her heart pumping, spikes of adrenaline shooting through her, Pearl pivoted and headed back toward the El. She hadn't anticipated how it would feel to see her mother. At least she was sure her mother hadn't seen her. She could write another email to say she just wasn't ready, that she needed more time. She'd just wanted her to know she was okay.

Inside the El station, Pearl wheezed, and her fingers shook so much she couldn't fit her card in the slot, couldn't face climbing the stairs or going back to her room alone. Heading back to Metropolis, she put her head down and darted past the window, forcing herself to walk in the front door, to make her way past the people standing in line for coffee, a handsome, black barista, some scruffy students on their computers, an older couple with matching Kindles, into the back room where her mother sat, shoulders hunched, squinting at the screen of her phone. Blood banging in her head, Pearl dragged herself until she stood in front of her mother and squeezed out the word, "Hey."

*** ***

WHEN ANDREA CAUGHT SIGHT OF the young woman, her head wrapped in an African scarf, she didn't recognize her, but then she heard her voice, and looked beyond the scarves and the African dress and launched herself to her feet, barking her shin on a chair, lurching over to grab Pearl into a hug. Under the heavy patchouli scent, Andrea could still smell her girl. She felt Pearl's face, gulping, trying not to cry, unable to speak, hugging her again. Pearl pulled back, then put her arms stiffly around Andrea. Andrea stood back, running her hands down Pearl's face, her shoulders. Pearl crossed her arms over her chest. She was breathing heavily and had gained weight, Andrea noticed. When she backed up to get a look at her, she saw that under the loose clothes, Pearl's weight had all gone to her middle. Pearl was pregnant. Andrea sucked in her breath, reached out her hand but pulled it back. Andrea felt faint and stumbled back to her chair. "Oh, Pearl. Where have you been?"

Pearl sat down across from her, still, Andrea could see, trying to shield her bulge.

"Are you okay, Mom?"

Andrea was crying now, unable to stop herself. "It's a shock to see you."

"I know."

"Oh, Pearl. Why didn't you call me?"

"I was afraid you'd be mad."

"Mad? Of course mad." She put her hand over her mouth, shaking her head. "Go ahead. Talk. I'm listening."

*** ***

TERRELL STOCKED THE SHELF WITH freshly roasted coffee beans, then made his first sweep of the rooms to gather up dirty cups and plates. A few minutes earlier, he'd seen an attractive young black woman rush in, wearing African clothes, and he wondered which country she'd come from. He'd never seen her before. She was curvy and dark with full lips and large eyes. She looked nervous, didn't even order anything, headed into the back room, probably late for a job interview. Not the way for a sister to get a job. A few minutes later, he saw her sitting at a table with a middle-aged white woman, and they were involved in a conversation. It didn't look like a job interview. The older woman was wiping her eyes, the younger woman had her arms crossed and was nodding her head. Were they lovers, hashing out a disagreement? Two friends? The white women wore drab pants and shirt and the younger one was swathed in bright African fabric, as different from each other as they could be. What was their connection? That's what he liked about working at Metropolis; every day, new people with new stories to imagine. The older woman put her hand out, and the younger woman took it, reluctantly. She ran her hand over the bulge of her stomach. The older woman was crying, but she didn't look unhappy. She ran her fingers through her hair, blew her nose on a napkin, and nodded as the younger woman talked. The younger woman looked nervous, kept fiddling with a frayed edge of her bag, shaking her head, retying her head scarf. Maybe it was a teacher and her ex-student, catching up on life after graduation. Or a case worker, checking in to see that her client was on the straight and narrow. Maybe the woman was trying to help the daughter of a friend get a job. Who knew what they were to each other?

Fomite

A fomite is a medium capable of transmitting infectious organisms from one individual to another.

"The activity of art is based on the capacity of people to be infected by the feelings of others." Tolstoy, *What Is Art?*

Writing a review on Amazon, Good Reads, Shelfari, Library Thing or other social media sites for readers will help the progress of independent publishing. To submit a review, go to the book page on any of the sites and follow the links for reviews. Books from independent presses rely on reader to reader communications.

For more information or to order any of our books, visit
http://www.fomitepress.com/FOMITE/Our_Books.html

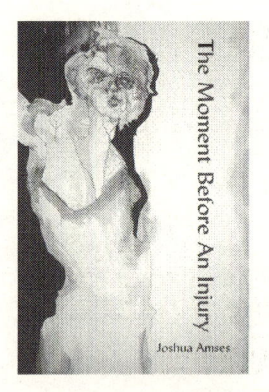

The Moment Before an Injury
Joshua Amses

Nothing Beside Remains
Jaysinh Birjépatil

The Way None of This Happened
Mike Breiner

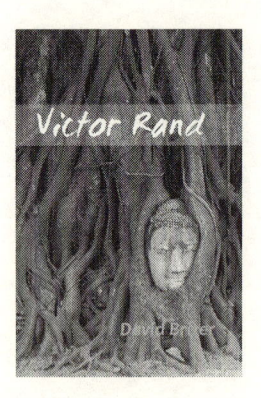

Victor Rand
David Brizer

Cycling in Plato's Cave
David Cavanagh

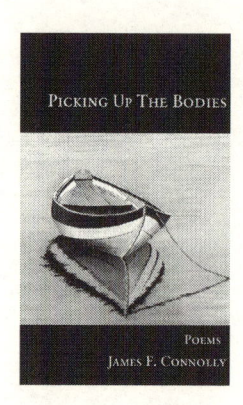

Picking Up the Bodies
James F. Connolly

Fomite

Unfinished Stories of Girls
Catherine Zobal Dent

Drawing on Life
Mason Drukman

Foreign Tales of
Exemplum and Woe
J. C. Ellefson

Free Fall/Caída libre
Tina Escaja

Sinfonia Bulgarica
Zdravka Evtimova

Derail Thie Train Wreck
Daniel Forbes

Where There Are Two or
More
Elizabeth Genovise

The Hundred Yard
Dash Man
Barry Goldensohn

When You Remeber
Deir Yassin
R. L. Green

Fomite

*A Guide
to the Western Slopes*
Roger Lebovitz

Confessions of a Carnivore
Diane Lefer

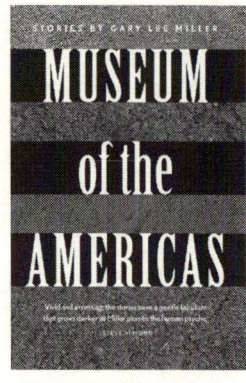

Museum of the Americas
Gary Lee Miller

My Father's Keeper
Andrew Potok

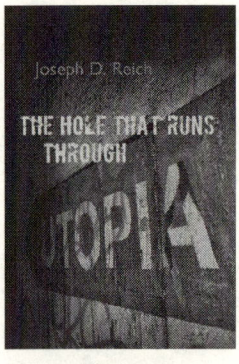

*The Hole That Runs
Through Utopia*
Joseph D. Reich

Companion Plants
Kathryn Roberts

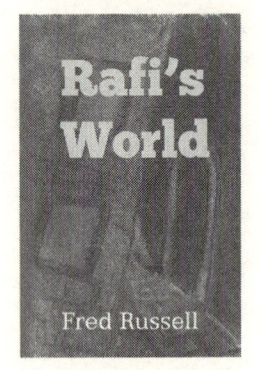

Rafi's World
Fred Russell

*My Murder
and Other Local News*
David Schein

Bread & Sentences
Peter Schumann

Fomite

Principles of Navigation
Lynn Sloan

Among Angelic Orders
Susan Thoma

Everyone Lives Here
Sharon Webster

The Falkland Quartet
Tony Whedon

*The Return of
Jason Green*
Suzi Wizowaty

*The Inconveniece
of the Wings*
Silas Dent Zobal

More Titles from Fomite...

Joshua Amses — *Raven or Crow*

Joshua Amses — *The Moment Before an Injury*

Jaysinh Birjepatil — *The Good Muslim of Jackson Heights*

Antonello Borra — *Alfabestiario*

Antonello Borra — *AlphaBetaBestiario*

Jay Boyer — *Flight*

Dan Chodorkoff — *Loisada*

Michael Cocchiarale — *Still Time*

Greg Delanty — *Loosestrife*

Zdravka Evtimova — *Carts and Other Stories*

Anna Faktorovich — *Improvisational Arguments*

Derek Furr — *Suite for Three Voices*

Stephen Goldberg — *Screwed*

Barry Goldensohn — *The Listener Aspires to the Condition of Music*

Greg Guma — *Dons of Time*

Andrei Guruianu — *Body of Work*

Ron Jacobs — *The Co-Conspirator's Tale*

Ron Jacobs — *Short Order Frame Up*

Ron Jacobs — *All the Sinners Saints*

Kate MaGill — *Roadworthy Creature, Roadworthy Craft*

Ilan Mochari — *Zinsky the Obscure*

Jennifer Moses — *Visiting Hours*

Sherry Olson — *Four-Way Stop*

Janice Miller Potter — *Meanwell*

Jack Pulaski — *Love's Labours*

Charles Rafferty — *Saturday Night at Magellan's*

Fomite

Joseph D. Reich — *The Derivation of Cowboys & Indians*

Joseph D. Reich — *The Housing Market*

Fred Russell — *Rafi's World*

Peter Schumann — *Planet Kasper, Volume 1*

L. E. Smith — *The Consequence of Gesture*

L. E. Smith — *Travers' Inferno*

L. E. Smith — *Views Cost Extra*

Susan Thomas — *The Empty Notebook Interrogates Itself*

Tom Walker — *Signed Confessions*

Susan V. Weiss — *My God, What Have We Done?*

Peter Mathiessen Wheelwright — *As It Is On Earth*

Made in the USA
Charleston, SC
09 June 2015